♥ *TENDE*

TENDER HEART

♥ *TENDER HEART* ♥

♥ *TENDER HEART* ♥

TENDER HEART

BY ANA P. CORMAN

♥ *TENDER HEART* ♥

Copyright © 1998, 2000 by Ana P. Corman
All Rights Reserved.
No part of this book may be reproduced, stored in a retrieval system, or transmitted by any means, electronic, mechanical, photocopying, recording, or otherwise, without written permission from the author.

ISBN: 1-58721-878-X

1stBooks – rev. 7/05/00

♥ TENDER HEART ♥
About the Book

Tender Heart is a contemporary lesbian romance novel. It is a fateful meeting of two tender women, a romance to soothe a painful past and a violent crime to test their love.

Dr. Megan Summers is a gifted neurosurgeon working in a trauma center in Austin, Texas. One fateful morning she exploded with anger and frustration at her colleague, Dr. Drake Darrow, while he was standing with his real estate agent, the breathtakingly beautiful, Rebecca Rhodes. Megan's fiery green eyes and emotional personality mesmerized Rebecca.

Megan was consumed with embarrassment for her volatile behavior as she sought out Drake and Rebecca to apologize. Drake sent Megan to a local café where he knew she would find Rebecca. Their meeting was intense and electrifying as the passionate chemistry flowed between them.

As their relationship slowly unfolded, Megan paid a surprise visit to Rebecca in her beautifully remodeled office. She ran into a very strange, eerie client of Rebecca's by the name of Sam Abbott. Megan learned from Rebecca and her assistant, Kyle that Sam Abbott had been trying relentlessly to wine and dine Rebecca. Rebecca had turned him down a thousand times and felt he'd finally got the message. Rebecca tried to reassure Megan that Abbott was harmless but definitely weird. Megan was not totally convinced.

A week into their relationship Megan and Rebecca shared a romantic lunch. Rebecca never returned to the office as Kyle expected and set off a horrific event of terror, gut wrenching fear and violence. Sam Abbott finally fulfilled his deranged wish of taking the one thing he felt belonged to him, Rebecca.

Tender Heart is a story that embraces the passion and sensitivity between women. It strikes the interest and compassion that people have to hear of others tragedies, personal struggles and triumphant. It displays the beauty of the human spirit and it's will to survive.

♥ *TENDER HEART* ♥

♥ TENDER HEART ♥

To my Catherine;

You are my soul mate and my love light. You feed my passion and nurture my imagination with the unconditional love of your tender heart.

♥ *TENDER HEART* ♥

♥ TENDER HEART ♥

Megan stopped in the doorway of the bathroom and leaned against the doorframe as she fully enjoyed the sight before her. Rebecca was sitting on the same spot on the vanity wearing a dazzling, gold colored, satin jacquard robe. She was leaning back against the mirror with her eye peacefully closed, her hands resting at her sides. The robe rested loosely above her knees and Megan admired her shapely, tanned legs. A gold satin belt gathered the robe at her slender waist. Megan's eyes were riveted to the gentle curve of Rebecca's breast beneath the slightly parted satin.

That's a beautiful look in your eyes, Dr. Summers."

Megan smiled sweetly and stepped toward this vision of loveliness. "It only reflects the incredibly beautiful woman that I'm looking at."

♥ *TENDER HEART* ♥

♥ *TENDER HEART* ♥
CHAPTER ONE

Megan snapped her bloody sterile gloves off and threw them in the nearest trashcan in disgust. She slipped out of her heavy lead apron and tore off her yellow gown and protective goggles. Ah, finally free to attack that itch on her nose that had been driving her nuts for the past fifteen minutes! She turned and stepped on the sink pedal and washed her hands vigorously beneath the soothing, warm water. Megan pulled out three sheets of paper towel and leaned back against the counter as the adrenal rush of the trauma room began to wane.

The trauma nurse reached over Megan's shoulder to dig into the cupboard for a bottle of sterile water. She closed the cupboard and smiled warmly at Megan.

"Excellent job, Dr. Summers. You're the best." Megan blushed slightly and smiled.

"Thanks, Sharon. I couldn't have done it without you." Megan watched Sharon pour the sterile water into the chest tube container while her residents finished suturing two chest tubes into their fourteen-year-old trauma patient's right side. Megan frowned at the strewn debris and bloody instruments that lay scattered throughout the trauma room. It looked like a glassed-in war zone rather than the center of a hustling E.R. department.

Megan looked over at the view box displaying her patient's collage of x-rays and frowned at the position of the bullets: one lodged in his brain and the destructive path of the two in his right upper chest.

Megan threw the paper towels in with her bloody gloves. She sighed and rubbed her weary neck. Would there ever be an end to senseless gang violence? An alarm sounded on the patient's cardiac monitor. Megan studied his vital signs continually displayed across the screen. She felt assured that he was finally stable enough to go to the operating room.

Megan watched Sharon and another nurse apply a dry dressing to the chest tube sites. The boy's right arm bore a huge

♥ TENDER HEART ♥

tattoo of the Virgin Mary. His last name was tattooed across his chest and the image of a blood-soaked hunting knife directly above his belly button. Megan shook her head at the contradictory messages of this young boy's tattoos.

Megan's handsome senior resident, Dean, stepped toward her and touched her arm warmly. "All we're waiting for is the orthopedic surgeon to come and assess his pelvic fracture and reset his fractured left arm. Then we can finally get him to the operating room," he said.

Megan frowned as she rubbed her throbbing temples. "I can't stay and wait for them, Dean. I'm already late for my first surgical case this morning and they've paged me three times to remind me of how tight our operating schedule is today. I don't need this added grief. And where the hell is Drake anyway? He told me thirty minutes ago that he would come in here and take over for me so I could get to the O.R." Megan released an exasperated sigh as she touched her resident's arm. "Dean, could you please stay with this patient until he's ready to come to the operating room?"

Dean smiled warmly at her. "Of course, Megan. Get to the O.R and I'll meet you up there once orthopedics are done."

Megan smiled brightly up at her senior resident. "I feel better knowing that you'll keep an eye on him for us. Meanwhile, I'll see if I can find Drake and kick him in the shins for not helping us out as he promised," Megan snapped. Dean's laughter boomed out as Megan headed through the trauma room doors.

"You go, girl," he shouted, as the doors swung back and forth.

Drake scrolled his signature across the final sheet and clipped his Mont Blanc pen to his lab coat pocket as Rebecca gathered all the sheets together.

♥ *TENDER HEART* ♥

"That's it, Drake. You're now the proud owner of your new dream home," Rebecca said, as she handed the papers to her assistant, Kyle.

Drake stepped forward and hugged her warmly. He leaned back and gently kissed Rebecca's forehead. "Thank you for everything, you two. I really mean that from the bottom of my heart," Drake said.

Holding on to his big, strong arms, Rebecca looked into her dear friend's sapphire blue eyes. His heart-stopping smile dissolved his trademark serious expression, highlighting his strong, dimpled chin, glowing tan and endearing sensitivity.

"Well, isn't this cozy," a voice called out. Drake, Rebecca, and Kyle turned to look across the nurse's station.

Megan walked stiffly towards them, fire in her eyes. She stepped within their intimate circle and took in the sight of this breathtakingly beautiful woman who reminded her instantly of Jaclyn Smith of the old show, "Charlie's Angels." Megan was enthralled by her aura of assertive dignity and exquisite amber, oval shaped eyes. Her thick, wavy chestnut brown hair cascaded down her slender back as her petite, artistic hands slid from Drake's and rested on the lapel of her onyx black, double breasted jacket. The matching thigh length skirt showcased graceful, shapely legs that instantly showered Megan in a quivering heat. Timidly tearing her eyes away from this mysterious, alluring stranger, she turned to Drake.

"It must be nice to have the time to socialize, Dr. Drake Darrow, when I have one kid in the trauma room waiting for me to remove a bullet from his brain and another patient lying on an operating room table waiting for me to remove his nasty brain tumor." Megan was seething with anger. But she stopped long enough to take a deep breath. "My O.R. schedule is packed, Drake, and you promised to take over for me in the trauma room so I could get out of there," Megan declared irritably.

Drake crossed his arms across his chest and tried hard not to smile at Megan's frustration. "Are you quite finished with your little temper tantrum, Dr. Summers?" Drake said sarcastically.

♥TENDER HEART♥

Megan's bright green eyes shot daggers right through him as she felt her anger bubbling in her stomach. "No! I'm not finished with my little temper tantrum, Dr Darrow. I needed your help in that trauma room. Instead, you're out here having a grand time while I'm trying to stop a fourteen-year-old boy from hemorrhaging to death from three different bullet wounds," Megan snapped.

Drake covered his mouth with one hand to conceal the smile he felt curling his lips as he watched this rare display of Megan's temper.

Megan looked over at a very still Kyle and Rebecca. She was captivated by the look of genuine concern in Rebecca's oval-shaped, amber eyes. Irritated by Drake's obvious enjoyment, Megan turned toward him.

"I don't have time for this shit, Drake. I expect that you'll supervise my trauma patient while I'm in the operating room. Do you think you could tear yourself away from your little social gathering and play trauma doctor?" Rebecca frowned at Megan's dripping sarcasm as she continued on her rampage. "Do you think you could do that for me, Dr. Darrow?"

Drake removed his hand from his mouth and frowned at Megan. "Yes, Ma'me! I promise to play E.R. physician slash trauma doc, and supervise your patient so you can take your toys and go play famous, highly acclaimed neurosurgeon," he ripped in.

Megan restrained herself from smacking Drake silly for his patronizing attitude; her anger burned at her stomach. "Good, then. I'm out of here. Thank you so much for your precious time, Dr. Darrow. I'm forever indebted to you." She shot him an icy glare and stormed toward the exit doors.

She heard Drake shout, "When you find your manners and social graces, Dr. Summers, do feel free to come back and apologize for your pathetic behavior!"

Megan stopped in the doorway long enough to give Drake a scowling look and gladly let the doors slam behind her.

♥ *TENDER HEART* ♥

Drake dropped his face into his hands and groaned in frustration, mumbling something that sounded like, "God, give me strength!"

Rebecca was mesmerized by Megan's stunning beauty and fiery personality. She stared at the swinging exit doors.

"Who was that?" she asked in amazement.

Drake smiled and shook his head. "That, my dear, is Dr. Megan Summers, neurosurgeon extraordinaire. She's one of the best neurosurgeons in the city and, I'd bet my life, one of the best in the country. She was highly recruited while she was in her residency in Boston. She's been here in Austin with us for two years now and has been an absolute pleasure to work with." Drake paused, "That is, until fifteen minutes ago."

They all laughed. Kyle rested his hand on Drake's shoulder and leaned closer. He stood an inch shorter than Drake's five foot ten inch frame and was built like a slender athlete. The blonde streaks through his auburn hair fell across his mischievous dark brown eyes as Drake admired his tailored, navy blue pinstripe suit.

"She's brilliant and gorgeous. I guess she has the right to be cranky once in a while," Kyle said in his lilting voice.

Drake frowned as he scratched his head and looked toward the trauma room. "That's just it . . . Megan and I instantly became friends the first time we met and she's always been a ray of sunshine. I've never seen her be cranky and I've seen her deal with a lot worse trauma's than this one," Drake said.

Rebecca looked back toward the exit doors. She clearly visualized Megan's fiery emerald green eyes and pillowy full lips as she vented with scorching anger. Regardless of her mood, her five-foot-eight inch frame moved through those doors with the grace of a dancer. She impressed Rebecca as a woman without fear of expressing her anger or passions.

"Our presence obviously pulled you away from your work, Drake. I'm sorry we caused you this stress. It's just that we needed your signatures today to get all your paperwork processed on time," she explained.

♥ TENDER HEART ♥

Drake smiled at Rebecca's apologetic expression, reached forward and gently touched her chin. "You're not responsible for what happened here, Rebecca. I was pulled away from the trauma room to do ten different things before you guys arrived, so don't feel responsible for Megan's fury. I'm the one that procrastinated on getting these forms signed and you guys have been kind enough to come out to the hospital so we can get this done. If anyone should be apologizing, it's Megan. I feel badly that I couldn't get back to the trauma room sooner but she knew I would get back to help her as soon as I could. Besides, she's outstanding in her field. I'm sure it's something other than work that's bothering her."

Rebecca felt an unusually warm concern for this captivating stranger.

The beeping of Kyle's pager broke into all their thoughts. He looked down at the display. "That's the office. We should probably go, Beck." Kyle extended his hand toward Drake and broke into his boyishly handsome smile. "Thanks for your time, Doc. I really enjoyed the show."

They all laughed as Rebecca hugged Drake warmly. "I'll have the final drafts done this afternoon, Drake. See you at five o'clock at our usual spot?"

Drake smiled and hugged her again. "Five o'clock it is. See you then."

"I'll probably be there earlier catching up on some paperwork, so just get there when you can, Drake," Rebecca said.

Kyle and Rebecca stepped towards the automatic doors.

Rebecca stopped and turned back towards Drake with an impish smile.

"Drake. When you talk to Dr. Megan Summers again, tell her she can hang her stethoscope on my bedpost anytime." Drake and Kyle burst into laughter.

"Forget it, Rebecca. I'll let you tell her that one yourself," Drake chuckled.

♥ *TENDER HEART* ♥

They all laughed as Rebecca blew Drake a kiss and followed Kyle out through the automatic doors.

Rebecca's body moved automatically forward but her mind was still inside that emergency room. She barely heard Kyle scream her name as he grabbed her by her slender waist and pulled her out of the way of a blaring, incoming ambulance. He caught his breath, held Rebecca by her shoulders and looked into her startled eyes.

"Girlfriend, will you please get your mind off that Dr. Megan Summers, and look where you're walking!"

Rebecca gave Kyle a guilty look and whispered, "Sorry."

He shook his head and laughed. "God, Beck. Your lesbian lust almost got you splattered all over this entrance way. How would you like me to explain that one to the grumpy Dr. Megan Summers?" Kyle started into his Nathan Lane impersonation: "Sorry, Dr. Megan, but you sent her into such a hormonal tizzy that she never even saw the ambulance coming. However, she wanted me to tell you that she thinks you're incredibly gorgeous and would love to come back in her next life as your stethoscope." They both burst into laughter as Rebecca playfully swatted Kyle's arm.

"Please don't tell me I was that obvious?" Rebecca said, defensively.

Kyle released a shocked laugh and gently took Rebecca's hand. "Girlfriend, the energy between you two was enough to propel the next space shuttle to Pluto and back." Rebecca burst into laughter as Kyle led her safely across the parking lot and into her silver Jaguar.

Megan entered the E.R. staff lounge and gently closed the door behind her. She looked across the room and saw Drake slumped into the couch with his Doc Martens-clad feet up on the coffee table, his eyes peacefully closed. His first reprieve today, a momentary escape from the rigors of emergency medicine that

♥ *TENDER HEART* ♥

he does so well. Megan tiptoed across the room and gently sat down on the coffee table, beside Drake's feet. The table creaked in protest. Drake slowly opened one eye. A smile lit up his face as Megan handed him an ice-cold can of Coke.

"A peace offering," she said, sheepishly.

Wordlessly, Drake cracked open the tab, taking a long, leisurely drink without taking his eyes off Megan's face. He sat up tall, set the soda on the coffee table, and slid over slightly to sit directly in front of Megan's apologetic smile. Drake rested his hands on Megan's knees and leaned forward, beaming into her with his loving, sapphire blue eyes.

"Peace offering accepted. Now, what the hell was that all about this morning, Dr. Summers? I've never seen you lose your cool like that before."

Megan dropped her face in embarrassment as her voice fell to a whisper. "I'm sorry, Drake. I was in a real bitchy mood and I didn't mean to take it all out on you."

Drake gently touched Megan's chin and raised her face to meet his eyes.

"I expected my knight in shining armor to come save me from that depressing trauma and he never showed up," Megan said softly.

Drake couldn't help but smile at his dear friend. "I'm sorry I didn't get you out of that trauma room sooner, Megan. I was saddened to hear that the kid died a few hours after surgery. We both know that his chances of survival were slim but if anybody was going to give him the best chance he could get it was you, Meg." Megan looked down at her hands in defeat.

He gently touched her chin and raised her eyes to meet his. "Somehow, I think that there's something else bothering you, Meg. It takes a lot more than a hectic day at the office to get you down." Megan felt embraced by the warmth of their friendship. She smiled and took a sip of Drake's Coke.

"It's just been a shitty day from the word 'go.' I was so tired when I went to bed last night that I forgot to set my alarm," Megan said.

♥ *TENDER HEART* ♥

Drake groaned as Megan continued.

"Exactly! My residents paged me an hour after I usually get here to ask me where the heck I was. Bed was not a good answer when they'd been to six trauma calls during the night and were dying to get rounds finished so they could get home to bed."

Drake laughed playfully at Megan's dilemma as he saw the scowl on her face.

"That's only the beginning, Drake. I'm already an hour and a half late as I zip into my parking spot and drive over a damn broken beer bottle and flatten both tires on the passenger side."

Drake dropped back onto the couch and burst into laughter.

Megan was indignant as she smacked his leg. "None of this is very funny, Drake. It all put me in a very pissy mood today."

Drake dried his eyes and leaned forward, resting his hands on Megan's knees. "You're right, Meg. It's not funny."

Megan watched with disgust as Drake rolled back onto the couch in a fit of laughter. Megan reached for the nearest magazine and proceeded to smack Drake with it about the head and shoulders till he seized the magazine from her and threw it on the floor. He forcefully grabbed her wrists, pulled her onto the couch beside him, and tickled her until she burst into laughter. Megan begged for mercy as Drake leaned back into the couch and let her catch her breath.

Megan slowly sat up and slid closer to Drake, resting her head on his shoulder as they both kicked their feet up on the coffee table. Drake wrapped his arm around Megan's shoulders as he watched a smile curl the corners of her mouth.

"Thanks, Drake. I needed that laugh."

Drake kissed the top of her chestnut brown head and held her close. "You're welcome. What are friends for?" He watched Megan play with a button on her lab coat and felt her body relax. "I'm sorry about everything that happened to you this morning. Do you have a ride home?" he asked.

Megan smiled and turned to face her dear friend. "I had two new tires put on my Expedition this morning, so I'm all set. Thanks for asking, Drake."

♥ TENDER HEART ♥

Drake watched Megan closely, wanting to understand her mood. "What else is bothering you then, Meg? Is it girl trouble?"

Megan laughed softly as she gave Drake a warm, shy look. "I don't have a girl to have girl trouble. You know that, Drake."

Drake smiled and reached for his can of soda, turning to Megan with a playful twinkle in his eyes. "Just thought I'd ask. Do you want me to rent you a girl to get you out of this pissy mood?"

Megan burst into laughter and playfully swatted Drake's knee. "No, thanks. I'll find my own girl, thank you very much," she said defensively.

Drake finished another sip of soda and handed the can to Megan. "All right, then. But don't say I didn't offer to help."

They smiled warmly at each other as Megan's thoughts floated to Drake's captivating female friend. She slowly twisted the tab around on the Coke and looked up into Drake's eyes. "I was really nasty to you in front of your friends, Drake. I'm really sorry. They must have thought I was a real bitch."

Drake laughed, remembering their comments on Megan's behavior. "No, neither one of them called you a bitch. However, they had some very interesting opinions about you that I'm sure they'll share with you themselves some day," he said, with an impish grin.

Megan gave him a questioning look and had to bite her lip to keep from asking Drake what exactly that beautiful woman had to say about her.

"I would have introduced you if you hadn't been in such a foul mood and stopped running off at the mouth," Drake said seriously. Megan dropped her eyes in quiet embarrassment. "Rebecca's my real estate agent. Remember I told you I had purchased a Victorian home that was newly renovated?" Drake had Megan's complete and undivided attention as she nodded her head yes.

"Rebecca's company buys these old homes and refurbishes them for resale. She's been doing this for about fifteen years now. My ex-wife, Karen, and I bought our first home from her

♥ *TENDER HEART* ♥

ten years ago. Since my divorce last year I've been looking to buy a new home. One day Rebecca called me and said, 'Drake, there's a house I want you to see that has your male ego written all over it.'" They both laughed as Drake's bright eyes danced with excitement.

"It has the coolest two-car garage, separate tool shed, woodworking shop attached to the garage, pool, outdoor change hut, greenhouse and huge vegetable garden. This place is my retirement dream home."

Megan smiled at his happiness. "Is there a house that goes with all these boy toys that you're so in love with?" she said playfully.

Drake laughed his deep, resounding laugh. "Oh yeah. Did I forget to mention the house? It's great too."

Megan smiled at Drake's excitement. "I'm so happy you've found the house of your dreams, Drake. I would love to see it, but don't plan on retiring too soon, mister. I need you around for at least another twenty years."

Drake smiled sweetly and hugged Megan close. "That's probably how much longer you and I will be busting our butts to try and save all these young trauma patients," he said sadly.

Megan basked in Drake's warmth as she mustered the courage to ask her next question. "Drake, why haven't you introduced me to Rebecca before? And who was the gentleman with her this morning? They seemed really close."

Drake listened to Megan's shy, subtle questions and remembered Rebecca's comment of where Megan could hang her stethoscope. "Rebecca's kept herself really busy lately. We've only seen each other a few times since you and I met, Meg. You've both had a lot going on in your personal lives. I was waiting for the right time to introduce you two, but it looks like fate has taken charge." Drake held Megan close. "Rebecca is very special to me and we've been friends since that first house," he explained. His eyes saddened as he looked deeply into hers. "Rebecca's life hasn't been easy, especially the past five years. She has such a strong spirit and has kept going during times that

♥ TENDER HEART ♥

would have devastated most people. Because she's endured so much and had to be so strong, it's hard to be able to help that woman. She can be such a stubborn pain in the ass at times."

Megan was completely engrossed in Drake's story of this interesting woman's life, surprised by her own need to know everything about that beautiful woman with the captivating amber eyes.

"The gentleman with Rebecca this morning was Kyle, her assistant. They've worked closely together since she started her company fifteen years ago." Drake laughed softly as he continued. "She calls him her Superman because he does such a great job of keeping everything in order for her. He calls himself her 'slave.'"

They both laughed softly. Drake could see the many questions in Megan's eyes. He smiled and leaned closer to Megan.

"Rebecca and Kyle are extremely close, and they'd do anything for each other. But that's as far as it goes between them. Kyle's gay. He's been with the same partner for five years now. Kyle's a great guy and so protective of Rebecca. She always said she'd be lost without him," Drake explained.

"I wasn't asking any personal questions about them, Drake. I was just wondering who they were," Megan said, softly.

Drake looked into Megan's eyes. "Oh, sure, inquiring minds want to know," he teased.

They both laughed as Megan lowered her eyes and admitted shyly, "I behaved very badly in front of them, Drake. I must have made them feel very uncomfortable as I was ranting and raving." Megan pulled at the button on her lab coat. "Drake, next time you see them will you tell them how sorry I am?"

Drake laughed and reached for his Coke in Megan's hand. "Forget it. I'm not doing your dirty work for you."

Megan gave him a surprised look as Drake took a swallow of his Coke and looked at his watch. "I'm supposed to meet Rebecca at the Java Cafe at five o'clock to sign the final draft of my ownership papers. It's three-thirty now. She said she'd be

♥ *TENDER HEART* ♥

there early getting caught up on some of her paperwork. Why don't you go and see if she's there and apologize yourself?"

♥ *TENDER HEART* ♥

♥ *TENDER HEART* ♥
CHAPTER TWO

Megan walked into the Java Cafe and was surprised at how busy it was at four o'clock in the afternoon. She stepped inside the doorway and was blanketed by the rich aroma of fresh coffee. Megan scanned the crowded tables and suddenly felt her heart race as she saw her. Rebecca was sitting at a table alone, deeply engrossed in writing notes on a legal pad of paper with a gold fountain pen. Her thick, rich, brown hair flowed beautifully beyond her shoulders, delicate beneath her cream silk blouse. Megan watched her as Rebecca set down her pen and removed her glasses. She was about to sip her coffee when their eyes met, communicating a profound intensity that sent both their pulses racing. Megan felt an incredible heat coursing through her veins as she smiled and struggled to regain her composure. She finally took a deep breath and headed toward the counter to order herself an iced mocha.

As she raised her coffee cup to her lips, Rebecca's eyes were riveted on Megan. She inhaled the rich, freshly ground aroma of the hot coffee and watched the tall, elegant woman standing with her back to her, awaiting her coffee. Rebecca admired her long, thick wavy brown hair, her sensual essence. Rebecca's eyes roamed freely over the rich, gray suede jacket that accentuated Megan's slender, athletic frame, and the black dress slacks that hinted at endless shapely legs. Rebecca took another sip of her strong coffee as she continued to watch Megan's every movement. Megan paid for her coffee and walked toward the counter of creams and sugars to search for a napkin. Megan stopped as she heard a sultry voice over her shoulder.

"Are you looking for these?" Megan turned as Rebecca offered her several napkins. Their eyes met with instant warmth and intrigue.

"Yes, I am. So you're the napkin thief around here," Megan accused playfully.

♥ TENDER HEART ♥

Both women smiled as Rebecca crossed her arms across her chest and leaned her hip against the counter. "Yes, I am. But I thought I'd better confess my sin and share some with you before you have another temper tantrum on me. I don't think I can handle that twice in one day," Rebecca stated strongly.

Megan looked down at her iced mocha and blushed a deep crimson red, embarrassed by her behavior earlier.

Rebecca inhaled sharply as she marveled at this woman's sensitivity and shyness.

Megan took a deep breath and looked into Rebecca's golden amber eyes. "I'm sorry about my temper tantrum this morning. I behaved pretty badly and the look in your eyes told me how unimpressed you were."

Rebecca forced herself to breathe as she thought; this gorgeous woman has no idea how impressed I truly am. Lost in Megan's beautiful green eyes, Rebecca reached forward and touched Megan's elbow, sending searing heat cascading through her entire being.

"There's nothing that impresses me more than hearing a woman voice her concerns and stand up for herself and what she believes in. I was unimpressed, Dr. Summers, because you would not shut up long enough for me to introduce myself." Megan laughed softly as Rebecca extended her hand. "Hi. I'm Rebecca Rhodes, and it's a pleasure to see you in a much friendlier mood."

Megan was floating in the warm pools of Rebecca's eyes as she luxuriated in the intense contact of her soft hand. Megan's smile danced across her eyes and warmed Rebecca's heart as she shook her hand firmly.

"Hello, Rebecca Rhodes. I'm Megan. You've obviously been filled in on the doctor part already. I hope Drake didn't say too many nasty things about me."

Rebecca laughed sweetly and hesitantly released Megan's soft, strong hand. "Let me see now, he called you neurosurgeon extraordinaire, outstanding in your field, a dear friend, and a pleasure to work with and, oh yes, a ray of sunshine."

♥ TENDER HEART ♥

Megan burst into gentle laughter as Rebecca accurately recounted Drake's every word. "Gee whiz! I should be mean to Drake more often so he'll continue to say such amazing things about me," Megan declared.

They both burst into laughter as Rebecca gently touched Megan's wrist. Megan's arm tingled and her heart skipped several beats as Rebecca motioned to her table.

"Would you care to join me, Megan, or are you meeting someone?" Rebecca found herself acutely aware of every gentle curve of this woman's sensuous lips and the velvet inflection of her deep, sexy voice.

"Actually, I had asked Drake to apologize to you for my bad behavior this morning. He flatly refused and told me that you'd be here, so I came looking for you." Rebecca was touched and smiled at the apology.

"So, you tried to hire a henchman to deliver your apology, did you?"

Megan blushed crimson red as she looked away from Rebecca and twirled the straw in her drink. "Yes, I did, but he basically told me to take a flying leap, so I figured I might as well bite the bullet and come apologize myself."

Rebecca's smile sent Megan's heart racing as she rested her hand on Megan's lower back, surrounding Megan in an incredible wave of warmth.

"I'm really glad you came to find me yourself, Dr. Megan Summers. You get a gold star for your honorable behavior." Megan couldn't stop smiling at this lovely woman's charming personality.

Rebecca guided Megan to her table by her elbow and gently sat down. She watched as Megan gracefully slipped out of her elegant suede jacket and draped it neatly across the back of her chair. She watched the muscles ripple across Megan's shoulders as her beautiful white dress shirt moved fluidly against her. Megan sat, then propped one foot on the rung beneath Rebecca's chair.

♥ *TENDER HEART* ♥

Rebecca forced her thoughts from the elegant frame beneath that stylish top. Rebecca watched Megan take a sip of her iced coffee and tried her best not to stare at those sensuous lips.

"What are you drinking?" Rebecca said, curiously.

Megan smiled at the intense look in those amber eyes. "It's an iced mocha. Have you ever tasted one?" Megan asked.

"No, actually. I've always been a big fan of hot coffee. I've never tried any of the iced coffees. Do you mind if I try a sip of yours?"

Megan placed her drink on a napkin and slid it directly in front of Rebecca. "Please, be my guest. It's such a smooth, refreshing drink compared to hot coffee, but still gives you the caffeine kick."

Rebecca smiled as she picked up the drink and took a sip. Rebecca's face lit up. "Wow! That's delicious. You're right, Megan. It's great."

Megan watched Rebecca take another sip, then another. "Hey, I thought you just asked for a sip, if I recall correctly," Megan complained.

Rebecca smiled at Megan's playful pout as she moved the drink beyond Megan's reach. "After the way you screamed at us today, the least you can do is share half of your drink with me," Rebecca scolded. Megan dramatically leaned back in her chair and groaned.

Rebecca burst into infectious giggles and continued to enjoy their iced mocha.

Megan savored the opportunity to watch Rebecca as she sipped on their drink. Her ash brown hair silhouetted the delicate features of her oval, amber eyes and highlighted her olive skin. Megan guessed she must be five-foot four inches tall with shapely feminine curves challenging Megan to draw her eyes away from Rebecca's. Megan finally cleared her throat and asked, "Are you going to torment me about my ten minutes of seething anger?"

Rebecca held the straw between her perfect white teeth and grinned. "I sure am."

♥ *TENDER HEART* ♥

Megan dropped her head onto her arm in defeat.

Rebecca basked in their intense warmth and restrained herself from reaching out and caressing this lovely creature's rich hair. Sipping the iced mocha, she watched Megan sit back in her chair and pout as her drink faded away. Rebecca gave Megan a sensuous smile; she ached to ease the sadness in that pouting lower lip.

"I'd love to hear about your day today, Dr. Megan Summers, and what it was that upset you so much this morning." Rebecca finished half of their drink and gently placed the tall glass in Megan's soft hand.

Megan gave her a joyous smile and took a big sip. She put the drink down and took a deep breath before telling Rebecca about her stressful morning and the death of her fourteen-year-old trauma patient.

As Megan finished her story, Rebecca rested her elbows on the table and leaned closer. "I'm so sorry about your patient, Megan. It must be devastating for you to work so hard to save their young lives, only to lose a few inevitably." Megan's eyes clouded with unmitigated pain and loss. "You had a terrible morning, Megan. You had a legitimate excuse to blow a fuse. However, I would prefer not to be the target of that temper ever again, young lady," Rebecca warned.

Megan blushed and played with the straw in her drink. "Thank you for understanding. Drake laughed when I told him my story."

Rebecca smiled and shook her head. "What did you expect, Megan? He's a man. I've never understood men and I have given up trying." They laughed warmly together as Rebecca leaned slightly closer, so close that Megan felt embraced by her subtle, intoxicating perfume. "Don't get me wrong, Megan. I love Drake dearly, but I think that men have a very warped sense of humor."

Megan smiled at the sparkle in Rebecca's eyes. "I couldn't agree with you more," she chuckled. Megan felt herself wanting to lean forward and be closer to this fascinating woman. "Drake has a very special place in his heart for you," Megan said,

♥ *TENDER HEART* ♥

luxuriating in the soft warmth in Rebecca's eyes. "He told me all about his new house. He's as excited as a kid on Christmas Eve. I think he's more excited about all the boy toys than the house itself."

Rebecca burst into laughter. "That's exactly what they are, Megan. Boy toys. I firmly believe that if men spent as much time with their partners as they do in their garages and woodworking shops then we would have a lot happier relationships out there."

"I couldn't agree with you more. Unfortunately people don't realize how precious time is with the ones you love," Megan said sadly.

Rebecca watched sadness settle on Megan's face as she twirled the remaining ice in her drink.

Megan looked back into Rebecca's loving eyes and said softly, "I've learned to appreciate the time that I share with the people I care about." She cleared her throat and quickly changed the subject to Rebecca's real estate business.

Rebecca noted the quick change in Megan's reaction and filed it away for later discussion. They became completely engrossed in a conversation about their respective careers.

Megan was enthralled by Rebecca's passion for her work and her deep desire to help people find their dream homes.

"Does your home fill all your dreams, Dr. Summers?"

Megan smiled as she looked down at the table and played with the corner of her napkin. "I've always dreamt about a big rock garden in my backyard with a fountain running through it and a huge pond at the base that I could fill with big, fat, happy goldfish," she said. Megan was momentarily lost in thought. "I can picture lounge chairs and a patio table around this pond where I can sit and watch the goldfish's gentle, random movement, and hide from the real world for a while."

Rebecca was enchanted by Megan's dream. She reached toward her and rested her hand on her arm. "What's stopped you from fulfilling your dream and putting that rock garden and pond in your backyard? Please don't tell me a man?" Rebecca suggested.

♥ TENDER HEART ♥

Megan looked away from Rebecca's intense, amber eyes that seemed to envelope her soul. "No, not a man."

Rebecca watched as clouds of sadness darkened Megan's beautiful eyes.

"I had a relationship that ended very badly a year ago. Ever since then my house has never felt the same. I feel restless and out of place in my own home," Megan explained.

Rebecca watched a deep frown crease Megan's forehead as her painful memories played over her face.

"Too many memories, I guess. I keep telling myself that I need to sell my house and start all over again so that I can get on with my life. Unfortunately, my way of dealing with those memories is to throw myself into my work. I've come to sadly realize that my work does not dissolve my pain. Every night I still have to return to this house that continually reminds me of the person I used to come home to," Megan whispered.

Rebecca ached to make the sadness in Megan's eyes disappear. She squeezed her arm and gently wiped away the single tear on Megan's cheek.

Megan closed her moist eyes and bit her lower lip in a feeble attempt to curb the tears straining to burst forth. The gentle caress of Rebecca's thumb across Megan's moist cheek instantly dissolved her emotional self-control. She struggled to regain her composure by taking a deep, emotional breath. Megan slowly opened her eyes and looked into Rebecca's amber eyes, all warmth and understanding.

Rebecca took a tissue and dried Megan's tears. The intensity between them escalated and crackled like explosive static as Rebecca longed to hold her close.

Megan was the first to look away. She looked down at Rebecca's hand on her arm and gently traced each finger.

Rebecca closed her eyes and fought to hold herself back from leaning into this woman and kissing her passionately as Megan's touch ignited every cell in her body. Rebecca slowly opened her eyes to see Megan watching her; their eyes met in an intimate, sensitive dance.

♥ TENDER HEART ♥

Megan slowly leaned closer to Rebecca, her heart pounding against her chest. "If you don't have any plans for tomorrow night, I would really like to make dinner for you at my place. I'd like to see you again and prove to you that I'm not the ill-tempered woman that you saw this morning," Megan said. "I promise not to throw another temper tantrum or any pots and pans."

Rebecca laughed sweetly and swallowed hard, trying to control her burning desire. She leaned back slightly to pull away from this woman's magnetic sensuality. "I would love to join you for dinner tomorrow night, Dr. Summers," Rebecca said, her voice strained. She looked away from Megan's incredible green eyes momentarily and tried to calm the effect they had on her heart. "I do believe you've already proven that you can be wonderful company," she added. Rebecca playfully looped her finger under the collar of Megan's top and pulled her close. "But don't you dare ever show me that temper again, Dr. Megan Summers. Otherwise, I'll build that goldfish pond for you and soak your temper in it."

They both laughed as Megan dramatically feigned a look of terror. "Don't do that! You'll kill all the goldfish," Megan said breathlessly.

Rebecca burst into laughter.

Megan felt completely enchanted by this breathtaking woman.

Rebecca moved her hand across the table and slid her pad of paper and fountain pen slowly toward Megan. Megan stared at them with a questioning look in her bright eyes.

"Directions. To your house, please," Rebecca said, sweetly.

Megan laughed at herself and the complete control that Rebecca had over her emotions as she blushed. "Oh, yeah," Megan said, as she took the beautiful fountain pen and asked where Rebecca lived and the location of her office, then drew her directions from both places. Rebecca marveled at her smooth, gentle strokes as she watched her strong feminine hands flow over the paper.

♥ *TENDER HEART* ♥

They went over the map together, exchanged phone and pager numbers, and decided on a time for dinner.

Megan leaned back in her chair and looked at Rebecca's bright, amber eyes. "Now, Ms. Rebecca Rhodes, tell me about your busy day," Megan said, as she basked in the sound of Rebecca's sweet, sultry voice. They talked as easily as two friends who have known each other forever.

♥♥♥♥♥♥♥♥♥♥

Drake walked toward their table with a huge smile on his face. "It's so nice to see my two favorite women getting along so well," he said.

Rebecca and Megan smiled warmly as Drake stood between them and leaned forward to kiss them both.

Drake looked down at their empty cups. "Can I get you lovely ladies another coffee? Hot or cold?" Both women politely declined as Drake bought himself a hot cup of coffee and sat down at their table.

Rebecca moved her papers out of his way and gave him a smile. "Is it five o'clock already?"

Drake took a sip of his steaming coffee and smiled at them both. "Five-thirty actually. Time flies when you're having fun," he said.

Megan looked into Rebecca's warm eyes. "It sure does," she whispered.

Drake set his coffee down. "I'm so glad you two had a chance to meet and spend some time together. But where's Kyle? I expected to see him here as well," he said.

Rebecca smiled and looked into Drake's warm, blue eyes. "Kyle and Scotty." Rebecca paused and looked at Megan. "Scotty is Kyle's lover. They're headed downtown to the symphony tonight," Rebecca explained.

Drake tilted his head and looked at Rebecca. "You gave up your symphony tickets to finish this paperwork with me, didn't you?"

♥ TENDER HEART ♥

Rebecca picked up her fountain pen and fiddled with the cap. "Yes, I did. Somebody had to finish all this paperwork with you tonight and Kyle's been run ragged all week. I felt he deserved a break." Rebecca laughed softly. She looked up into Megan and Drake's eyes. "After all, I have to make sure my Superman gets a balanced diet of work and play. Otherwise, he gives me his Nathan Lane-whining, whimpering routine for days and complains of being unfairly treated. He's even threatened to report me to the Labor Relations Board and Human Rights Commission for assistant abuse. He can be such a nagging wife sometimes," Rebecca revealed as she wrinkled her tiny nose.

They all burst into laughter as Drake touched Rebecca's arm warmly. "Any regrets at being the one left behind tonight?" he said.

Rebecca gave Drake a magnificent smile and looked over at Megan's beautiful eyes. "Not one," she announced happily.

Megan smiled deeply as she leaned back in her chair and struggled to look away from Rebecca's mesmerizing eyes. She nervously cleared her throat and tried desperately to control the swell of emotions in her chest.

"That was a very loving thing you did, Rebecca. You gave Scotty and Kyle your symphony tickets and allowed them to have their evening together," Megan said emotionally.

Rebecca could feel Megan's intensity, and remembered what she had said about valuing time with the people she cared about. She tilted her head toward her. "Do you enjoy classical music, Megan?" she asked.

Megan's smile lit up Rebecca's heart as Drake laughed. "Are you kidding? Every time I walk into this woman's office I feel like I've stepped into an Itzhak Perlman concert," he filled in.

Megan laughed softly as Rebecca was thrilled to hear that they enjoy a similar taste in music. Megan looked lovingly into Rebecca's amber eyes and smiled. "Does that answer your question?"

Rebecca beamed her a breathtaking smile. "It sure does," Rebecca said.

♥ TENDER HEART ♥

Megan hesitantly looked down at her gold watch. Sliding her chair back, she looked from Drake to Rebecca. "I should go and let you guys finish your business." Megan stood and slipped her arms into her suede jacket.

"Don't feel you have to leave, Meg," Drake said.

"You're welcome to stay, Megan," Rebecca added urgently.

Megan smiled at them both warmly and carefully tucked her chair back in. "I would love to stay with you both but I'm meeting someone for dinner."

Rebecca's heart dropped; her face was filled with disappointment. Drake smiled and leaned back, crossing his arms across his chest. "Oh, I see. You're shunning us for a hot date. So, tell us Meg, what's her name?" he teased.

Megan blushed, touched by Rebecca's obvious disappointment. "She's someone very special to me, Drake, and that's all I'm going to tell you. The rest I'm going to leave to your overactive imagination."

Drake laughed as he rose from his chair and took Megan into his arms, hugging her warmly.

Drake took his seat as Megan stepped toward Rebecca and took her hand, guiding her to her feet. Their eyes locked in their own, intimate connection as Megan held both Rebecca's hands softly in her own. "Thank you for the opportunity to apologize, and thanks for drinking half of my iced mocha on me."

Rebecca laughed as she squeezed Megan's hands gently. "Thank you for delivering the apology in person and introducing me to that delicious drink of yours. Most of all, thank you for the opportunity to get to know you." They stood staring into each other's intense eyes, neither one wanting this beautiful moment to end.

"If your date has a hard time handling your temper, just come back here and I'll be glad to straighten you out," Rebecca stated playfully.

They both laughed as Drake added, "Too late for that, Rebecca. Megan's never been straight a day in her life."

♥ TENDER HEART ♥

Megan blushed as Rebecca leaned intimately close. "I hope that wasn't supposed to be a secret?" she whispered.

Megan laughed and felt overwhelmed by this woman's close proximity as she leaned against her ear. "I hoped you had figured it out by now," Megan whispered seductively.

Unable to control her intense desire to touch this woman any longer, Rebecca leaned her cheek against Megan's and took her in her arms.

Rebecca's gentle, throaty moan echoed throughout Megan's soul, igniting her passion. Megan's hands caressed Rebecca's lower back as Rebecca held her close; luxuriating in the warmth of her slender, firm body.

Rebecca tilted her head and leaned her forehead against Megan's soft cheek. "Have a wonderful date," Rebecca whispered, half-heartedly.

Megan smiled at the look on Rebecca's face and playfully toyed with her emotions. "I definitely will. Thank you."

Rebecca looked sadly down at their entwined hands, and rubbed her thumbs lightly across the back of Megan's hands. "I look forward to seeing you tomorrow night," she whispered. They hesitantly pulled away.

Megan's smile completely tilted Rebecca's world. "I certainly look forward to seeing you tomorrow night, Rebecca Rhodes." Megan gently traced her finger along Rebecca's soft cheek and watched the passion cloud her amber eyes as Megan's desire spun out of control. Megan took a deep breath and slowly stepped back.

"Good night," she said, as she headed toward the exit door of the cafe. She stopped momentarily in the doorway and gave Rebecca a seductive wink, then left with a gentle wave of her hand.

Rebecca remained standing after Megan had left, staring at the door as if waiting for her to return. Drake laughed and leaned toward her, taking her by the arm and guiding her back into her chair.

♥ TENDER HEART ♥

She finally looked at Drake with huge, astounded eyes. "She's incredible, Drake. She knocks my socks off."

Drake burst into laughter and leaned forward on the table. "With that hug you both just shared, I'm sure she would like to remove more than just your socks," he confirmed.

Rebecca blushed and stared toward the exit door as visions of the beautiful Dr. Summers swam before her eyes; she could see Megan's full lips smile seductively before her.

Drake took another sip of his coffee, thrilled for what could possibly be. He set his cup down and leaned closer to Rebecca. Gently, he touched her chin, guiding her face toward him. "You're both incredible women, Rebecca. Listen to your heart and go for the happiness that you finally deserve."

Rebecca slipped her hand into Drake's and held it tight as he wiped away the tears tumbling onto her cheeks.

♥♥♥♥♥♥♥♥♥♥

Rebecca threw her paperback book on the couch beside her, giving up on trying to absorb what she was reading. She ran her fingers through her hair and stared off through her bay window for the hundredth time. Her mind zoomed in several aimless directions like an erratic pinball. She curled her feet under her and reached for her glass of white wine. The telephone startled her. Who would be calling her at ten-thirty at night? She reached for the receiver with her left hand. Rebecca set down her wine glass as she answered softly, "Hello?"

Rebecca's heart thudded against her chest.

"Good evening, Ms. Rebecca Rhodes. I hope I didn't wake you."

Rebecca felt her smile could light up the entire house as she hugged the phone close and felt her entire body respond to the deep, sexy voice that had consumed her every thought since the Java Cafe.

"No, you didn't wake me, Dr. Megan Summers. I've been incredibly awake since the moment I met you this morning,"

♥ *TENDER HEART* ♥

Rebecca said with excitement. "I'm thrilled to hear your voice, Megan."

Rebecca sensed Megan's illuminating smile curl her full lips as Rebecca hugged the phone.

"How was your date this evening?" Rebecca asked, hesitantly.

Rebecca felt consumed by a selfish jealousy that she knew she had no right to feel. She knew Megan was toying with her emotions as she waited an eternity to reply.

"Fabulous! Do you want to hear all about it?"

Rebecca frowned at Megan's enthusiasm; all she felt was disappointment. "Not really," she said dejectedly.

Megan burst into playful laughter. "You're such an honest woman, Rebecca Rhodes. Your personality warms me inside out and I like that."

Rebecca couldn't help but smile.

Megan decided to put Rebecca's mind at ease. "It's not what you think, Rebecca, so stop sounding so adorably sad. The woman I went out to dinner with tonight happens to be someone that I love very dearly. She's beautiful, bright, witty, charming and also happens to be my younger sister."

Rebecca laughed in surprise and felt overwhelmed with relief. "Your sister! Why didn't you tell me at the cafe you were going out to dinner with your sister? You could have saved me a lot of grief, Megan Summers, and you know it," she said.

Megan's laughter filled Rebecca's heart. "You never asked," Megan offered, tauntingly.

Rebecca released an exasperated breath and rolled her eyes. "Megan Summers, you're such an imp! You purposefully tormented me with your date tonight." Rebecca could hear Megan laughing. She swung her legs off her white leather couch. "Let me tell you about my evening, Dr. Summers. I haven't been able to get one thing done because my mind is completely consumed by thoughts of you. I've been sitting here on my couch in front of a warm fire with a glass of wine and my book and read the same damn page ten times and I have no idea what I've read."

Megan laughed softly, feeling encompassed by Rebecca's passion. "You've been equally distracting this evening, my friend. My sister, Madison, was telling me about her day and when I began to ask her a question I called her Rebecca." Megan chuckled. "That went over really well. She threw her napkin at me and said, 'Who the hell is Rebecca?'"

Rebecca laughed as she felt Megan's embarrassment.

"We spent the rest of the evening talking about you and the whole time I was wishing you were with us."

Rebecca was captivated by Megan's tender warmth. "I wish I'd been there too," she said softly.

They both hesitated.

Megan held the phone close as constricting warmth burned in her chest. Rebecca awakened a surge of desire and want so intense like Megan had not experienced in a long time. "That warm fire and glass of wine sound very romantic," Megan said.

Rebecca smiled deeply and leaned back into the couch. "It would be if you were here," she whispered.

Megan groaned. "Rebecca, I'm going to hang up on you if you don't stop driving me crazy like this," she said.

Rebecca laughed as she enjoyed Megan' frustration. "Drive you crazy! Who's the one that made me believe she was on some hot date and then dares to call me this late at night with that sweet, sexy voice that melts me instantly."

"I miss you," Megan whispered.

Those words catapulted their way throughout Rebecca's heart and brought tears to her eyes. "I miss you too, Megan," she said intensely.

Rebecca gently wiped at her eyes. "Tell me about your sister, Madison."

Megan took a deep breath and tried to control her racing heart. "Madison is a sweetheart. She's twenty-eight years old, ten years younger than me. Our father is an airline pilot and our mother is an entertainment director for a large hotel chain. Kids

♥ *TENDER HEART* ♥

were definitely my father's idea and not my mother's," Megan said.

"What do you mean?" Rebecca asked.

Megan explained, "My mother is a dedicated, glamorous, career woman. She just had kids to please my father. With their careers taking them away from home most of the time, Madison and I were raised by nannies and each other. We never had a so-called 'family life,' we only had each other. We've always been extremely close and I love her very much."

Rebecca felt Megan's profound love for her sister. "What does Madison do for a living?" Rebecca asked.

"She's an incredible architect. Madison and her lover, Shawna, recently moved into the new house she designed. They hated the color of their bedroom so they had it repainted this week. They've been staying with me because Madison is allergic to the smell of paint and perfumes."

"Are they still there with you?"

"Yes, they are. They think they'll go back home the day after tomorrow. They went to bed around ten o'clock and I've been sitting on my back deck pretending to watch goldfish swim around in my imaginary pond." Megan loved the sound of Rebecca's gentle laughter and felt embraced by her warmth. "Actually, I've been staring up at the stars with the phone in my hand, dying to call you. I thought it was too late but I couldn't stand it any longer and just had to call," Megan admitted.

"I'm so glad you called, Megan. I can't tell you how much it means to me to hear your voice," Rebecca said tenderly.

"Now it's your turn, Ms. Rhodes. Tell me about your dysfunctional family."

Rebecca burst into laughter. "How did you know my family was so dysfunctional? Have you done an FBI background check on me already?"

"I haven't had a chance to contact the FBI, but all I know is that I want to know everything there is to know about you. And I don't know anyone that has grown up in a so called normal, 'Leave It to Beaver'-type family," Megan said, chuckling.

♥ *TENDER HEART* ♥

"You have no idea what dysfunctional is till I tell you about my family, Megan."

They both laughed.

Rebecca could hear Megan shift the phone to her other ear. "You have my complete and undivided attention, Rebecca, so feel free to tell your story."

Rebecca smiled and sank back into her couch. She couldn't remember the last time she'd talked about her traumatic childhood with anyone. She felt completely embraced by Megan's warmth and love. "Let me begin by telling you that we have a few things in common. We're both thirty-eight and I also have one sister. Her name's Lindsay, and she's twenty-three years old. My mother was older when she was pregnant with Lindsay, so Lindsay was born with Down's syndrome. She's been tested at the functional level of a ten year old."

Megan gasped, devastated by Rebecca's story. "Oh, Rebecca, I'm sorry."

"Don't ever apologize for Lindsay, Megan. I can't wait for you to meet her. She's one of the greatest gifts in my life. I wish everyone could have the pure innocence and unconditional love of Down's syndrome kids."

"I've had a few patients with Down's syndrome, and each and every one has never ceased to amaze me with their openness, honesty, and desire to love and be loved," Megan said.

"That's a perfect way to describe Lindsay. I give her credit for being a lot brighter than a ten year old and she never fails to put a smile on my face." Rebecca felt pure love at her thoughts of her precious Lindsay.

"Your parents must be very proud of you and Lindsay," Megan said.

Rebecca took a deep breath and frowned. "My parents never had the pleasure of knowing Lindsay. My father was an alcoholic and very emotionally and physically abusive. My mother did her best to protect me and many times we would hide out at my father's brother's house. Unfortunately, my mother fell in love with my uncle and became pregnant by him. He's Lindsay's father.

"I was fifteen at the time and all I can remember was my father's rage. When Lindsay was born and diagnosed with Down's syndrome my father saw it only as further humiliation. Lindsay had been home one week when I heard a gun go off and ran into my parents' bedroom. I stood in the doorway as I saw my father shoot my mother repeatedly then point the gun in Lindsay's crib. I screamed, 'No!' and my father turned and stared at me in the doorway."

Megan clutched the phone tightly in fear as if she was standing in that doorway with Rebecca. She held her breath as she heard a sob catch in Rebecca's throat.

"He took the gun and aimed it at his own temple and said, 'Good-bye,' then fired. My parents both died that night in their bedroom and left Lindsay and I behind." Rebecca's tears flowed freely as she reached for a tissue.

"Oh my God, Rebecca. I'm so sorry. I had no idea what you had been through. Drake said you'd had a hard life, but that's an absolute nightmare. What happened to you and Lindsay?"

Rebecca dried her eyes and took a deep breath. "Lindsay's real father, my uncle, took us in and treated us like his own kids. He was married a few years later and both my uncle and his wife have been wonderful to us both. They've been so good with Lindsay and continue to love her and care for her. Five years ago I found a private school that caters to the mentally challenged. Lindsay goes there three days a week and gets incredible love and nurturing from the teachers. It gives my aunt and uncle a break and I'm continually amazed by the things that Lindsay has learned there." Rebecca took a deep breath and dried her eyes.

Megan could hear her sniffle. "I wish I could be there to hold you and dry your tears," Megan whispered.

Rebecca struggled to stifle the sob in her throat. "I wish you were here too, Megan. You could be warmed by my fire and share my glass of wine with me."

"I'm so sorry for everything you've been through, Rebecca."

♥ TENDER HEART ♥

Rebecca took a sip of her wine. "Don't be sorry, Megan. I truly believe that everything happens for a reason. I am blessed to have Lindsay for a sister, and my aunt and uncle have been wonderful parents. I don't think that I've had a hard life like Drake said. I've just been given little challenges along the way."

Megan felt moved by this woman's positive attitude and strong spirit. "You certainly are a special woman, Rebecca Rhodes. That's an incredible childhood story. It means a lot to me that you shared your pain with me. I know it must have been hard for you to do that."

Rebecca could feel Megan's compassion and understanding as she hugged a pillow to her chest. "You have this incredible warmth about you, Megan, that makes me feel so safe and comfortable to open up my heart to you. That's not an easy thing for me. As a child I lived with so much shame because of my father that I kept everything inside. I was terrified to speak of what was going on in my family and after my parents' tragic death I never wanted to be a burden to my aunt and uncle. I kept everything to myself and just tried to be a good girl. There are very few people that I feel comfortable with to share my true feelings with, but you, Megan, just tear down my walls with one whisper of that incredible voice."

"Rebecca, did your father ever sexually abuse you?"

Rebecca closed her eyes as she took a deep breath. She wished she could be in Megan's strong arms. "I have a lot of things to be grateful for, Megan, and one of them is that he never stooped that low. He smacked me around a lot when he was drunk but he never touched me in a sexually inappropriate way."

Megan felt overcome with relief as tears stung her eyes at Rebecca's devastating childhood. "I'm so grateful that he didn't hurt you that way, Rebecca. I'm just sorry for all the other ways that he did hurt you."

Rebecca hugged the pillow tight. "We both share experiences of childhood pain, Megan, and look how we turned out anyway."

They both laughed softly.

♥ TENDER HEART ♥

Megan looked up into the ebony night sky strewn with shimmering stars. "I wish you were here with me, Rebecca," she whispered.

Rebecca felt embraced by Megan's love and tenderness. "I feel like I've been right beside you the whole time, Megan."

Megan felt overwhelming warmth in her heart. "You're quickly becoming very special to me, Rebecca Rhodes."

Rebecca leaned back into the couch and glided her thumb across the lip of her wine glass. "You're very special to me, Dr. Megan Summers, and I'm so excited about seeing you tomorrow night."

Megan was completely aroused by Rebecca's sultry voice and struggled to control the fluttering in her stomach. "I can't wait to see you, Rebecca."

They both sat in peaceful silence as they hesitated to say good-bye.

"Speaking of tomorrow night, Rebecca, do you like seafood?" Megan asked.

"I love seafood, especially shrimp," Rebecca said, excitedly.

"Good, because I was going to dip my fishing pole into my imaginary pond and see if I could catch us a couple of goldfish for supper tomorrow night."

Rebecca fell back into her couch and laughed until tears streamed down her cheeks.

Rebecca wiped at her eyes with a tissue and finally caught her breath. "Thank you so much for that laugh, Megan. I really needed that after our family discussion."

Megan stared out over the deck lights illuminating her backyard. "You're very welcome, my dear. I love to hear you laugh. I could spend the rest of my life listening to your laughter."

Rebecca held the phone close and listened to Megan's gentle breathing. "Do you realize, my dear Dr. Megan, that it's almost midnight?"

♥ *TENDER HEART* ♥

Megan was shocked as she looked at her watch and groaned. "I hope that doesn't mean that you're going to say good night," Megan pleaded.

"What time do you have to get up in the morning, Megan?"

"Five o'clock," she whispered.

Rebecca gasped, "Megan, you only have five hours till you have to get up. I feel so badly for keeping you on the phone like this."

"I've thoroughly enjoyed this time with you, Rebecca, besides, I haven't had a nibble on my fishing pole yet. Please stay and talk to me till I at least catch our supper."

Rebecca's laughter warmed Megan's heart. "I want you to put your fishing pole away, young lady, and tuck yourself into bed, or I will come and tuck you in myself," Rebecca said playfully.

"Don't tease me like that, Rebecca. You come over here and tuck me in and I can promise you that you'll be sharing my pillow with me."

Rebecca released a gentle sigh and hesitated briefly. "Your pillow is only the beginning of what I want to share with you, Dr. Megan Summers."

Megan groaned with pure sexual frustration as they both felt the intensity and depth of their love. "Rebecca, I need to say good-bye so I can go dip my overheating desire in the pond with my goldfish."

Rebecca laughed softly and tilted her head. "I'd rather you dipped your desire into my pond," she said seductively.

Megan groaned, "Stop it! I can't take this sexual teasing any longer. You have a lot of nerve tormenting me like this over the phone, young lady."

Rebecca burst into infectious giggles. "You deserve to be tormented, Dr. Summers. You made me mope around my house all evening wondering who exactly your date was tonight and if it was someone special in your life."

"I was pretty bad about that wasn't I?" Megan said, sheepishly.

♥ *TENDER HEART* ♥

Rebecca laughed and held the phone close, wishing it were Megan she was holding. "You were awful, Megan. Now it's my turn to get even."

They both laughed warmly as they felt their incredible connection and hated to end their time together.

"Thank you for sharing yourself and your childhood with me, Rebecca. I really enjoyed talking to you."

Rebecca stared into the dying embers of her fire. "It's been my pure pleasure, Megan. You're a very special woman and I can't seem to get enough of you. I hate to say good-bye to you but I want you to get some sleep."

"All right, if we have to," Megan said, sighing.

"Good night, Megan. Sleep tight," Rebecca whispered.

"Good night, my friend. Sweet dreams," Megan whispered, as they both reluctantly said good-bye.

♥ *TENDER HEART* ♥
CHAPTER THREE

The residents and ICU nurses surrounded Megan as they proceeded through their morning rounds. Megan's senior resident, Dean, explained the history of their next patient. "Thirty-five-year-old white female, involved in head-on motor vehicle accident with drunk driver last night at approximately eight-thirty in the evening. She was an unbelted, front-seat passenger and ejected through the windshield." The residents and nurses grimaced. "She was unresponsive at the scene, intubated and airlifted to our facility," Dean explained.

Megan stepped away from Dean's side and stood at the patient's bedside. She began to assess the patient's level of consciousness as Dean continued. "She remains completely unresponsive to painful stimuli and pupils are fixed and dilated. She has no gag, cough, or corneal reflexes. When she arrived in our trauma room the nurses noted a pool of blood between her legs. When we assessed her we saw that she had aborted a twenty-six-week-old fetus," Dean said, grimacing.

Everyone in the room gasped as Megan looked up from the patient into Dean's sensitive eyes.

Dean had to momentarily look away from Megan's warm, caring eyes and take a deep breath. "She has three other kids at home under the age of ten. Her husband's parents are taking care of the kids. Her husband is devastated and has been here at her bedside all night. The driver of the vehicle was our patient's sister and she died at the scene. She was thirty years old. The drunk driver walked away with a bump on his head, and this is his fourth drunk driving offense."

Megan shook her head in disgust and turned to the nurse caring for the patient. "How were her vital signs overnight?"

The nurse tucked a loose strand of auburn hair behind her ear and looked at Megan with saddened eyes. "We had trouble with her blood pressure being low when she first came in, but we gave her four units of packed red blood cells, two units of fresh

♥ *TENDER HEART* ♥

frozen plasma and bolused her with two liters of lactated ringers. Her vital signs have been stable since then but she remains completely unresponsive," the nurse explained, as she slipped her pen into her breast pocket.

Megan looked up at the patient's cardiac monitor and checked her vital signs. The residents and nurses watched in respectful silence as Megan leaned toward the patient and gently continued her thorough assessment. They all watched her expertly test the patient's pupillary response, gag, blink, and cough reflexes.

Megan unfolded her stethoscope from her lab coat pocket and listened to the woman's heart sounds and breath sounds. She laid her pen across the patient's nail bed and pressed down firmly, trying to elicit any response to the painful stimuli. There was no response. This thirty-five-year-old mother of three lay like a lifeless rag doll. The only sound heard in the room was the hissing of the ventilator.

Megan shook her head and folded her stethoscope neatly into her pocket. "What did you see on her CAT scan, Dean?"

Dean looked from the patient to Megan. "Massive subarachnoid hemorrhage with midline shift. It's up on the view box, Dr. Summers. Come have a look."

Megan began to follow Dean out of the patient's glassed-in room when she stopped in the doorway. She placed her hand on the shoulder of the nurse caring for the patient and looked at the whole group. "Good job stabilizing this patient, guys. You all did a terrific job." Their faces lit up at Megan's glowing compliment as they all watched her follow Dean to the view box.

Megan flipped the light on the view box and stood facing the images of her patient's traumatized brain. With her residents standing on either side, Megan asked them what they saw and gently walked them through the patient's injuries. Megan faced them and paused to take a deep breath. "I would like to speak to the patient's husband so we can decide how far to go with medical treatment, considering the patient's grave condition and

♥ TENDER HEART ♥

extremely poor prognosis. We need to test her for brain death and see how the family feels about organ donation."

Annie, the charge nurse in the Neurosurgical Intensive Care Unit, poked her head around the corner from the nurse's station. "Sorry for interrupting, Dr. Summers, but I have Dr. Darrow on the phone for you. Do you want me to take a message?" she asked.

"No, it's okay Annie, we're done here. I'll talk to Dr. Darrow." Megan gave her residents final instructions, and then headed for the phone in the nurse's station.

Megan cradled the phone against her ear and hit the flashing red light. "Good morning, Dr. Darrow. How can I be of service to you?" she said.

Drake burst into his deep laughter. "Well if you're in the business of granting wishes how about arranging for me to have a month off where I can bask on the golden shores of a pacific island with a steady supply of margarita's and beautiful women," Drake teased.

They both laughed.

Megan shook her head. "Drake, I need to find you a good, straight woman."

"I'm taking an official hiatus from relationships, Meg. Karen caused me enough heartache to last a lifetime," Drake said, seriously.

Megan's memories of Drake's ex-wife, Karen, leaving him for his best friend caused a tight band around her heart. Drake loved Karen deeply and had been devastated to find out about her affair.

"Did you get to work on time, Dr. Summers, without flattening any tires this morning?" he said.

Megan blushed as she tucked her hand into the pocket of her crisp, black pleated slacks. "Yes, sir, I did," she said shyly.

Drake smiled at the softness in his dear friend's voice. "Good. I'm happy to hear that. Now, the reason I called you, Dr. Summers, is to tell you that I have a special delivery down here

♥ TENDER HEART ♥

in the E.R. for you. If you have a minute, why don't you come down and get it."

Megan was surprised and intrigued. "A special delivery for me? What is it, Drake, and who is it from?"

"Bring your beautiful self down to the E.R., Dr. Summers, and see for yourself."

♥♥♥♥♥♥♥♥♥♥

Megan walked briskly through the bustling emergency department and was greeted with bright smiles and enthusiastic waves by all the staff. She walked toward the nurse's station. Drake was on the phone, talking with an ambulance crew at an accident scene. He smiled at Megan and motioned toward the staff lounge. She leaned into the nurse's station and kissed Drake's cheek; he reached up and gently touched her chin. Megan's face beamed with warmth as she turned the corner into the staff lounge.

Megan's heart somersaulted as she smiled from ear to ear. Sitting on the table was a tall, iced mocha from the Java Cafe. She stepped closer to the table and saw a pretty yellow card beside the drink, addressed to Dr. Megan Summers, in the beautiful flow of a fountain pen. She picked up the card and sat in the nearest chair. She turned the card over to open it and saw a gold star on the flap. Below the sticker the words: "a gold star for your honorable behavior." Megan burst into laughter as visions of Rebecca's smiling, playful eyes filled her mind. She reached for the iced mocha and took a big sip, luxuriating in the cold, refreshing flavor. Visions of Rebecca's full, sensuous lips around the straw of their drink ignited her awakened passion.

Megan set her drink down and tore open the card. The front was a serene picture of two women sitting by a pond in deep conversation. Megan was moved by the peacefulness of the two women and the intensity in their eyes. A narrow piece of paper fell from the card into her lap. She picked it up and began reading.

♥ *TENDER HEART* ♥

REBECCA COUPON

This coupon entitles, Dr. Megan Summers, to spend tomorrow evening at the symphony with Rebecca Rhodes. Dinner at a romantic, candlelit restaurant will also be provided prior to the symphony on the one condition that Dr. Megan Summers promises to be on her best behavior and leave her temper at home. Not redeemable with other coupons or other women. This coupon expires immediately if the answer is not YES. Reply expected ASAP.
I miss you.
Love, Rebecca xoxo

Megan burst into laughter as she read the coupon again and again. Rebecca's sense of humor and romanticism touched Megan profoundly. She thought of how thrilled she would be to go to the symphony and out for a romantic dinner with the woman who had captivated her heart and soul.

Megan set the coupon down on the table and turned her attention to the note Rebecca had written in the card. She marveled at her beautiful, flowing penmanship as she began reading.

My Dearest Megan:

Thank you for your lovely company at the Java Cafe and the heartwarming conversation on the phone. I can't tell you how much it meant to me that you called.

I wanted to buy you an iced mocha to start your day off with a bang, especially since I did not leave you with many hours to sleep last night. I figured I owed you an iced mocha anyway after the way you whined and complained that I

♥ *TENDER HEART* ♥

drank most of yours. Did they not teach you how to share in kindergarten, Dr. Summers?

I would love to take you to the symphony tomorrow night. I can't promise that Itzhak Perlman will be there but I think you will enjoy it nonetheless.

When I saw this card I immediately thought of you and your goldfish pond. I hope that someday we will sit on the edge of your pond together and watch the goldfish and their gentle, random movement and escape from the real world together.

You stir things in me that I have never felt before, Megan. You are a tender heart.

Have a wonderful day and know that I am thinking about you.

Love, Rebecca   xoxo

Megan's eyes were moist as she gently closed the card and stared at the picture. She slowly traced the outline of each woman with her finger as she whispered to herself, "You move me, Rebecca Rhodes," and visualized herself and Rebecca sitting together, lost in each other's eyes.

Drake walked into the lounge with a big smile, sipping on his hot coffee. "How do you like the gifts that Rebecca brought us this morning?" he said brightly.

Megan shyly looked away and reached for a tissue in her lab coat pocket.

Drake was instantly concerned and pulled a chair up beside her. "Are you all right, Meg?"

Megan laughed softly and wiped away her tears. "I'm more than all right, Drake. I'm completely, head over heels, in love with Ms. Rebecca Rhodes," she admitted.

Drake burst into laughter. "That's the most wonderful news I've heard in a long time!"

"When was she here, Drake? Why didn't she page me?"

♥ *TENDER HEART* ♥

Drake smiled at Megan's disappointment and leaned closer. "She was here about twenty minutes ago. We called the NICU and Annie told us you were in the middle of rounds. Rebecca said not to interrupt you and asked me to make sure you received your gift."

Megan lowered her eyes and frowned.

Drake touched her chin and raised her face to meet his warm, blue eyes. "Your Ms. Rhodes had the same look on her face that you do right now," he said.

Megan reached forward to tug on the lapel of Drake's crisp white lab coat. "Next time, Drake, make sure she interrupts me," Megan said.

Drake laughed and leaned back in his chair. "Okay, Meg. Next time I'll stop the earth's rotation to make sure you both don't miss each other because I can't stand to see this sadness in both your lovely faces."

Megan laughed softly and felt consumed by her deep feelings for Rebecca. She reached for her iced mocha and held it in her hands. Drake watched her play with the straw. She looked into Drake's eyes. He reached forward and took her hand. Megan entwined her fingers in Drake's strong hand.

"She's incredible, Drake. She's won my heart so completely. I can't get enough of her and I ache to be with her and talk to her."

Drake smiled at Megan's deep love and set his empty cup on the table. "I can tell you that the feelings are mutual. Rebecca told me herself, you knock her socks off."

Megan laughed as Drake smiled.

"After you stormed out of the E.R. yesterday, she said to tell you that you could hang your stethoscope on her bedpost anytime."

Megan blushed as a smile lit up her face. "I hope to hang more than just my stethoscope on her bedpost," Megan confided shyly.

♥ *TENDER HEART* ♥

Drake burst into laughter as Megan took a sip of her iced mocha, trying her best to shake off her sensuous visions of Rebecca.

Drake reached for Megan's hand and held it softly. "You both mean so much to me, Megan. You're both very special and I'm thrilled to see you two so enamored with each other."

Megan smiled and ran her thumb down her moist cup. "I'm certainly enamored with that beautiful woman."

Drake leaned back in his chair as Sharon, the E.R. nurse appeared in the lounge doorway. "Hi, Dr. Summers. Sorry for interrupting, guys, but the helicopter just landed on the roof with our trauma patient, Drake. Should be here in five minutes," she announced.

Drake frowned and looked down at his watch. "Thanks, Sharon. I'll be right out," he said. He stood, picked up his empty coffee cup from the table.

"What's the trauma, Drake?" Megan said.

Drake threw his coffee cup in the nearest trashcan. "Eighteen-year-old kid on roller blades tried to race a dump truck through a yellow light. Guess who won?" he said, rolling his eyes.

Megan groaned in disbelief.

"The kid's barely got a pulse or blood pressure, so he sounds pretty bad. Nothing like starting your day off with a level one trauma," Drake said, as he leaned forward and kissed Megan softly. "See you later, beautiful," he whispered.

Megan smiled and watched him head for the door.

She was absorbed in Rebecca's card as Drake looked back at the serene expression on her face. "Meg." Megan looked up and was surprised to see Drake still standing there. "Go knock her socks off," he teased.

Megan blew him a kiss and watched him wave as he headed out the door.

♥♥♥♥♥♥♥♥♥♥♥

♥ *TENDER HEART* ♥

Megan gently closed her office door behind her and tossed her empty coffee cup into the trashcan. She slipped into her plush office chair, picked up the phone, and dialed Rebecca's office number for the first time.

A secretary answered. "May I tell her who's calling?"

Megan smiled playfully and stared at the card on her desk. "Tell her it's a secret admirer who's a big fan of goldfish."

The secretary burst into laughter. "I'll certainly tell her that. Please hold." Celine Dion's silky voice filtered through the phone.

The song was abruptly cut off by an excited, sultry voice. "Well, hello there, secret admirer. Could this person who loves goldfish also enjoy sharing iced mochas and the music of Itzhak Perlman?" Rebecca asked.

Megan laughed and held the phone close. "Shucks! What gave me away?"

Rebecca laughed softly.

"Am I interrupting anything important, Rebecca?"

"Not at all, Megan. You're timing is perfect. I was just staring out my window and admiring the view as I thought of you."

Megan felt warmth cascading throughout her entire body as she thought of Rebecca. "Thank you for the delicious treat and the beautiful card. I would absolutely love to turn in my Rebecca coupon for a romantic dinner and evening at the symphony with you."

Rebecca twisted her right hand around the phone cord. "I would be delighted to take you out tomorrow night, Dr. Summers."

Megan felt embraced by an intense warmth as she ached to reach out to Rebecca.

"I would have loved to deliver your gift in person, Megan, but I didn't want to interrupt your morning rounds. I was disappointed that I couldn't see you. I really miss you," Rebecca said.

♥ TENDER HEART ♥

"I miss you too, Rebecca. Next time, Rebecca, please page me directly. If I can't see you at least I can talk to you. Promise you'll do that for me?" Megan pleaded gently.

Rebecca leaned her head back against her executive chair and closed her eyes, lost in Megan's sensuous voice. "Use that sad voice on me, Dr. Megan Summers, and I would promise you the world." Rebecca purred. "I promise to page you directly from now on, Megan, no matter what my needs," Rebecca teased, seductively.

"Your needs are very important to me, Rebecca."

Rebecca laughed softly as she deepened her sexy, sultry voice. "Well then, Dr. Summers, you'd better meet me on your pillow immediately."

Megan groaned in sexual frustration as she closed her eyes and held the phone tighter. "Stop doing this to me over the phone. You tease me and taunt me then leave me aching for you," Megan scolded.

Rebecca twirled the phone cord in her hand. "Tell me where it hurts, Dr. Summers, and I'll kiss it better for you."

Megan dramatically dropped her head onto her desk and let the phone fall to the floor as she groaned with explosive lust.

Rebecca burst into laughter at Megan's response, realizing that this woman had awakened a playfulness in her that she never knew existed. "Megan? Megan? Are you still there? Are you okay?"

Megan finally retrieved the phone. She ran her hand through her hair in frustration and sat back in her chair. "No, I'm not okay, Ms. Rhodes. You're such a tease."

Rebecca felt her desire soar as she ached to hold Megan close. "I really enjoy you, Megan Summers. You're so much fun."

Megan laughed sweetly, fondly remembering their conversation the previous night. "My priority with you, Ms. Rhodes, is to ensure that we create all the fun and laughter that you missed growing up."

♥ *TENDER HEART* ♥

Rebecca was deeply moved by Megan's words as she felt tears blur her vision. "That would take a lot of catching up, Megan, but if anyone can do it, it would be you."

Megan felt Rebecca's anguish in her words and ached to reach out and hold her. "I really look forward to seeing you later, Rebecca."

Rebecca smiled and wiped away her tears. "I can't wait, Megan. Is there anything that I can bring with me?"

"Just yourself and your beautiful smile," Megan said.

They both enjoyed the warmth between them and the gentle hesitation.

"I really love this card, Rebecca, and I just want you to know that I skipped a few grades in public school so I must have missed that lesson on sharing."

The sound of Rebecca's sweet laughter invigorated Megan's soul.

"That's obvious, Dr. Summers. But fret not, I offer myself to you as your private tutor on the joys of sharing. My payment plan is very simple. An occasional iced mocha and the pure pleasure of your exhilarating company."

Megan couldn't help but smile at Rebecca's charming personality and bubbly wit. "That's one payment plan that I look forward to fulfilling," Megan said, sweetly. Megan twirled her coupon in her hand. "I love my Rebecca coupon. I was wondering if there are other Rebecca coupons that I could look forward to in the future?"

"I plan on filling your dreams with my Rebecca coupons."

Megan dropped her head back against her chair and sighed with pure pleasure as her pager disrupted their conversation. Megan looked down at her pager and frowned. "I hate to end this precious time with you, Rebecca, but Drake is paging me to the E.R. I should go, unfortunately."

"Go and dazzle them with your brilliance, darling," Rebecca said in admiration.

"I'll try and call you later, Rebecca, and if you need me for anything please don't hesitate to call," Megan said, seriously.

♥ *TENDER HEART* ♥

"Then I would be paging you every fifteen minutes, my darling, and your patients would never see you," Rebecca said, tenderly.

Megan laughed softly as they hesitantly said good-bye and promised to call each other before leaving work.

♥ *TENDER HEART* ♥
CHAPTER FOUR

Rebecca guided her sleek, silver Jaguar into Megan's circular driveway and felt her heart race at the thought of seeing her again. She parked her car in front of the three-car garage and took in the sight of her beautiful Spanish-style villa.

Rebecca grabbed her purse from the passenger seat and stepped out of the car, slinging the purse over her shoulder. She reached back behind her seat and used both hands to pull out a large gift bag. She hit the automatic lock, shut her doors, and activated the alarm.

Rebecca was awestruck by the elegant stone archway before her and walked through into a cozy courtyard blanketed by ivy and vibrant flowering bushes of oleander and bougainvillea. She walked toward the elegant, glass double doors and into Megan's breathtaking home. The high cathedral ceilings made the rooms appear endless as Rebecca was drawn to the sunken living room adorned with Santa Fe style couches and light pine furniture. A modern entertainment center and huge stone fireplace adorned one end of the room and divided the living room and elegant dining room. The centerpiece of the dining room was a long mahogany table that could comfortably seat ten people. Rebecca was in awe of the chic, cozy design as she stared out the floor to ceiling windows that framed the wall beyond the dining room.

Just as Rebecca set down her purse and gift bag, she saw Megan.

Megan stepped out of her kitchen and walked towards her, overwhelmingly beautiful in a pair of brown, plush suede pants and cream-colored, ribbed turtleneck. Rebecca felt a staggering excitement in her chest and had to remind herself to breathe as she watched Megan approach with a glowing smile.

Their eyes never wavered as Megan openly admired Rebecca's elegant, slender frame dressed in khaki pleated trousers and matching silk, striped shirt. Megan's heart

♥ *TENDER HEART* ♥

catapulted her forward; she melted into Rebecca's arms and knowing of no place where she would rather be.

Rebecca held her tight as she leaned against her cheek and moaned, throaty and passionate. "God, I missed you," Rebecca whispered, breathlessly.

Megan let her hands roam freely across Rebecca's silk-covered back. "I thought I was going to burst waiting for you to get here. I've never felt this excitement waiting for someone in my entire life," Megan said, in a smoky voice.

Rebecca nuzzled into Megan's neck and inhaled the subtle scent of her perfume as she heard a gentle sigh escape from her throat.

"You are so beautiful, Rebecca, and you feel so wonderful."

Rebecca gently rubbed her cheek against Megan's and leaned back slightly to look into her passionate eyes. "You continue to make little sounds like that and we're going to be eating dinner over your pillow," Rebecca said, quietly.

Megan burst into laughter and rested her hands on Rebecca's slender waist.

Rebecca reached up and gently traced Megan's cheek and jaw as Megan closed her eyes and melted to her touch. "You are so beautiful, Megan Summers."

Megan opened her eyes and stared into Rebecca's golden eyes.

Rebecca gently touched a spot over Megan's heart with one finger. "An incredibly beautiful and intelligent woman with such a tender heart. Where the heck have you been all my life?" Rebecca scolded playfully.

Megan laughed softly and floated her hands over Rebecca's slender hips and up her back. Her hands glided into Rebecca's rich, thick hair as she held her head gently in her hands. Megan slid her thumbs over Rebecca's cheeks, watched her close her eyes, and luxuriated in the sight of her sensuous, moist lips.

Rebecca opened her eyes filled with seductive passion and slid her hands onto Megan's lower back, gently pulling her closer until their hips met in an intimate union. Rebecca looked deeply

♥ *TENDER HEART* ♥

into Megan's eyes moist with passion and love, no longer able to restrain her desire for this woman. She leaned toward her moist, slightly parted lips and softly brushed her lips against Megan's. She released a gentle moan as Rebecca leaned back slightly and saw the undeniable passion in her eyes.

Megan trailed a finger slowly along Rebecca's cheek and across her moist lower lip as she watched her close her eyes and meet her fingertip with her tongue. A wave of heat washed over Megan's entire body and engulfed her most sensitive areas as she leaned toward Rebecca. Their lips united slowly, softly as they both gasped and held their breath. Megan leaned back slightly and stared deeply into Rebecca's eyes, needing and wanting her with an intensity that threatened to consume her entire being.

Rebecca threaded her fingers deeply into Megan's thick, rich hair and guided her a breath closer. "God, Megan, please kiss me again."

Megan needed no further encouragement as she took Rebecca's lips with unbridled passion. Megan groaned with ecstasy as she touched her tongue to Rebecca's lips and found her way into her awaiting, sweet mouth. Their tongues caressed and probed as they impatiently tried to taste and consume each other.

Megan glided her hands down Rebecca's silky back and onto her hips, pressing their hips intimately tight. Rebecca gasped and finally had to lean back as they both struggled to gain their equilibrium.

Rebecca leaned her forehead against Megan's cheek and held her tight as they both struggled to catch their breath.

Megan slowly turned her head and kissed Rebecca's forehead, allowing her lips to linger.

Rebecca glided her hands along Megan's lower back and hips. "That, Dr. Megan Summers, was incredible!"

They both leaned back slightly and smiled, never moving from within their intimate contact.

♥ TENDER HEART ♥

Megan gently caressed Rebecca's cheek and jaw and lovingly watched her moist lips. "Your lips melt me, Rebecca Rhodes. I want to share kisses with you for the rest of my life."

Rebecca closed her eyes as she luxuriated in Megan's gentle touch. "See how much fun sharing can be," Rebecca said, playfully.

Megan laughed sweetly as Rebecca touched her chin and guided her face gently toward her. Megan inhaled sharply as their lips met and slowly, seductively tasted and explored each other. Megan felt Rebecca's tongue along her lower lip as she rested her hand against the back of her head, gently guiding her closer, opening her mouth and allowing Rebecca to explore her completely. Their gasps exploded within their throats as their tongues chased and played, sending their desire into an uncontrollable frenzy.

Megan hesitantly leaned her cheek against Rebecca's and tried to catch her breath. "Oh my God, Rebecca. You're incredible," Megan moaned heavily.

Rebecca smiled and took a deep breath, her hands lingering along Megan's back and hips. "I think I'm ready to meet your pillow, how about you?" Rebecca said.

Megan leaned back and laughed. "And miss the special goldfish dish that I slaved over for you? No way. I have full intentions of meeting the needs of your tummy before any of your other needs are met," Megan chuckled.

Rebecca dropped her head onto Megan's shoulder in defeat. "If I eat all my vegetables will you promise to make love to me for the rest of my life," Rebecca pleaded.

Megan laughed softly and held Rebecca warmly in her arms. "If and only if you eat all your vegetables like a good little girl." They both burst into laughter as Megan gently kissed Rebecca's warm, full lips.

"I love you," Megan whispered, as she stared deeply into Rebecca's golden eyes.

Rebecca lifted her head back and looked lovingly into Megan's beautiful green eyes. She reached up and caressed

♥ *TENDER HEART* ♥

Megan's face as tears tumbled onto her cheeks. "I love you with all my heart, Megan Summers. I can't tell you how much your love means to me."

Megan gently wiped away Rebecca's tears, tilted her chin up and kissed her softly. They held each other tight, luxuriating in their newfound love. Megan handed Rebecca a tissue, watched her lean back slightly and dry her eyes. Rebecca's smile exploded in Megan's heart as they looked longingly into each other's passionate eyes.

Megan held her close and looked down into the gift bag on the floor. She looked back into Rebecca's golden eyes and smiled. "What's this?"

Rebecca reached up and gently touched Megan's face. "I brought you a surprise," Rebecca said.

Megan smiled enthusiastically and tried to peek inside the bag again. "Another gift. Boy, I need to have temper tantrums in the E.R. more often if you're going to keep spoiling me like this," Megan said, impishly.

Rebecca burst into laughter. She met Megan eye to eye and held her face firmly in her hands. "All you will ever get for another temper tantrum is a good spanking, Dr. Megan Summers, so watch it because I won't hesitate to turn you over my knee."

Megan glided her hands over Rebecca's hips and sensuously onto her back as she kneaded her firm muscles. "You're really turning me on, Ms. Rhodes. Stop teasing me with promises of incredible pleasure." They both burst into laughter as Megan leaned toward Rebecca and took her lips with astonishing desire and need. Megan leaned her forehead against Rebecca's and closed her eyes, trying to slow her breathing. "You have the most amazing lips, Ms. Rhodes."

Rebecca reached up and traced her finger seductively along Megan's moist lower lip. "Please take me to your kitchen so we can inhale your special goldfish dish and I can take you to your bed and make passionate love to you."

♥ TENDER HEART ♥

Megan moaned erotically as Rebecca reached for her purse and handed it to Megan. She bent down, picked up the gift bag, and entwined her hand in Megan's as they walked into her kitchen.

Rebecca was impressed by the spaciousness of Megan's kitchen. Pine cupboards covered one wall and were accented by Spanish tiled countertops that embraced the kitchen in a u-shape. Standing alone in the center of the kitchen was a solid pine island and freestanding indoor grill and stove unit. The floor to ceiling window extended from the dining room and encased the kitchen in the golden hue of the early evening sun. The ambiance in the kitchen invites you to come in and play. Rebecca turned and rested her hand on Megan's arm. "You have a gorgeous home, Meg."

"Thank-you," Megan said, as she pretended to use both hands to hoist Rebecca's purse onto the counter. She smiled as she basked in Rebecca's sweet laughter. "Your purse weighs a ton, Rebecca. What do you have in here?"

Rebecca laughed and playfully rolled her eyes. "The usual: my phone, pager, wallet, keys, and my gun," Rebecca explained.

Megan stopped dead in her tracks. "You carry a gun?" Megan said in shock.

Rebecca smiled and set down her gift bag. She lovingly rested her hands on Megan's slender waist and guided her to sit on a padded kitchen stool. She stepped intimately between her legs and rested her hands on her strong shoulders. "Unfortunately, I have no choice, Megan. Women in real estate are very vulnerable," Rebecca said, as she gently caressed the frown on Megan's forehead. "As a real estate agent I show people into vacant homes. My particular types of homes are usually four to ten thousand square feet and isolated on large properties away from other homes and people. Imagine a woman alone in an empty house with a guy who has other motives than buying a house," Rebecca said carefully.

Megan's eyes filled with concern and worry. "I never thought of that, Rebecca," she said with alarm.

♥ *TENDER HEART* ♥

Rebecca continued, "There have been some horror stories over the years of women being raped and murdered by men that purposefully prey on the vulnerability of real estate agents. I've always made it a policy that all my agents, male or female go out in pairs to protect them from the lunatics out there. When Kyle first started working for me he would always volunteer to come show homes with me to be my sole protector and we have been inseparable since."

Rebecca laughed softly and shook her head. "It's kind of funny actually because Kyle is such a big teddy bear. He runs at the sound of any barking dog and can't even bring himself to kill a spider. He's terrified of guns, even though Scotty is a homicide detective for the Austin Police Department and makes him carry a gun in the glove compartment of his car. He refuses to go into his glove compartment because he knows the gun is there," Rebecca chuckled.

They both laughed softly as Rebecca gently held Megan's concerned face in her hands. "My comfort comes in knowing that Kyle is with me and his presence would always deter some deranged man from trying anything. If they did try anything, I always know I have my gun with me. I've never had to use it, thank God, and Scotty always makes sure we go out to a shooting range every couple of months," Rebecca explained, holding Megan close and desperately wanting to ease her discomfort. "Please don't be worried, Megan. I have never had an incident in fifteen years with any of my agents and I am always very careful with my gun," Rebecca said, as she leaned up and kissed Megan's soft lips. "I know that you must see the horrors of guns in the trauma room but in my line of work it's a necessity that I carry one," Rebecca explained.

Megan leaned her forehead against Rebecca's. "I've never held a gun and I have no idea how to even handle one," Megan said, with concern.

Rebecca smiled and kissed Megan's forehead. "I would love to have Scotty teach you, Megan. We could go to the shooting range together and teach you how to handle my gun, so we can

♥ *TENDER HEART* ♥

both feel comfortable with having it in our home," Rebecca offered carefully.

"I'd like that," Megan said honestly. "I'm grateful that you're protected and I'm grateful that Kyle pretends to take good care of you."

They both laughed as Megan gently reached toward Rebecca and touched her face. Rebecca closed her eyes and leaned her face into Megan's hand, melting to her gentle touch.

"So help me, if any guy hurts you I'll take my scalpel and amputate his balls and feed them to the neighborhood dogs," Megan threatened fiercely.

Rebecca burst into laughter and leaned into Megan's arms, basking in her love. Rebecca leaned up and kissed Megan softly, adoring her tender moans and ignited by her gentle lips. Rebecca leaned back and looked into Megan's passionate eyes. "Take me to those vegetables before I burst at the seams," Rebecca said impatiently.

Megan laughed sweetly.

Rebecca inhaled the delicious aroma of dinner and looked around the spacious, sun-filled kitchen. "You really do have a breathtakingly, beautiful home, Megan."

Megan smiled and tried to playfully peek in her gift bag. "Thank you. I'm glad you like it," she said distractedly.

Rebecca smiled at Megan's childlike enthusiasm and guided her face back to meet her eyes. "I would love a guided tour later but you'd better make your bedroom the last stop. Once the door to that room is closed behind us we won't be coming out for a while," Rebecca said seductively.

They both smiled and gave each other a passionate look as Megan tried again to reach down for her bag.

Rebecca laughed, entwined her fingers in Megan's hands and held them close to her chest.

Megan sighed with frustration and leaned her forehead against Rebecca's. "What did you bring me, Rebecca? The suspense is killing me," Megan whined.

♥ TENDER HEART ♥

Rebecca laughed and leaned toward Megan, kissing her sweet, playful lips. Rebecca probed her deeply with burning desire then abruptly withdrew her playful tongue. Megan groaned impatiently and leaned closer for more as Rebecca held her face securely in her hands. Rebecca stared at her moist, sensuous lips and grinned with devilish delight. "You can't have it all, my sweet Megan. It's either a kiss or the gift . . . what's your pleasure?"

Megan stared into Rebecca's passionate eyes. "I want you, Rebecca Rhodes. God, I want you."

A rush of scintillating heat cascaded down from Rebecca's chest to her thighs. She moaned ever so softly and took Megan's lips with the hunger of a sex-starved teenager.

Megan held Rebecca tight in her arms and gently caressed her back as they both struggled to catch their breath. Megan nuzzled her face into Rebecca's neck and tried to part the gift bag with her foot and sneak a quick peek.

Rebecca trailed her tongue along Megan's tiny earlobe then firmly clamped it between her teeth.

"Ouch!" Megan squealed.

Rebecca gently sucked on the injured lobe and caressed it with her tongue. "Oh, I'm sorry, darling. I thought for a moment there you were distracted by something other than me," Rebecca whispered into her ear. Megan's soft laughter was laced with guilt. Rebecca took her glowing face in her hands and kissed her with aching, insatiable desire.

Rebecca loved the gentle gasp that escaped from Megan's moist lips as she leaned back and looked into her passionate green eyes. Rebecca gave her a beautiful smile and reached down into the gift bag as Megan squirmed with eager anticipation. Rebecca removed the tissue paper covering the top of the bag and reached deep inside, pulling out a large, clear goldfish bowl, and setting it on the counter in front of Megan.

Megan clapped her hands with delight. Rebecca reached inside the bowl and pulled out a water-filled plastic bag holding a single, disoriented goldfish. Rebecca handed the bag to Megan and watched the expression of happiness shimmer in her emerald eyes.

"Rebecca! You bought me a goldfish," Megan shouted.

Rebecca gave her a glowing smile and kissed her softly. "I just wanted to start your dream in motion. This little fish is just one small step toward your goldfish pond," Rebecca said softly.

Megan hugged her tight and kissed her. Megan held up the bag and watched the little goldfish bob around in the bag with each movement. "You are incredible, Rebecca Rhodes. I love you so much."

Rebecca's smile illuminated her beautiful face as she leaned toward Megan and kissed her softly, slowly, igniting their burning passion and intensifying their need. Rebecca leaned back and caressed Megan's glowing face. "I love you, Dr. Megan Summers." Rebecca smiled and kissed the tip of Megan's nose and reached for the goldfish bowl. "I'd better rinse this bowl so our little friend can escape that plastic bubble and swim freely in her new home," Rebecca said.

Megan watched the little goldfish with childlike amazement as Rebecca took the bowl and headed to the sink. "How do you know it's a her?" Megan asked.

Rebecca smiled as she finished rinsing and filling the bowl. She reached for a dishtowel and stepped back toward Megan. "I think it's a her because as I stood before the tank trying to pick out the most beautiful tangerine-colored fish for you, this little one kept swimming up to the glass and blowing me kisses," Rebecca claimed.

Megan burst into laughter and stared at her new little pet. "Rebecca. You bought me a lesbian goldfish. How wonderful!"

They both laughed as Megan twirled the fish and Rebecca filled the base of the bowl with beautiful colored stones. "Tangerine. I think that would be a great name for our little wet friend. What do you think, Rebecca?"

Rebecca laughed and stepped intimately between Megan's legs, gently taking the bag from her hands. "I think that's a

♥ TENDER HEART ♥

wonderful name, and just for the record, I want you to know that Tangerine isn't the only one that's wet."

A glorious smile burst across Megan's face as Rebecca gave her a seductive grin. She gently untied the bag and poured Tangerine into the bowl. "Welcome to your new home, little Tangerine. You couldn't have asked for a better mommy," Rebecca said, as she watched the goldfish swim with reckless abandon.

Megan wrapped her arms around Rebecca's waist as she watched her dry her hands on the dishtowel.

Rebecca leaned toward Megan and kissed her softly. "There is one thing that Tangerine asked me to bring to your attention, Dr. Summers." Megan watched Rebecca lean into the gift bag and pull out a post-it note. Rebecca slid the fish bowl directly in front of Megan and stuck the post-it note to the front of the bowl. Megan burst into laughter as she read,

NO FISHING ALLOWED! TRESPASSERS WILL BE SPANKED!

Megan guided Rebecca into her arms and hugged her tight as they basked in their playful, loving ambiance. "Thank you for my special gift, Rebecca. I'm touched by your incredible kindness and I promise to retire my goldfish fishing pole."

They both laughed warmly as Rebecca caressed Megan's smiling face. They stared into each other's eyes as Megan leaned toward her. Their lips united as they explored their gentle passion and Tangerine explored her new world.

Rebecca leaned back and traced Megan's chin with her finger. "I bought you one other thing," she said softly. She momentarily stepped away from Megan and reached down into the gift bag. She pulled out a container of fish food and a net and placed them beside the fish bowl. "Those are for Tangerine, and this is for you." Rebecca handed Megan a beautifully wrapped gift box. Rebecca stepped back between Megan's legs and

♥ TENDER HEART ♥

watched her tear open the gift with excitement. Rebecca smiled deeply as she watched Megan carefully hold up her gift.

"It's a dream catcher," Megan said in amazement.

Rebecca leaned closer to Megan and tenderly touched her face. "May all your dreams come true, Megan."

Megan set the beautiful dream catcher down on the counter and pulled Rebecca closer as tears filled her eyes. "They're beginning to materialize like I never imagined," Megan said tenderly. She leaned toward Rebecca and kissed away her tears as she held her face in her hands. "Thank you for the beautiful gifts, Rebecca. You completely astound me."

Rebecca gave her a stunning smile as she leaned closer. "You're so welcome, my love," Rebecca whispered as she claimed her lips with burning, hungry passion.

Rebecca leaned back and stared into Megan's moist eyes as she saw movement from the corner of her eye. She looked over Megan's shoulder and smiled at a beautiful young woman with the same captivating green eyes and sensuous lips as Megan's. The woman stood leaning against the doorframe with her arms across her chest, smiling warmly.

"You must be the much talked about Rebecca Rhodes that has turned my sister's heart inside out, upside down, and made her forget my name."

They all laughed as she stepped into the kitchen and Megan turned to smile at her sister.

Rebecca stepped away from Megan and took her sister's hands in her own. "You must be Madison, the woman that caused me nothing but grief last night when Megan told me she was going out to dinner with a very special woman," Rebecca said.

Madison burst into the same joyous laughter as Megan's and smiled at her sister. Madison squeezed Rebecca's hands and looked deeply into her beautiful eyes. "Hello, Rebecca Rhodes. It's so nice to finally meet you," Madison said, as she looked from Megan to Rebecca and smiled at the crackling intensity between them. "You are truly as beautiful as Megan said."

♥ *TENDER HEART* ♥

Rebecca blushed and smiled sweetly at both women. "Hello, Madison Summers. It's a pleasure to meet you. Megan's told me so many wonderful things about you. Her love for you is incredible," Rebecca said.

Madison looked from Rebecca's golden eyes to her sister's beaming smile. "Yes, she loves me so much that she forgot to wake me from my nap." Madison scowled at Megan as Megan hid her face in her hands.

"I'm so sorry, Madi. Time seems to have escaped me," Megan said defensively, as she looked over at Rebecca. "I was rather distracted," she admitted.

Madison pulled a smiling Rebecca into her arms and hugged her tight. "Yes, I noticed that when I walked into the kitchen," Madison said sternly, as she looked into Rebecca's face and held her close. "Do me a favor, Ms. Rhodes, and try not to be so damn distracting okay?" Madison warned.

Rebecca gently kissed her cheek and grinned. "I'll try, Madison, but I can't make you any promises."

Madison hugged her close as they all laughed.

"Madison, look what Rebecca brought me," Megan said enthusiastically.

Madison looked onto the counter. A smile lit up her face and she turned to Rebecca. "I can't believe you bought her a goldfish. She's always talked about putting a goldfish pond in her backyard."

Rebecca blushed sweetly and stood close to Madison. "Yes. I know."

Madison looked into Rebecca's loving eyes as Megan slipped off her stool.

"Madison, meet my lesbian goldfish, Tangerine. Tangerine, this is my lesbian sister, Madison." They all laughed at Megan's formal introduction.

Madison stepped closer to the fish bowl and smiled. "Priscilla would love to have you for lunch, little Tangerine," Madison said.

♥ *TENDER HEART* ♥

Megan laughed at the bewildered look on Rebecca's glowing face. "Priscilla is Madison and Shawna's white Persian cat," Megan explained.

Rebecca became instantly indignant as she stepped toward Madison and swatted her bottom. "Madison Summers, don't you dare let Priscilla anywhere near Tangerine or I'll send my two cats, JC and Penney after you," Rebecca warned.

Madison laughed and touched Rebecca's arm. "I knew there was something wonderful about this woman. She's a cat lover."

They all stood close together as Rebecca entwined her hand in Megan's.

"What does JC stand for?" Megan asked.

Rebecca smiled and squeezed Megan's hand. "I have no idea. I'd have to call the department store to find out. One morning I found them both as kittens huddled under my car on a JC Penney bag."

Megan and Madison burst into laughter as Madison put her arm around Rebecca's shoulders. "She's beautiful, brilliant, and a cat lover. What more could a woman ask for," Madison affirmed.

Madison looked down at her watch and smiled. "Speaking of incredible women, I'd better get going or Shawna is going to trade me in for a more punctual wife," Madison said playfully.

Rebecca smiled and rested her hand on Madison's arm. "When am I going to meet your Shawna?" she asked.

Madison smiled and looked from Megan to Rebecca. "Tonight. Shawna and I are going to her parents' place for dinner, and then we'll be back here after that. I can't wait for Shawna to meet you," Madison exclaimed.

Rebecca smiled and squeezed Madison's arm. "I can't wait to meet the woman that is fortunate enough to have won your heart," Rebecca said affectionately.

Madison smiled and kissed Rebecca's cheek. She stepped toward Megan and smiled. "I'll tell Shawna's parents that you passed up an invitation to have dinner with them in order to spend the evening with this gorgeous, delightful woman. I'm sure they'll find some way to understand."

♥ TENDER HEART ♥

They all laughed as Megan hugged Madison tight and kissed her softly. "Give them my love, Madi, and please drive carefully."

Madison smiled and stepped into Rebecca's arms. "It's been a pleasure meeting you, Rebecca."

Rebecca smiled and hugged her tight. "It's been a pleasure meeting you, Madison. You're as wonderful and as beautiful as your sister."

Madison hugged Rebecca tight as Megan smiled at their warmth.

"Madison, will you please go cuddle with your own wife and leave mine with me," Megan scolded.

Rebecca turned quickly to look at Megan as a feeling of bliss and peacefulness surrounded her as Megan called her her wife.

Madison playfully stepped away and gave them both a beautiful smile. "Cuddling with my wife is what fills me with pleasure."

Megan and Rebecca smiled and stood close together by the kitchen island. They watched Madison grab her jacket and wave as she headed out the door.

♥♥♥♥♥♥♥♥♥♥

Rebecca helped Megan hang her new dream catcher by her panoramic kitchen window and they both found Tangerine her own special place on the Italian tiled kitchen counter.

Megan pulled a chair out for Rebecca at the glass-topped table and guided her to have a seat. The floral print place settings and matching pink linen napkins awed Rebecca. "This is beautiful, Megan. I love the pastel colors in your place settings. This all feels so intimate and romantic. You went through a lot of trouble for me and I want you to know that I'm truly touched."

Megan leaned forward and kissed Rebecca's forehead. "I was really excited to do this for you. Please don't thank me till you have at least tasted the goldfish filets."

♥ *TENDER HEART* ♥

Megan reached towards the kitchen island and grabbed the bottle of chilled white wine. She turned and handed the bottle and corkscrew to Rebecca. "Will you please do us the honors, Madame?"

Megan stepped towards the kitchen counter and retrieved two glass bowls of fresh garden salads. She placed them both on the place settings and took her seat.

"This looks mouth watering good, Megan."

"It's just something I whipped together from the seaweed I pulled up on my fishing pole."

Megan burst into laughter at the look of astonishment on Rebecca's face as the wine cork bounced off her shoulder.

Megan handed Rebecca her homemade oil and vinegar dressing and watched her shake it with enthusiasm. "Tell me about your day, Ms. dream maker?" Megan said.

Rebecca liberally doused her salad and handed the crystal decanter to Megan. "It was nuts. Kyle and I showed four homes to an elderly couple that want to buy a home for their daughter as a wedding gift. Can you imagine your parents buying you a home as a wedding gift?"

Megan stopped her fork full of salad in mid air. "Hardly. Besides, my parents will have to wait several life times if they are waiting for me to get married."

They both burst into laughter.

"And how was your day, Ms. healing hands?"

Megan was touched by Rebecca's interest in her work. "It was really busy. I didn't have any surgeries scheduled so I saw patients in my office and attended to all the needs of the patients on the floor, unit and emergency department." Megan told Rebecca about a few of her more interesting patients. Rebecca asked some excellent questions as she watched Megan clear their empty salad bowls. She returned to the table and ceremoniously presented Rebecca with a dish of shrimp fettuccini.

Megan slipped into her seat beside Rebecca and spread her pink linen napkin on her lap. She leaned intimately close to

♥ TENDER HEART ♥

Rebecca and tapped one of her shrimp with her fork. "Those aren't really shrimp."

Rebecca gave her a dubious look. "Let me guess. Goldfish," Rebecca said.

"No, wise guy. JC Penney catfish."

Rebecca burst into laughter at Megan's beautiful sense of humor. She speared one of the shrimp and seductively fed it to her, lost in the vision of Megan's tongue and lips enjoying the delicious treat.

"Tell me, Dr. Summers, how did such a beautiful, vivacious woman decide to become a neurosurgeon?"

Megan hesitantly looked away from Rebecca's intense eyes and twirled her fork in her creamy pasta.

"When I was ten, my best friend, Nancy, was diagnosed with leukemia. She spent the best part of two years in and out of the hospital for chemotherapy treatments. I would go with her as often as I could. While she was having her treatments I would read to her or we would play cards or a board game if she were up to it. I watched while all the doctors and nurses fought for Nancy's life only to have her die before her thirteenth birthday. I was inspired by what they all did. I knew that someday I would like to be the best doctor I could be to help save people like Nancy."

Rebecca reached for Megan's hand and entwined their fingers tightly. "You're an incredible woman, Dr. Summers. I bet that Nancy is really proud of you."

Megan set her fork down and cradled Rebecca's soft hand in both of hers. "Now it's your turn. Tell me what inspired this deep need to find people their dream homes and become a dream maker?"

Rebecca stared into Megan's bright eyes as she felt the tingling excitement of Megan's thumb caressing the palm of her hand. "When my parents died, I lost them and the only home that I knew. I realized that a place to call home gives me a sense of security and belonging. Even though my uncle was wonderful, I always felt like a visitor in his home. A home filled with warmth,

♥ *TENDER HEART* ♥

love and laughter is so important to me because of what I lost in my childhood. Now, I spend countless hours finding the ideal home for people and encourage them to fill it with love and laughter."

"Is your home filled with love and laughter, Rebecca?"

Rebecca stared deeply into Megan's eyes. "Presently it's filled with only my warmth and the love that I ache to share with you, Megan."

Rebecca leaned closer to Megan's shimmering eyes and moist lips. She slowly, hesitantly brushed her lips against Megan's and basked in Megan's husky, gasping moan. She watched in rapture as Megan looked at her with smoky eyes. Rebecca glided the soft pad of her thumb across Megan's moist lower lip. She replaced her thumb with her own tongue as she gently traced Megan's lip and kissed her deeply and sensuously.

Rebecca leaned her forehead against Megan's and struggled to catch her breath.

"We better get back to our goldfish fettuccini before it gets cold, Megan. I would hate to be responsible for ruining all your hard work."

Megan kissed Rebecca softly as she threaded her hand gently through her thick hair.

"After that kiss, nothing could taste as good as you, my darling."

They both slowly leaned back and reached for their forks.

Megan dug into her pasta as she basked in the loving presence of this woman that captivated her.

Megan cleared their dishes as Rebecca wiped her mouth with her linen napkin. "That was truly a scrumptious meal, Megan. You can cook goldfish fettuccini for me any time."

"I knew I could make a believer out of you," Megan said, as she placed a hot, bakery fresh, apple crumb pie before Rebecca.

A little while later Rebecca set her dessert spoon down on her empty plate and leaned back in her chair. She settled her hands on her tummy and beamed Megan a satisfied smile. "That

♥ TENDER HEART ♥

was absolutely delicious, Megan. Please feel free to feed me for the rest of my life."

Megan stood and reached for Rebecca's plate. "I plan on it," Megan said, as she kissed Rebecca softly and headed towards the kitchen sink.

Rebecca stood and gathered the rest of the dishes and placed them on the counter beside the sink. Megan rinsed the dishes and began placing them in the dishwasher as she watched Rebecca clear off the rest of the table. Rebecca returned to the counter and placed the salad dressing in the fridge.

"What's wrong, Megan? You're frowning. Did I do something wrong?"

Megan slowly closed the dishwasher and reached for a dishtowel to dry her hands.

"You didn't do anything wrong, Rebecca. It just feels strange to have another woman cleaning up in my kitchen with me since . . . my relationship ended. I haven't enjoyed a meal like this with another woman in a long time."

Rebecca slowly reached for Megan and held her face gently in her hands. "Well, if I do this with you often enough I hope I can make that strange feeling go away and with it chase away your sad feelings. I plan on staying in this kitchen and helping you clean up years worth of dirty dishes."

Megan glided her hands onto Rebecca's slender waist and pulled her into her arms and held her tight.

Megan kissed Rebecca tenderly on her neck and cheek before finding the lips that she ached to taste. Megan glided her tongue gently over Rebecca's and devoured her eager, sweet mouth that tasted like warm apples.

Megan rested her forehead against Rebecca's and inhaled deeply. "Incredible. You're truly incredible, Ms. Rebecca Rhodes."

Rebecca nuzzled her warm, moist lips against Megan's ear and sighed delightfully.

"Would those ravishing lips care for more wine, my darling?" Megan said.

♥ TENDER HEART ♥

"Yes, please, as long as that wine comes with more of you."

Megan smiled impishly as she hesitantly slipped from Rebecca's arms and refilled her wine glass. She handed Rebecca her glass of wine and placed her own in the sink.

"Are you not having another glass, Megan?"

"I would love to share another glass of wine with you but I'm on call tonight, so one's my limit."

"Can I please have your pager, Megan, so I can bury it in the freezer with all the goldfish fillets."

"I can't tell you how many times I've been tempted to do that myself, beautiful lady. Now come with me. I don't plan on wasting one minute of my precious time with you." Megan took her by the hand and guided her into her sunken living room.

Rebecca sat on the semicircular white couch facing the fireplace. She watched Megan expertly light a romantic fire. Rebecca's gaze caressed Megan's slender frame then traveled around the cozy room decorated in soft cream colors. Two Victorian wing chairs filled the corner of the room before a floor to ceiling bookcase filled with medical textbooks, bestseller fiction, biography, and how-to garden books. Several paintings adorned the walls of women walking along a beach and sitting comfortably on a front porch. The thick beige carpeting embraced the room with warmth.

"This is a really lovely room, Megan. Do you sit in here often?"

Megan added another hardwood log to the fire and stood to brush off her hands.

"As much time as I can. I love this room. It makes me feel so at peace."

"I can feel that. This room is very warm and sensuous. Just like you."

Megan slipped in beside her. Their eyes met in a passionate play of desire and excitement. Megan rested her arm around Rebecca's slender shoulders, leaning toward her and slowly, seductively, watching her eyes dance with vitality and arousal. Megan leaned close enough to feel Rebecca's breath on her moist lips as she hesitated, feeling Rebecca hold her breath. "I love you, Rebecca," Megan whispered softly.

Rebecca's eyes were moist with raw emotion as she reached up and touched Megan's beautiful face. "I love you immensely, Megan," Rebecca said as their lips met in a desirous, hungry kiss. Rebecca melted into Megan's arms, holding her tight, their bodies consumed by a raging heat.

Rebecca leaned back and rested her forehead against Megan's cheek as Megan wiped away her fallen tears.

"You're not used to people telling you they love you, are you, Rebecca?"

Rebecca sat back and dried her eyes, as she felt enveloped in Megan's loving warmth. She looked down at their entwined hands and hesitated as she caught her breath. "No, those are not words that my parents or partners shared freely, unfortunately."

Megan handed Rebecca several tissues and gently caressed her beautiful face. "Tell me about the partners that were fortunate enough to win your tender heart," Megan said soothingly.

Rebecca smiled and dried her eyes as she leaned intimately into Megan's arms. She looked down into her hands and twisted the edge of her tissue, hesitating. "You'll be rather surprised to know that I was married at the age of twenty because that's what I thought I was supposed to do," Rebecca said, as she looked into Megan's warm eyes. She smiled and entwined their hands gently together. "I sadly watched for ten years as my husband turned into an abusive alcoholic like my father," Rebecca said.

Megan's heart constricted as she felt Rebecca's deep pain and inner turmoil. Megan held her close and wished she could wash her pain away.

"Five years ago he was flying his Cessna plane over a New Mexico development site, surveying the land for property development for me. He crashed into a satellite broadcast tower and died at the scene. His blood alcohol level was very high and they found several bottles of whiskey in his plane. I begged him not to drink when he flew but that obviously fell on deaf, drunk

♥ *TENDER HEART* ♥

ears like all my other pleading." Tears collected in Rebecca's eyes as Megan squeezed her hands.

"I'm so sorry, baby," Megan whispered.

Rebecca took a deep breath as Megan handed her more tissues and watched her dry her eyes. Rebecca stared into the soothing, relaxing fire as her memories stirred emotions long cemented in her heart. "It was a really rough time in my life. I was starting to feel like anyone that I cared about would be taken away from me by some horrible tragedy," Rebecca said. Rebecca looked into Megan's warm, loving eyes. "I couldn't stand the thought of attracting another alcoholic into my personal life, so I vowed to stay away from relationships and threw myself into my work. I spent a year alone, struggling to get my life back together and understand what was important to me."

Megan reached up and brushed away a stray strand of hair from Rebecca's forehead and gently trailed her fingers along her damp cheek.

Rebecca leaned her face against Megan's hand. "Then I met Maggie. She's a real estate agent who came to work for me at that time and introduced me to the true meaning of love. For three years I shared a level of intimacy and communication with her that I never knew existed. There's something so special about the intrinsic bond between women that feels so right in my heart," Rebecca said, emotionally.

Megan smiled and slowly ran her fingers through Rebecca's thick hair. "What happened between you and Maggie?"

Rebecca looked down at Megan's strong feminine hand entwined in hers and felt her loving warmth and understanding. "Maggie's dream was to open her own real estate company in Hawaii. My life and my business are here in Austin. So one year ago she had to make a choice. I lost her to her dream. I never felt such intense emotional pain in my entire life as I did when Maggie left me." Rebecca bit her lower lip in an attempt to control her tears. She looked away from Megan and toward the fire.

♥ TENDER HEART ♥

Rebecca looked back into Megan's beautiful eyes and took a deep breath. "If I had to do it again I wouldn't change a thing. Maggie gave me a renewed zest for life and awakened my natural desires to be with a woman. I would never stop anyone I cared about from fulfilling her dreams for my own selfish needs. I was proud of her for making the right decision. She has a new partner now and her business is doing really well. She's very happy and we stay in touch, so that makes me happy."

Rebecca's smile slowly returned to her eyes as Megan gently ran her finger along her cheek and jaw. Rebecca closed her eyes, delighting in Megan's sensuous, feathery touch.

"You are an exceptional woman, Rebecca Rhodes, that for some reason has traveled a very bumpy road."

Rebecca slowly opened her eyes. "I've learned so much about myself and others along the way, Megan. I just pray that what I've learned will enrich our relationship."

Megan smiled and watched as Rebecca leaned toward her and gently brushed her lips against hers, slowly, seductively, eliciting the gentle moans that burned straight through her entire being and fanned a raging fire throughout her tingling body.

They melted into each other's arms, tasting the wine on each other's tongues. Megan held Rebecca tight in an embrace of comfort and awakening. Rebecca leaned back and tenderly traced her finger along Megan's cheek and full lower lip. She marveled at her incredible beauty and intense green eyes.

"Tell me about the woman you used to come home to," Rebecca whispered.

Megan smiled and softly kissed Rebecca's wandering fingertip, relishing in her gentle, erotic gasp. "Holly and I met eleven years ago when I was a resident in Boston. I found her at my computer at work installing a new program that the hospital had purchased. I was livid that she got into my office computer without my permission because it was loaded with confidential patient information." Megan frowned and looked down at their entwined hands. "I threw one of my now-famous temper

♥ *TENDER HEART* ♥

tantrums and she gathered her things and left my office faster than a frightened rabbit," Megan said, shamefully.

Rebecca laughed softly and leaned back against the couch.

"I spent the next week trying to track her down to apologize," Megan said.

Rebecca smiled, captivated by Megan and her story.

"We fell in love and spent ten wonderful years together, or so I thought." Megan looked away from Rebecca's tender eyes and watched the blue flames embrace the firewood as her memories assaulted her heart.

Rebecca watched a single tear trail down her cheek and gently wiped it away. Rebecca touched Megan's chin tenderly and guided her eyes back to meet hers. "What happened between you and Holly, sweetheart?"

Megan reached for several tissues and turned back to face Rebecca's loving, golden eyes. "The last two years of our relationship Holly was promoted within her computer company. She started going away a lot on overnight business trips, which was unusual because Holly hated to fly and her company knew that. This particular trip she told me she was going to be gone for a week in Atlanta. In the middle of the week I received a phone call from a woman named Karen, someone I only knew as a co-worker of Holly's. She told me that she and Holly were in Banff, Alberta, and that Holly had been seriously injured in a ski accident."

Rebecca closed her eyes and whispered emotionally, "Oh no, Megan."

Megan shook her head as if to rid herself of her horrible memories and pain. "You can imagine the million questions that were running through my mind at the time. I was sick with worry and filled with anger and betrayal as I boarded the next flight to Banff. I found Holly in a Trauma Intensive Care Unit, unconscious with a severe concussion, fractured right leg and ruptured spleen. She was unconscious for two days as I sat by her bedside, and Karen reluctantly admitted to me that she and Holly had been having an affair for the past two years!

♥ TENDER HEART ♥

Obviously, the business trip to Atlanta was a cover-up for their ski vacation in Banff. Who knows how many other trips she lied to me about."

Rebecca watched the tears tumble onto Megan's cheeks. She handed her several tissues and watched her dry her eyes and take a deep breath. "You can imagine the look on Holly's face when she woke up and saw Karen and I sitting at her bedside. She quickly realized that hitting that tree was a much more pleasant experience than what she was about to encounter," Megan said sadly.

Rebecca laughed softly and leaned closer as she entwined her hand in Megan's.

"I spent a week with her till I felt comfortable that Holly was receiving the proper treatment and was going to be okay. We talked and cried in that hospital room till there were no more tears left. When I asked Holly how she could destroy our relationship like this, she told me that I was too focused on my career and made her feel like she didn't matter to me anymore. She told me Karen made her feel special and needed, the way I once did." Tears streamed down Megan's cheeks as she looked down at their hands and tried to control her anguish.

Rebecca squeezed her hands warmly and gently wiped away her tears. "Did you put your career first before your relationship?" Rebecca said, carefully.

Sadness clouded Megan's glistening green eyes as she turned to look at Rebecca. "Besides me, you're the only person that has ever asked me that question, and the answer is as painful as her being unfaithful. I took Holly's love for granted and I have learned from my mistakes. I loved her very much and painfully let her go. Holly and Karen have been together since and now live in Dallas. I feel sick about the way our relationship ended, and I'm terrified of failing again," Megan said, as she looked at Rebecca with huge, emerald teary eyes.

Rebecca let her fingers linger on Megan's moist cheek and brushed away a loose strand of hair from her face. "You didn't fail, Megan. You obviously learned from that relationship and

♥ TENDER HEART ♥

that's what all these painful events in our lives are all about. You're being made to feel like you're totally responsible for the deterioration of your relationship when Holly was the one who chose to deal with it by walking away from you instead of talking."

Megan inhaled a deep emotional breath and looked down at their hands. "I feel like I let Holly and our relationship down," Megan admitted sadly.

Rebecca smiled and touched Megan's chin, guiding her face back up to meet her eyes. "Stop beating yourself up, Megan. You're not the one that had the affair that ended your relationship. Things might have been different if Holly had chosen to talk to you, but she didn't. She chose the cheap way out. We're all adults, Megan, and have to live with our choices and our mistakes."

Megan smiled and nuzzled into Rebecca's soft neck. Rebecca pulled Megan into her arms as they basked in each others comforting warmth. Rebecca kissed Megan's damp cheek and gently caressed her hair.

"I'm so sorry this all happened to you, sweetheart. But I must admit that I'm also grateful to have the opportunity to love you," Rebecca said.

Megan gently kissed Rebecca's neck and tasted her skin as stirring moans escaped from her lips. Rebecca tilted her head back and ran her fingers through Megan's thick, lush hair as Megan's lips traveled to her throat, igniting an erotic tingling in her breasts and down to her thighs. Rebecca's desire consumed her as she held Megan's face in her hands and looked into the eyes of this captivating woman and devoured her full, sensuous lips.

Megan chased and toyed with Rebecca's tongue as she slowly slid her fingers along the inside of her thigh. The sexual energy was explosive as Megan leaned Rebecca back on the couch and they both jumped at the sound of the phone. Megan rested her forehead against Rebecca's and tried to catch her breath as the phone continued to ring. Megan growled with

♥ *TENDER HEART* ♥

frustration and reached for the cordless phone on the coffee table. "This number is no longer in service so good-bye," she bellowed.

Rebecca giggled at Megan's response and frustration as they both sat up together. Megan heard a sweet giggle on the other end of the phone and frowned.

"Madison! Your timing leaves a lot to be desired, young lady," Megan shouted.

"You're the first woman to accuse me of that, Megan," Madison said.

Megan couldn't help but laugh at her sister's charming personality.

"Shawna and I just wanted to call and let you know that we're on our way home in case you guys were naked on the kitchen floor or something," Madison said, as she giggled.

Megan burst into laughter and looked into Rebecca's seductive eyes. "Madison, I ache to have this gorgeous woman naked in my bed so you two better hurry and get here before you walk into an empty house and find a 'do not disturb' sign on my bedroom door."

Rebecca laughed and signaled for the phone. Megan handed it to her. "Madison, please hurry. Your sister and I are in rather an amorous mood," Rebecca said.

Madison's laughter filled the phone as Rebecca ran her fingers along Megan's cheek, down her throat and between her sexy breasts.

Megan closed her eyes and felt Rebecca's fingers trail to her abdomen as the heat from her touch ignited her burning desire.

"You're my kind of girl, Rebecca Rhodes. See you in fifteen minutes," Madison said. They both said good-bye as Rebecca asked them to drive carefully, and then replaced the phone in its cradle.

Megan took Rebecca's hands and entwined their fingers, sharing a feeling of passion and warmth. "Do you notice that you hold the phone to your left ear, which is so unusual for a right-handed person," Megan said. She saw the sudden look of sadness and discomfort in Rebecca's beautiful, almond-shaped eyes.

Rebecca looked away from Megan, consumed by painful memories.

Megan was astounded by her profound reaction. She gently cupped her chin in her hand and raised her face to see her big tears. "What's wrong, sweetheart? Did I say something that hurt your feelings?" Megan said with concern.

Rebecca smiled and snuggled closer into Megan. "No, sweetheart. It's nothing like that. Six months before my husband died I noticed I was having trouble hearing people on the telephone when I listened with my right ear. I would automatically switch to my left ear and it would be clear as a bell. At first I thought it was the phone line till Kyle started teasing me that I needed to get my hearing checked because I wasn't hearing half of what he was saying to me. It concerned me enough to talk to Drake about it and he sent me to an ear, eye, nose, and throat specialist. The specialist checked me out and sent me to your fellow neurosurgeon, Dr. Erica Beaumont."

Megan was visibly stunned by Rebecca's story. "Why? What did they find?"

Rebecca smiled softly and looked into Megan's intense green eyes. "They discovered on my MRI that I had an acoustic neuroma the size of a marble," Rebecca said.

Megan looked at her in total disbelief.

"I asked Dr. Beaumont what the heck an acoustic neuroma was, and she explained that I had a brain tumor on my eighth cranial nerve that innervated the hearing in my right ear and that's why I was losing my hearing. She tried to reassure me that it was a benign brain tumor but the location of it makes it difficult to remove. Within a week I had brain surgery and she was able to completely remove the little pest. It's been five years since my diagnosis and I haven't had any evidence of recurrent growth. At the time they said I lost twenty percent of the hearing in my right ear and it still remains a habit for me to use my left ear when I'm on the phone."

♥ *TENDER HEART* ♥

Megan was shocked. She gently glided her fingers behind Rebecca's right ear and felt the scar on her scalp.

Rebecca took Megan's hand and kissed the palm, smiling and leaning her cheek into her hand. "That's not a story I share with a lot of people. I'm grateful that my hair covers my scar," Rebecca said softly.

Megan's expression was wrought with concern; she was overwhelmed by the hardships in Rebecca's life. "Why, sweetheart? An acoustic neuroma is not something to be ashamed of," Megan said.

Rebecca smiled and held Megan's hand close. "The responses of the people in my life at the time certainly made me feel like it was. The day of my surgery my husband went out and doubled my life insurance policy because he was convinced that this was the end of me."

Megan rolled her eyes and groaned at the man's insensitivity as Rebecca gazed toward the crackling fire. "When Maggie and I started spending a lot of time together I told her about my tumor and I was even more disappointed by her reaction. She felt extremely uncomfortable touching my face and head. She treated me like I was some porcelain doll that would crack at any moment if not handled properly."

Megan laughed softly and traced her finger along Rebecca's ear and cheek. "That's why you melt every time I touch your beautiful face," Megan said tenderly.

Rebecca smiled and kissed Megan's hand. "I've never been touched the way you touch me," Rebecca whispered passionately.

Megan glided her hand into Rebecca's hair and rested it on the back of her head, pulling her closer to her lips. "I'm so sorry for everything you've had to deal with without me," Megan whispered.

Rebecca smiled and gently traced Megan's lower lip. "Yeah. Where were you five years ago when my acoustic neuroma and I needed you," Rebecca scolded.

♥ *TENDER HEART* ♥

Megan smiled and kissed her forehead. "Unfortunately, I was in Boston doing my residency. I really wish I'd been here for you, Rebecca."

Rebecca smiled and nuzzled into Megan's neck. "I feel so blessed to have you now, Megan, and to have the opportunity to fall in love with you."

Megan held her close and kissed her warm cheek. "Rebecca, I'm going to ask you to do me a favor."

Rebecca leaned back and looked into Megan's serious eyes.

"I want you to try and start listening with your right ear again so we can assess your degree of hearing loss. Have you had your hearing tested since your surgery?"

Rebecca's face was consumed by guilt as she blushed shyly. "No, I was supposed to but I never went to the appointment."

Megan gave her a stern, scowling look and sighed. "Rebecca!"

Rebecca grimaced and toyed with the collar on Megan's turtleneck. "Well, I was afraid they would tell me I'd have to wear a hearing aid, and I'm too young for that nonsense," Rebecca said, bashfully.

Megan laughed softly and pulled her back into her arms. "I'm going to make you an appointment to have your hearing tested and I promise you that I'll be there with you so you don't have to be frightened. If and when you're ever told you need to wear a hearing aid, I'll buy you one that is so tiny that it fits right inside your ear and you and I will be the only ones that will know you're wearing one. Meanwhile, I want you to try and get back in the habit of using your right ear on the phone. That way we can stimulate your hearing and you'll know if things change again. It's important so we can be alerted to any recurrent growth of your acoustic neuroma," Megan said.

Rebecca squished her face like a beautiful child told she had to eat all her broccoli.

Megan burst into laughter and held Rebecca tight. Rebecca reached up and caressed Megan's face. Megan leaned toward her and united their lips in a gentle, sensuous kiss.

♥ TENDER HEART ♥

The front door slammed. Megan and Rebecca looked up and saw Madison descend into the living room toward them, holding the hand of a beautiful Hispanic woman with an infectious smile. Rebecca was captivated by what a beautiful couple they made together. Shawna stood slightly shorter than Madison, with midnight black, flowing long hair that framed her exquisite olive skinned face.

Megan and Rebecca stood as Madison happily introduced Rebecca to Shawna. They all hugged and kissed each other.

Madison held up her bag of Hershey's Kisses and smiled with glee. "My Shawna bought me a treat. Does anyone want a kiss?" Madison announced happily.

Rebecca smiled playfully and reached inside Madison's bag. "I love Hershey's Kisses, and I would love one of your kisses," Rebecca said.

Madison gave her a beautiful smile and kissed her softly. Megan and Shawna rolled their eyes and laughed. "You know, every time you buy her those chocolate kisses, Shawnie, she offers a kiss to every woman she sees," Megan scolded.

Shawna laughed as she watched Madison and Rebecca settle into the plush couch together, smiling as they unwrapped their treats. Shawna smiled at Megan and slipped into her loving arms. "I certainly don't blame her for offering Rebecca a kiss. Megs, you've had this incredibly gorgeous woman in your house all evening and you're both still fully dressed. What's wrong with you? Have your hormones completely lost their senses or what?"

Megan released a frustrated groan as she squeezed Shawna tight. Shawna playfully cried for help as Madison snuggled in beside Rebecca.

"Megan! Stop taking your sexual frustrations out on my wife. Let her go, please. I have plans for that beautiful body later," Madison stated firmly.

Megan finally let Shawna go as Rebecca tilted her head back and looked into Madison's radiant green eyes. "How did you meet that beautiful woman, Madison?" she said.

♥ *TENDER HEART* ♥

Rebecca popped a Hershey's Kiss into Megan's mouth, luxuriating in the light touch of her tongue against her fingertip. Rebecca had to tear her eyes away from Megan's seductive smile; she barely heard Madison.

"I'd love to share our story with you, Rebecca," Madison said as she extended her legs onto Shawna's lap. Shawna gave her a beautiful smile as Madison scowled at Megan. Rebecca smiled as she watched Megan bury her face in a pillow. Rebecca laughed at their antics as Madison rested her arm around Rebecca's slender shoulders.

"Two years ago I came to spend a few days with Megan while Holly was away on one of her supposed business trips." Madison's voice was dripping with sarcasm as Megan gave her a maternal, scolding look. "Megan had been at the hospital all day and all night doing emergency surgery when I awoke to the most horrific crash outside the house. I looked out my bedroom window and was terrified as I realized Megan had fallen asleep at the wheel and crashed her Blazer into the tree in the front yard. I ran to her and found her with a big gash in her head and her face covered in blood. I called 911 and they rushed her back to the hospital. Thank God Drake was in the emergency room at the time. He checked her out thoroughly and x-rayed her tough skull. Drake arranged for a plastic surgeon to sew up her splintered coconut."

Rebecca gave Megan a horrified look as Megan buried her face back in the pillow.

"Megan promised me that she would never again drive after spending that many hours at the hospital," Madison said sternly. Everyone looked at Megan as she lifted her embarrassed face from the pillow.

"Sweetheart! We could have lost you," Rebecca gasped.

Megan entwined her hand in Rebecca's. "I know. That was pretty stupid of me to drive when I knew I was beyond exhaustion. I just wanted to get home," Megan said.

Rebecca touched Megan's face tenderly and reached for her scar as Megan guided her hand to her forehead. Rebecca

♥ *TENDER HEART* ♥

frowned with concern as she traced her fingertip along the three inch jagged scar.

Madison and Shawna watched their tender display as Shawna gently squeezed Madison's legs. "I brought Megan home the next day and tucked her into bed, then went to the nearest car rental place to rent Megan a vehicle while hers was being repaired." Madison gave Shawna a magnificent smile as she recalled their first meeting. "The woman who rented me the vehicle was my Shawna. She was so sweet and helpful. We talked for the longest time and she told me she was working there to put herself through university as a computer graphics designer. I thought she was amazingly gorgeous and just treated me with the same kindness she treats everyone else," Madison said.

Megan and Shawna burst into laughter at Madison's innocence. Megan leaned closer to Shawna and continued. "Two weeks later, I returned the rental and Shawna was so blatantly disappointed that I was the one that returned the vehicle and not Madi," Megan scoffed. "Imagine a woman being disappointed to meet me," she said in animated disbelief.

They all burst into laughter as Shawna leaned her head on Megan's shoulder.

"I wasn't disappointed to meet you, Megs. I just had a huge crush on your sister. I even made sure that I was scheduled the day that the vehicle was to be returned so I could see Madison again," Shawna explained, shyly.

They all laughed as Madison gave Shawna a seductive wink.

"Shawna was so smitten by Madison that I asked her if she had a business card she wanted me to pass on to Madi. Shawna's face lit up brighter than a Christmas tree as she handed me her business card with her home phone number on the back. I came home and handed Madi the card and said, will you please phone this woman before she spontaneously combusts. You made quite an impression on her," Megan said, rolling her eyes.

They all laughed together.

♥ *TENDER HEART* ♥

"Madison called her that day and three days later I learned, much to my horror, that they're sleeping together," Megan stated, as she playfully smacked Madison's legs. "You little hussy! I thought I raised you better than that," Megan said sternly. "I'm a firm believer in getting to know somebody before you sleep with her," she affirmed.

They all burst into laughter as Madison gave Megan a joyous smile. "Sleeping with Shawna was a marvelous way to get to know her." Madison declared.

Rebecca smiled at the beautiful women around her. "Good for you, Madison. That's such a beautiful story, except for the part of Megan meeting the tree," Rebecca said, as she reached up and touched Megan's chin, smiling seductively. "I'll try to remember that you need to know someone before you sleep with them," Rebecca said, slowly.

Madison and Shawna cheered as Shawna said, "Oh, Megs. You just dug yourself a deep hole on that one."

Shawna filled them in on their evening with her parents and Megan told her how she met Rebecca. Shawna watched Madison yawn as she lovingly caressed her legs. "Ready to go to bed, sweetheart?"

Madison smiled at the woman she loves. "Sure am, darling. We need to pack our stuff as well. The painters said it is safe for us to go home tomorrow, Meg. Can you handle the privacy or would you rather we stayed another week?" Madison teased.

They all burst into laughter as Megan swatted her with her pillow. "I'm sure Rebecca and I will have no trouble entertaining each other, but thank you so much for your thoughtfulness, Madison."

Madison leaned toward Rebecca and kissed her good night. Just then the phone rang. Shawna handed Megan the cordless phone as they all listened to her conversation. They all watched Megan massage her temple.

"I understand, Dean. I just hope that the woman I'm with will understand," she said sadly. Megan handed the phone back to Shawna and buried her face in her hands.

♥ *TENDER HEART* ♥

Rebecca ran her fingers through Megan's lush hair. "I get the sinking feeling that I might be parking my pillow with Madison and Shawna tonight." Madison and Shawna burst into cheers and wild applause as Megan raised her face and gave them both an evil look.

"What's happening at the hospital, sweetheart?" Rebecca asked disappointment etched in her sultry voice.

Megan sat back on the couch and looked into Rebecca's eyes. "I admitted an eighteen-year-old trauma patient today that was roller blading to school and thought it would be fun to try and race a dump truck through a yellow light." Everyone groaned at her images of this disaster. "He suffered a serious head and spinal cord injury. I was hoping to let him stabilize overnight before I took him to surgery, but it seems he's developed a blood clot on his spinal cord and is no longer moving his arms. I need to get back to the hospital and operate on him before he suffers permanent damage to his spinal cord."

Rebecca rose and extended her hand to Megan, guiding her to her feet. "Come on then, my precious Dr. Summers. That young man needs you."

They all rose. Madison and Shawna hugged them both good night, promising to see each other soon. Megan gathered the wine glass as they watched Madison and Shawna head towards their bedroom.

Rebecca gathered her purse, stopped to feed Tangerine and blew her a kiss good night. She walked with Megan to the front door and helped her slip into her jacket. Rebecca smiled at the disappointment on Megan's face.

"I'm sorry to end our evening like this, Rebecca. This doesn't happen very often."

Rebecca wrapped her arms around Megan's neck and guided her intimately close. "Megan, I had a wonderful evening with you and I would have loved to spend the night. However, I have a very strong feeling that we'll be spending a lifetime of nights together, so please don't look so sad. Besides, this will give you

♥ TENDER HEART ♥

more time to get to know me. I'd hate to have to call you my little hussy," Rebecca said, with an impish grin.

They both burst into laughter as Megan playfully toyed with a button on Rebecca's beautiful silk blouse. "I promise to make this up to you."

Rebecca gave her a glowing smile and kissed her tenderly. "I'm going to hold you to that promise, Dr. Summers." They both smiled as Rebecca seductively slipped her leg between Megan's thighs and made intimate contact.

Megan gave her a passionate, rousing look, glided her hands onto Rebecca's slender waist, and pulled her in tight.

"Do me a favor, Dr. Summers, and pack yourself an overnight bag for tomorrow. When we get home from the symphony I'm going to tear your clothes off and send you soaring so high that you'll need a compass to find your way back."

Megan tilted her head back and released an erotic moan as Rebecca escalated her desire. "Rebecca Rhodes, you set me on fire."

Rebecca entwined her fingers in Megan's hair and rested her hands on the back of her head, gently guiding her closer. Their lips met slowly, seductively, igniting their burning passion and feeding the insatiable desire they had for one another.

Megan leaned her forehead against Rebecca's and held her close. "Was that as good as your Hershey's Kiss?" Megan asked playfully.

Rebecca gave her a beaming smile and whispered against her moist lips, "Better than a million Hershey's Kisses," as she took her lips with impatient urgency.

Megan leaned back and slowly caught her breath. "Thank you for a wonderful evening with you and my slippery dream pet, Tangerine."

Rebecca's lips curled into a beautiful, radiant smile. "Thank you for such a delicious meal and the pure pleasure of your extraordinary company."

♥ *TENDER HEART* ♥

They both smiled as Megan leaned closer and teased Rebecca with soft, brushing kisses, hating the thought of letting her go. "Oh, Rebecca. Do me a favor," Megan said suddenly.

Rebecca smiled and watched Megan walk into her hall closet. "I would do anything for you, my love," Rebecca said.

Megan returned within seconds with a black stethoscope in her hand and a sheepish smile on her face. "Will you please hang this on your bedpost for me?" Megan asked.

Rebecca took the stethoscope and blushed deeply as she gave Megan a sweet, shy look. "I guess Drake told you," Rebecca whispered.

Megan laughed and kissed her blushing cheek. "He sure did and I told him that I hope to hang more than just my stethoscope on your bedpost."

Rebecca gave Megan a glowing, seductive smile and rested her hand sensuously on her abdomen. "I was so attracted to you the moment I saw your gorgeous face, Dr. Summers."

Megan laughed sweetly and leaned intimately close to Rebecca's moist, sensuous lips. "You were so beautiful standing in that E.R. And so damned distracting when I wanted to be angry and couldn't tear myself away from your mesmerizing eyes."

Rebecca smiled and gently ran her fingers between Megan's breasts and up to her chin. "You'd better walk me to my car, Dr. Summers, before I can no longer restrain myself and make love to you right here, right now."

Megan leaned forward and lightly brushed her lips against Rebecca's. She held the front door open for her and saw her safely to her Jaguar.

♥ *TENDER HEART* ♥

♥*TENDER HEART*♥
CHAPTER FIVE

Rebecca and Kyle left the boardroom together in animated conversation and headed toward Rebecca's office. Kyle opened the door for her as Rebecca stopped in the doorway. "I'm really pleased with the results of the staff meeting this morning, Kyle. Our home sales from last year have nearly doubled and everyone seems to be working really hard for our clients."

"That doesn't surprise me, Beck. You work your butt off around here to meet the client's needs and it shows in the number of homes you sell. Everyone who works for you sees that and respects you for your high standards and diligent work ethics. You motivate everyone with your actions, Rebecca. You should be very proud of yourself and the success of this company as a whole."

"Are you looking for a raise again, Kyle?"

Kyle rolled his eyes and pointed into the office. "Shut up and get in. The day is young. We have work to do if you want to continue to be one of the best real estate agents in the city."

Kyle followed her in and closed the door behind him. Kyle loved what Rebecca had done to her office. He squinted as he saw the noonday sun struggle to squeeze between the slanted blinds covering the panoramic window. The sunlight cast a striped pattern throughout Rebecca's spacious corner office. The huge glass topped, mahogany desk stood nestled at the juncture of the windows, allowing Rebecca a breathtaking view of the city.

Center stage in the office, Rebecca created a sitting area with plush, overstuffed cream couches. Beyond the couches, a round, mahogany worktable, big enough to seat twelve people comfortably, was covered with architects sketches and blueprints of remodeling plans currently in progress in Rebecca's homes. Kyle smiled at the pastel pink walls trimmed with a border of delicate red roses. He was lost in the warmth of Rebecca's décor when he finally realized Rebecca had stopped dead in her tracks.

♥ *TENDER HEART* ♥

Kyle stepped behind her and rested his hands on her shoulders. Rebecca stared at her polished mahogany desk and saw a single red rose lying across an iced, cafe mocha from the Java Cafe. Beside the iced coffee lay a pretty pink card and two glimmering Hershey's Kisses.

Rebecca walked slowly toward her desk with tears in her eyes. She picked up the delicate rose and inhaled its fragrant scent. She reached for the card and smiled at her name written beautifully in Megan's penmanship. Rebecca hugged the card to her chest as tears spilled onto her cheeks.

Kyle came to stand beside her. "Let me guess. Our gorgeous, grumpy, Dr. Megan Summers was here," Kyle said happily.

Rebecca gave him a glowing smile as her phone rang. She set the card down and pressed the speaker button on her phone.

Diane said, "Rebecca, I have a woman on the line for you that says she's Tangerine's mom."

Rebecca burst into a huge glowing smile as Kyle laughed and slipped out of Rebecca's office with a wave good-bye.

Diane laughed softly and added, "Someday I'd like to know this woman's real name. She's so much fun to talk to."

Rebecca laughed softly, clicked off the speakerphone and reached for her cordless phone. "She really is a lot of fun, Diane, and I'll make sure you meet her someday. Please put her through." Rebecca heard the connection click through and felt a tingling excitement in her chest. "Well, hello, Tangerine's mom."

"Hello, JC and Penney's mom. How are you, Ms. Rhodes?"

Rebecca smiled and leaned against her antique, executive mahogany desk. She buried the toes of her Italian leather shoes into the plum carpeting. "I would be a lot better if I'd seen you when you dropped off my special gifts. When were you here, Megan? Why didn't you have them pull me out of my staff meeting?" Rebecca said.

Megan laughed softly and felt embraced by Rebecca's excitement. "First answer one question for me, my love. What ear are you holding the telephone to?"

♥ *TENDER HEART* ♥

Rebecca's face flushed with sheepish guilt as she quickly switched the phone to the other ear.

"My right ear." They both laughed together as Rebecca felt warmed by Megan's caring.

"Thank you for switching ears, Rebecca. Can you hear me okay?"

"I can hear you fairly well. Now it's your turn to answer my questions, Dr. Summers."

"I arrived in your beautifully remodeled mansion about fifteen minutes ago. I escaped from the hospital after my last surgical case this morning because I just had to bring you those gifts and put a smile on your beautiful face. They couldn't tell me how long you'd be in your staff meeting, so I placed your gifts on your elegant desk. Your office is beautiful, Rebecca. I love the rich mahogany furniture you have. It gives your office a feeling of warmth and professionalism."

Rebecca smiled and stared at her pretty pink card. "Thank you, Megan. I wish I were here to show you around my office. And I want you to know, Meg, my thoughts of you, always put a smile on my face."

"I left another surprise outside your door, Rebecca. Did you see it?" Megan asked.

Rebecca frowned and held the phone close. "No. I didn't. The only other surprise I want is you, Megan."

"Please put down your phone and peek into your hallway for me, Rebecca."

"All right, Megan. I'll go look. Hang on one minute please."

"I'll wait for you forever," Megan whispered, as she heard Rebecca place the phone on her desk.

Rebecca whisked her office door open and stepped into the hallway, then emitted a euphoric scream as she ran and jumped into Megan's arms.

Megan held her tight and laughed at her incredible response. Rebecca leaned back and held Megan's face in her hands and kissed her with burning passion as Kyle and other agents stepped out into the hallway to see what the scream was all about.

♥ *TENDER HEART* ♥

Kyle leaned his head against the doorframe of his office and placed one hand over his heart. "Jesus, Beck. You scared me to death with that scream," he scolded.

Rebecca leaned back slightly from Megan's warm, moist lips and blushed beautifully as she saw all the smiling faces in the hallway. Rebecca cleared her throat and gave Megan a beaming smile. She placed her hand on Megan's lower back and guided her closer to the awaiting crowd, introducing her to everyone.

Rebecca guided Megan toward Kyle as Kyle extended his hand warmly. "Hello, Doc Grumpy. Nice to see you again," he said teasingly.

Megan blushed sweetly and continued to hold Kyle's hand in hers. "I'm sorry about the other day, Kyle. I behaved pretty badly in front of you and Rebecca. I hope you can find it in your heart to forgive me."

Kyle looked from Megan to Rebecca's dazzling smile. "How can you help but fall in love with a woman like that? You're lucky I'm not a lesbian, Beck, or I'd be giving you some stiff competition," he challenged.

They all burst into laughter as Megan entwined her hand in Rebecca's and basked in her loving touch. "You have such a beautiful office, sweetheart. I just love what you've done to this house," Megan said in awe.

Rebecca smiled and squeezed Megan's hand. "Did you get much of a chance to look around?" Rebecca said.

"Actually, I did, and when I was downstairs admiring your reception area I ran into a really strange man that instantly gave me the creeps," Megan said. She could clearly visualize the tall, muscular man with the bleached blonde hair, steely gray eyes and s-shaped scar on his left cheek.

Rebecca and Kyle became gravely concerned and exchanged a knowing glance. "Did he say anything to you, darling?" Rebecca asked as an involuntary shiver chilled her to the bone.

Megan frowned and looked at them both. "No, he didn't. It was just the way he looked me up and down and lingered with his eerie eyes. Who is that guy? I don't like the feeling I got from him at all."

Rebecca exhaled a concerned breath and ran her hand through her hair. "His name is Sam Abbott and unfortunately he is a client of ours. We've been trying to find him a home for the past three months. He never likes anything we show him and he is becoming a big waste of my precious time," Rebecca said carefully.

Kyle leaned back against the doorframe and tucked his hands into his pleated trousers. "We call him the Stalker because he always shows up here unexpectedly and gives us all the creeps. Unfortunately, he has a big crush on Rebecca and has been trying relentlessly to get her to go out with him. She has told him flat out 'no!' a thousand times and we think he's starting to get the message."

Megan turned to Rebecca with a look of deep concern in her eyes.

"Don't be worried, darling. We had Scotty do a background check on him and he came up clean. Kyle and I always show him our homes to keep an eye on him and just make sure he behaves himself. He's harmless but definitely weird," Rebecca said, trying to allay Megan's fears.

Megan reached toward Rebecca's face and gently caressed her soft cheek. "Just be careful when he's around, okay, sweetheart? The guy's obviously not playing with a full deck," Megan said seriously.

Rebecca leaned her face against Megan's hand and smiled beautifully. "I promise to be careful around him, love."

Kyle stepped away from the door and closer to Megan. "I should go, ladies. I have messages to return and a husband to call." Kyle took Megan's hands and held them softly. "You've made Rebecca very happy, Megan. I love the smile that lights up her face every million times she mentions your name in a conversation."

♥ *TENDER HEART* ♥

They all laughed as Megan looked at Rebecca shyly. "I love her very much, Kyle, and I hope to keep that smile on her face for many, many years."

Kyle pulled Megan into his arms and hugged her close as Rebecca smiled and watched their loving embrace.

"Hey, you. I'm the one she came to hug. Time's precious so get out of my way, Superman," Rebecca threatened.

Kyle burst into laughter as he stepped towards his office and watched Rebecca playfully lure Megan into her office.

♥♥♥♥♥♥♥♥♥♥

Megan had just completed her rounds in the Neurosurgical Intensive Care Unit. She stood outside the room of the eighteen-year-old boy that she had operated on late the previous night and talked to his parents and girlfriend. Megan had successfully removed the blood clot from his spinal cord and prevented any permanent damage. She had fused the fractured bones in his neck with a piece of bone graft from his own hip and placed him in halo traction. She inserted a tracheostomy tube to facilitate suctioning and better ventilation of his lungs.

Megan updated the family on his condition and made it very clear to them the seriousness of his injuries and the long road of rehabilitation ahead. Megan answered all of the family's questions and did her best to reassure them that their son was getting the best care possible.

She headed toward the nurse's station and stopped outside the room of the woman who had been ejected through the windshield. The hospital Chaplin stood with all the family members around the bedside and led them in prayer. Megan felt their grief and anguish as they bowed their heads. She wished she could answer their prayers but knew that nothing more could be done.

Megan took the eighteen-year-old boy's chart off the rack in the nurse's station and wrote a progress note. She closed his chart and checked her watch. Two o'clock in the afternoon, only

♥ *TENDER HEART* ♥

three hours since Megan left Rebecca's office. She smiled as she thought of their passionate kisses and ached to hold Rebecca's warm, slender body in her arms. Megan ran her hand through her hair and felt overwhelming joy at the thought of starting a relationship with that special lady.

Megan stood and replaced the chart on the rack as her pager chimed at her waist. Unclipping it from her belt, she read the message: "Please call Kyle. ASAP!" and Rebecca's office number below. Megan's heart filled with concern as she picked up the nearest phone and was immediately put through to Rebecca's office.

Kyle quickly answered the phone with obvious distress in his voice.

"Kyle, what's wrong?" Megan said.

"It's Rebecca, Megan. We were going over some blueprints at her work table and I didn't see her reach for her glasses when I turned the print over and caught her right eye with the corner of the paper," Kyle said, in a torrent of raw emotion.

Megan listened intently as she heard Kyle take a deep breath.

"She's in terrible pain, Megan, and can't even open her eye. I told her I wanted to bring her in to you and Drake, but she's being such a stubborn pain in the ass and won't listen to reason. She thinks this is just going to go away. Please help me with her, Megan," he pleaded.

Megan took a deep breath as her mind raced in fast forward. "Kyle, you're going to put Rebecca in your car and bring her straight to the E.R. I'll meet you there, okay?"

"Okay, Megan, but try and convince Beck of that."

Megan's concern grew as she struggled to maintain her usual calm. "Put her on the phone, Kyle." Megan could hear soft voices in the background as Kyle handed Rebecca the phone. Megan melted as she heard that sultry sad voice.

"Hi, baby," Rebecca said.

Megan held the phone close and leaned against the counter. "Hi, sweetheart. Don't think for one second that your sweet voice is going to stop me from being stern with you, my little lover. I

♥ *TENDER HEART* ♥

want you to listen to me, Rebecca. We need to assess your eye and make sure that no damage has been done to your cornea. I want you to do your best to keep your right eye closed and you are going to be a good girl and let Kyle bring you into the E.R. so I can assess your eye properly."

"I just want this terrible pain to go away, Megan."

"Then let Kyle bring you in so I can help take that pain away for you, Rebecca."

"I don't really have time for this, Megan. I have appointments this afternoon and I'm sure this pain will go away soon."

Megan inhaled a frustrated breath and tried to control her mounting impatience. "Rebecca Rhodes, your vision is much more precious than your afternoon appointments! There is no further discussion here, young lady. You're going to go with Kyle or I'm coming to get you. Those are your only two options."

"You're a big bully, Dr. Summers. I guess Kyle and I will see you in fifteen minutes."

Megan smiled at Rebecca's playful frustration. "Good girl. You'll be handsomely rewarded with a gold sticker for your honorable behavior and maybe even a Hershey's Kiss," Megan said.

"I don't want Hershey's Kisses. I want your kisses," Rebecca snapped.

Megan laughed at Rebecca's defiance as a blanket of warmth encompassed her heart. "My kisses belong to you, Rebecca Rhodes. Now bring your beautiful golden eyes to me and remember that I love you."

"I love you too, Meg." They both said good-bye as Kyle grabbed Rebecca's purse and carefully guided her to his Ford Explorer.

♥♥♥♥♥♥♥♥♥♥♥

♥ *TENDER HEART* ♥

Megan and Drake watched as Kyle pulled up to the E.R. doors. Megan helped Rebecca out of his Explorer. Kyle went to park as Drake and Megan guided Rebecca to an empty examination room. Megan kissed Rebecca softly and sat her on the edge of the stretcher. Megan and Drake carefully examined her injured eye.

Megan turned the light off on the ophthalmoscope and slipped it back into its bracket on the wall. She gently placed the soft pad of her thumb on Rebecca's right eyelid and guided it closed. "Sit back and relax, sweetheart, and keep your right eye closed. I'm going to page Dr. Laura McKean, the ophthalmologist," Megan said as she stepped toward the wall phone.

Dean walked into the room and was introduced to Rebecca by Drake as she explained what had happened to her eye. Kyle joined them in the room and heard Megan talking on the phone to the ophthalmologist. A few minutes later Megan hung up the phone and heard Rebecca arguing with Kyle and Drake.

"Don't cancel our afternoon appointments, Kyle. I'll be out of here in a few minutes," she went on irritably.

Megan had heard enough and was slowly losing her patience.

Drake stepped toward her and shook his head. "I told you she can be a pain in the ass sometimes." Drake reached for Dean and Kyle and guided them out of the examination room.

Megan gave Rebecca a glaring, no-nonsense look and stood directly in front of her angry face, placing one hand on each knee.

Rebecca sat quietly with her hand covering her right eye, knowing that she was about to learn how far she could push Megan's patience.

"I've heard enough denial from you, young lady. This is very serious, Rebecca, and you're going to be here longer than a few minutes while we assess your eye. In the meantime, Kyle is going to cancel the rest of your appointments for this afternoon and tomorrow," Megan said sternly.

♥ *TENDER HEART* ♥

Rebecca's pain and frustration hit a boiling point. "No, Megan! You have no right to tell him to do that. I've just scratched my eye, for God's sake. You guys act like I severed a limb," Rebecca said defensively.

Megan's need to make this woman understand tore her apart as she felt her anger burn.

"I have every right to do what I think is in your best interest, Rebecca. I love you and I want you to let me take care of you and your eye."

Rebecca looked deeply into Megan's moist eyes as she gently placed her hand on top of Megan's.

Megan took a deep breath and, overwhelmed by her love for this woman, she softened her tone. "You have injured your eye, Rebecca, and what it needs is rest. You can't go about your usual business with one eye patched. It greatly diminishes your visual capacity and puts a terrible strain on your left eye. If we don't take care of this properly, Rebecca, you could seriously cause further damage to your eye. I won't let that happen regardless of how angry you are with me for caring about you."

Tears streamed down Rebecca's cheeks as she leaned her forehead against Megan's strong shoulder. "I'm sorry, Meg. It hurts so much and I'm scared."

Megan wrapped her arms around this gentle woman she loved so deeply.

Megan took a tissue from her lab coat pocket, wiped away Rebecca's tears, and tenderly kissed her forehead. "I know you're scared, baby, but please let me help you," Megan said.

Rebecca reached up and touched her fingertips to Megan's lips. She guided her face toward her, gently meeting her lips. Megan's soft moans escaped from her throat as Rebecca looked at her with playful passion and kissed her again, whispering softly against her lips, "Beautiful bully."

Megan smiled sweetly and brushed her lips against Rebecca's. "You don't really think I'm a bully, do you?"

♥ *TENDER HEART* ♥

Rebecca tried to hide her smile and leaned her forehead against Megan's. "No. I'm just not used to someone caring about me like you do."

Megan smiled and kissed Rebecca's forehead. "Well, get used to it, Madame, because you're stuck with me for the rest of your life," Megan said seriously.

Rebecca gave her a glorious smile and caressed her face. "It would be an honor and a pleasure to be stuck with you, Dr. Megan Summers."

Megan leaned forward and kissed her softly as they heard a knock at the door. Rebecca playfully straightened the collar on Megan's lab coat as Megan gave her a flirtatious wink. "Come in," Megan said.

Drake opened the door and introduced the ophthalmology resident, Dr. Laura McKean, who greeted them all warmly. "I'm going to leave you guys in the capable hands of Dr. McKean. Kyle has gone to take care of your paperwork, Rebecca, so he'll be here in a few minutes," Drake explained, as he leaned toward Rebecca and kissed her damp cheek. "Be a good girl or I'll come back in here with the biggest, sharpest needle you've ever seen in your life," he threatened.

Rebecca recoiled in mock terror and buried her face in Megan's neck. "Don't let him hurt me, Megan. Please don't let him give me a needle."

Megan laughed softly and swatted Drake's arm. "Get out of here, you. You're scaring her to death."

Drake laughed and headed out of the room as Dr. McKean smiled and closed the door behind him.

Dr. McKean stepped beside Megan and placed her hand warmly on her back as Megan introduced her to Rebecca. "Thanks so much for coming down to see Rebecca, Laura."

Laura gave them both a warm smile as she placed her hand affectionately on Rebecca's shoulder. "I'm glad I can help, Meg."

Laura turned to Rebecca. "Kyle told me what happened, Rebecca. Does your eye still hurt?"

♥ *TENDER HEART* ♥

Rebecca frowned and wiped away the tears that continued to drain from her right eye. "Just a little. Certainly not as bad as when it first happened."

Megan moved to Rebecca's side and entwined her hand in Rebecca's. Rebecca gave her a loving smile and squeezed her hand. Dr. McKean reached for the ophthalmoscope. Dr. McKean turned off the light and spent the next fifteen minutes assessing Rebecca's eye. She finished and traded places with Megan so she could also have a good look.

Dr. McKean flipped the light on and had Rebecca lie back on the stretcher. She instilled several different drops in her eyes. "Does that relieve the pain at all, Rebecca?"

"It sure does. Those drops have brought the pain from a raw, burning sensation to a dull ache."

Dr. McKean sat on the edge of Rebecca's stretcher and handed her several tissues while the drops bathed her eye.

"Rebecca, you have several minor, corneal abrasions and need to keep an eye patch on your eye for the rest of the day. You can remove it when you go to bed tonight and I'll give Megan your eye drops so she can instill more drops when you remove the eye patch. Your eye will be back to normal in twenty-four hours as long as you keep the eye patch on, use the eye drops, and promise to get some rest."

Rebecca frowned and looked from Megan to Laura. "Yes, ma'am."

Megan and Laura laughed softly at Rebecca's reluctant surrender as they applied a tight eye patch over her right eye. Megan helped Rebecca to sit up on the edge of the stretcher and stood back to admire their handiwork. Laura smiled and rested her hand warmly on Rebecca's shoulder.

"Tell me, Meg. How did you meet this beautiful woman?"

Rebecca blushed and entwined her hand in Megan's as Megan told Laura their story. Laura smiled and leaned her hip against the stretcher. "I need to spend more time around Drake," Dr. McKean said. They all burst into laughter as Rebecca gave Megan an endearing smile.

♥ *TENDER HEART* ♥

Rebecca took Laura's hand and squeezed it warmly. "Thank you for all your help and kindness, Dr. McKean," Rebecca said.

"It's been my pleasure, Rebecca. Megan would do the same for my partner. If I had a partner," Laura said, hopelessly. They all laughed softly as Laura gathered her equipment, then hugged Rebecca and Megan before she headed out the door.

Megan held Rebecca's face in her hands and smiled. "You look so beautifully dangerous," Megan whispered, sensuously.

Rebecca frowned as she looked into Megan's loving eyes. "Does this mean we can't go to the symphony tonight, Meg?"

Megan kissed the patch over Rebecca's eye and smiled. "I love the way you say 'Meg,' and unfortunately the symphony is out of the question. You need to rest your eye, Rebecca."

Megan's heart burst with love for this extraordinary woman as she watched the beautiful pout form on her lower lip. Megan gently glided her finger along that pouting lip and leaned intimately close to Rebecca's face. "Don't be sad, darling. I still have my Rebecca coupon and I plan on turning it in as soon as your eye is ready." Megan gently brushed her lips against Rebecca's and luxuriated in her eager responsiveness. "Instead of the symphony we're going to spend the evening relaxing at your house. That's if JC and Penney will have me," Megan said.

Rebecca rested her forehead against Megan's and toyed with the buttons on her beautiful, coral green blouse. "That'll be questionable after I tell them how you yelled at me," Rebecca said with huge, sad eyes.

Megan burst into laughter and held Rebecca close. "You're damned lucky I was afraid somebody was going to come back into this examination room, Ms. Rhodes. Otherwise, I would have taken you over my knee and spanked your sexy, stubborn behind."

Rebecca ran her fingers into Megan's thick, beautiful hair and pulled her intimately close to her lips. "Stop teasing me with promises of pure pleasure," Rebecca said in a thick, sultry voice. They both burst into laughter as Rebecca guided Megan closer and claimed her lips with sensuous, burning passion.

♥ TENDER HEART ♥

Megan leaned her forehead against Rebecca's. "I'll have Kyle take you home, where I expect that you will put your feet up and get some rest. Is that clear, Ms. Rhodes?"

Rebecca frowned and traced her finger along Megan's collar and neck. "Yes, ma'am."

Megan smiled and basked in Rebecca's feathery touch. "I should be done here in the next two hours and then I'll meet you at your place. When I get there I'll take care of dinner and you."

Rebecca smiled and reached up to touch Megan's face. "Don't forget that overnight bag," Rebecca said, seductively.

Megan laughed softly and leaned toward Rebecca's lips. "Packed and waiting at the door." Rebecca's smile warmed Megan's heart as their lips united in a kiss of passionate need and burning desire.

Drake knocked loudly on the door and stepped right in with Kyle behind him. Both men smiled at each other as Drake stepped beside Megan and watched them shyly move apart. "Gee, Meg. That's quite the bedside manner. No wonder your patients love you to pieces." Everyone burst into laughter as Megan stood back and allowed Drake to give Rebecca a warm hug.

Megan saw the swarming emotions in Kyle's eyes and stepped toward him.

"I'm so sorry, Megan. I feel sick about what happened," he said, shamefully.

Megan pulled him into her arms and hugged him tight. "It was an accident, Kyle. You have nothing to apologize for. I'm just sorry that Rebecca gave you such a hard time. It meant a lot to me that you paged me right away."

Kyle smiled and looked into Megan's beautiful green eyes. "I'm so glad she met you, Meg. You're very good to her and she has had such painful relationships in the past. In the fifteen years I've known her I've never seen her so happy and so in love as she is with you. You've touched her heart and soul in places I don't think anyone's been able to reach. I'm so happy to have you in

♥ *TENDER HEART* ♥

our lives so you can help me take care of that stubborn pain in the ass."

Her own tears blurred Megan's eyes as Kyle's words moved her. "I will always love her and take care of her, Kyle. I can promise you that."

Kyle hugged her as Rebecca watched their loving embrace. "Kyle! Are you making my lover cry?" Rebecca said, accusingly.

Kyle and Megan smiled at each other as Megan dried her tears.

"I may make her cry, but at least she doesn't have to yell at me for being a stubborn little shit," Kyle hissed.

Rebecca squished her face and stuck her tongue out at Kyle as they all laughed.

Megan reached into the breast pocket of her lab coat and pulled out her business card. She turned it over and wrote her pager and home numbers on the back and handed it to Kyle. "Don't ever hesitate to call me, Kyle, for anything, anytime."

Kyle smiled and looked down at the business card. "Thanks, Meg. I won't. Now I won't have to beg and plead with Rebecca to give me your number so I can call and tattle on her."

♥♥♥♥♥♥♥♥♥♥

Kyle started up his Explorer as Megan helped Rebecca into the passenger seat and clicked her seatbelt into place. Megan rested her hands on Rebecca's thighs and gave her a warm smile. Rebecca toyed with a pearl button on Megan's elegant blouse. "I'm going to miss you, Meg. Come home to me as soon as you can."

Megan leaned closer and kissed her softly. "I'll be there as fast as I possibly can. I promise. I need to finish my rounds on the Neurosurgical ward and check on the boy I operated on last night. Then I should be free to run into your arms."

Rebecca brushed her lips lightly against Megan's. "I love you, Dr. Summers."

♥ *TENDER HEART* ♥

Megan kissed her with sensitive, feathery, arousing excitement. Megan leaned back and ran her fingers through Rebecca's thick hair with burning desire. "I love you, Rebecca Rhodes."

Kyle leaned back into his seat and sighed heavily. "Will you two just rent a room for God's sake! You're starting to steam up the windows and you're making me very jealous over here."

Megan and Rebecca burst into laughter as Megan reached over and squeezed Kyle's hand. "Good bye, Kyle, and thanks for everything," Megan said.

"Good-bye, sweetheart. Go give your lips a rest while I take our one-eyed wonder home and settle her in," Kyle teased.

Megan turned and winked seductively at Rebecca. "Little does he know that my lips have only just begun."

Rebecca's face glowed with happiness as Megan gave her one last kiss and gently closed her door. She headed toward the E.R. doors and waved as she watched them drive away.

♥ *TENDER HEART* ♥
CHAPTER SIX

Megan knocked lightly and proceeded through Rebecca's ornate, stained glass doors and into the front foyer of her Georgian estate. She stopped to admire the twelve-foot high beam ceilings and domed skylight that filtered in rays of the setting sun. Megan stepped out of her black leather loafers and slipped them beneath the white wicker loveseat adorned with big fluffy, flowery pillows.

She balanced a dozen pink roses in her arms as she stepped out of the foyer and into the spacious, bright living room. Two matching white leather saddlebag couches sat before a massive stone fireplace. The dusty rose area rug enhanced the oak hardwood floors that shone under the direct track lighting. Megan's eyes instantly traveled to a marble statue of two feminine hands entwined. Megan stepped towards the oak coffee table and ran her fingertips over the cool surface of the statue, as she felt embraced by the warmth and gracefulness of this room. Hand painted borders of entwined ivy graced the archway above the fireplace and wound around a seascape painting of brilliant blues and greens. Megan visualized Rebecca spending countless hours in this room as she headed toward the sultry voice in the kitchen.

Kyle saw her coming first. "Hey, doc," he shouted affectionately.

Rebecca whipped her head around and squealed with delight as Megan set down her gift and caught her in her arms. Megan spun her around before she set her down, held her face in her hands and kissed her softly.

Kyle grabbed his leather jacket and car keys and stepped toward the girl's warm embrace. "I have to go to the office and tie up some loose ends," he said.

Megan touched his arm warmly. "My sister, Madison, and her girlfriend, Shawna, are bringing over enough Chinese food to

♥ *TENDER HEART* ♥

feed an army. Why don't you get Scotty and come back for dinner," Megan suggested.

Kyle's smile was heartwarming as he squeezed Megan's hand. "I'd really like that. I know that Scotty would like to see Rebecca and he's been dying to meet you."

Kyle kissed them both good-bye and headed for the door. "Kyle," Megan called out.

Kyle turned and looked into Megan's loving eyes.

"Thanks for everything."

"She owes us, Megan. Big time."

Rebecca laughed softly and leaned into Megan's arms. "Oh, the two of you can't help but love me and my stubbornness."

Kyle stepped back toward Rebecca and leaned intimately close to her face. "I do love you, Rebecca, but your stubbornness we can do without. You're lucky I didn't have on those Superman boxers you bought me for Christmas. Otherwise, I would have picked you up and flown my Lois Lane to that E.R. kicking and screaming." They all burst into laughter. Kyle kissed the tip of Rebecca's nose and waved as he headed to the front foyer.

Megan held Rebecca close. "Did you really buy him a pair of Superman boxers?" Megan asked with amusement.

Rebecca laughed sweetly and nodded her head yes. "Scotty calls Kyle his 'Man of Steel' when he puts them on," Rebecca grinned.

They both laughed as Megan shook her head. "Say no more."

Rebecca kissed Megan softly. They both suddenly looked down and smiled at a big, fluffy, orange and white cat rubbing herself continuously against Megan's legs in a figure eight pattern. Megan laughed softly and bent down.

"Penney, I see you're busy introducing yourself to my lover," Rebecca chuckled.

Laughing, Megan gathered Penney into her arms and stood next to Rebecca. "You're a beautiful kitty, Penney. I hope you don't mind making room for me in your life." Megan gently caressed Penney's head and face as the cat buried her furry face into Megan's chest and went limp.

♥ *TENDER HEART* ♥

Rebecca laughed as she heard Penney's purr of pure ecstasy. "Looks like your touch has the same effect on Penney as it has on me," Rebecca said, with a seductive smile.

Megan leaned intimately close to Rebecca's sensuous lips and luxuriated in the pure passion in her smile. "I love the sounds that you make when I touch you," Megan whispered.

Rebecca gently touched Megan's chin and guided her face closer as she kissed her with smoldering passion. Penney lifted her head and gave Rebecca an evil look and a discontented squeak for distracting Megan from her massage. They both laughed and watched Penney nuzzle her face into Megan's hand and lick her fingers.

Rebecca laughed and rolled her eyes. "It looks like Penney won't mind at all making room for you in her life," Rebecca said. They both laughed as they heard the crinkling of paper behind Rebecca. They both looked toward the source as Megan set Penney down on the floor, much to her disapproval.

"Hey there, you little fur ball. Those roses are not for you," Megan declared.

Rebecca laughed as she watched Megan walk toward JC and scoop the beautiful tabby kitty into her arms. Megan picked up the exquisite bouquet of long-stemmed pink roses and baby's breath and handed them to Rebecca. "These, Madame, are for you."

Rebecca gave her a joyous smile and touched each of the delicate flowers. "They're gorgeous, Megan. Thank you."

Megan set JC down on the back of Rebecca's elegant white leather couch and took her into her arms. Rebecca leaned up and kissed Megan softly. A tear trickled down Rebecca's cheek. Megan wiped the tear away and held her close in her arms. "Hey, you're not allowed to cry or you'll get your eye patch all soggy," she said tenderly.

Rebecca laughed and looked at the beautiful bouquet in her arms. "I never received flowers from my husband or Maggie," Rebecca said in a choked voice.

♥ *TENDER HEART* ♥

Megan smiled and kissed Rebecca's forehead. "I see. Well, I hope you don't mind, but I have this burning desire to grow you a whole rose garden."

Rebecca laughed softly and set the roses down on her oak kitchen table. She turned toward Megan and entwined her hands in her hair and kissed her with slow tenderness. "You are an extraordinary woman, Megan Summers, and I'm so grateful to have you."

Megan smiled and glided her hands along Rebecca's slender waist and pulled her intimately against her. "I love you, Rebecca, and you are my greatest gift."

Rebecca smiled and leaned toward Megan, brushing her lips lightly and pulling away. Megan groaned with sexual frustration as she slid her hands along Rebecca's slim-fitting, aquamarine sundress, up her back and into her hair, resting her hands on the back of Rebecca's head. She pulled her closer as their lips united in a burning kiss of fiery passion.

Megan held Rebecca tight in her arms. "How is your eye, sweetheart?"

"It feels much better, Meg. I'm ready to tear off this silly eye patch any time now."

Megan gave her a scolding frown as she kissed her forehead. "Be patient, Rebecca. We'll be taking if off before you know it."

Rebecca sighed irritably and leaned her head on Megan's shoulder. "I'm so glad you're here, Megan."

Megan caressed her silky hair and held her close. "I'm really happy to be here with you, Rebecca. You have a gorgeous home. I love what I saw as I walked in here."

Rebecca raised her head and kissed Megan's cheek. "Let's get those gorgeous roses in a vase and then I'll show you around the rest of the house."

Megan picked up the bouquet of pink roses and entwined her hand in Rebecca's and guided her towards the gray and white speckled counter. Megan set the roses on the countertop as Rebecca reached on her tiptoes into the hand carved oak cabinets

♥ *TENDER HEART* ♥

and produced a tall crystal vase. Megan took the vase from her and set it beside the flowers.

"Thank you, Rebecca," Megan said, as she rested her hands on Rebecca's slender waist. She guided her to sit on the countertop, admiring the way her aquamarine sundress glided against her slender curves. Megan stood intimately between Rebecca's legs and slipped out of her stylish black, double breasted jacket, pulled a letter-size envelope out of the inside pocket, and handed it to Rebecca.

Rebecca watched her drape her jacket across the back of one of her high backed, velvet lined, oak chairs. She began to roll up the sleeves of her white, cotton dress shirt that accentuated her feminine curves beautifully as Rebecca admired the sleek curves of her form fitting jeans. Rebecca looked down at the envelope and smiled at the shiny gold sticker awarded to her for her honorable behavior, her name written beautifully across the envelope.

Rebecca squealed with delight and held the envelope up for Megan to see. "Look, baby. I got a gold sticker, just like you!" They both laughed as Megan kissed her glowing face and began placing Rebecca's roses in her crystal vase. Rebecca leaned back and openly admired Megan's form-fitting jeans and slender, muscular frame. "You're so sexy in those jeans, Dr. Summers, and I love your tight ass."

Megan laughed and gently brushed Rebecca's chin with a delicate rose. "You're supposed to be opening your envelope, Ms. Rhodes. Not looking at my jeans."

Rebecca loved the gentle shyness in Megan's smile and leaned toward her sensuous lips. "Those jeans and what's in them belong to me now, so I can look at them all I want my sweet, shy, little lover."

Megan smiled sweetly and leaned closer to Rebecca, taking her lips with a hunger that melted away every ounce of her shyness.

Rebecca sat up properly and gave Megan a provocative, beddable look as Megan leaned against the counter to catch her

♥ TENDER HEART ♥

breath. Rebecca glided her fingertips across Megan's blushing cheek. "I love your passionate response to our kisses, Megan. You're a very sensuous woman."

Megan gently taped the envelope in Rebecca's hand. "Please open that and read it before I tear that sexy dress off of you and make love to you right here in your kitchen."

"Promises, promises," Rebecca teased, as she tore open the envelope with excitement and burst into laughter. "Look, sweetheart. I got a Megan Coupon!"

Megan smiled as she watched her unfold the single sheet of paper and read it out loud.

MEGAN COUPON

This coupon entitles Ms. Rebecca Rhodes to spend the weekend in San Antonio with Megan Summers. Dinner at several romantic, candlelit restaurants will be provided with long moonlit walks. On the one condition that Ms. Rebecca Rhodes promises to be on her best behavior and leave her stubbornness at home. Not redeemable with other coupons or other women. This coupon expires immediately if the answer is not yes.

Reply expected ASAP.

I love you. Always.
Your Meg   XOXO

Megan finished arranging the roses and was drying her hands on a hand towel as Rebecca turned to her with utter disbelief. "Megan! Are you really taking me to San Antonio for the weekend?"

Megan laughed softly and stepped between Rebecca's legs, gliding her hands along her thighs and onto her hips, pulling her intimately against her. "Yes, I am, my love. I got someone to cover for me at work tomorrow and I'm off this weekend, so as of this very moment, I'm completely yours."

Rebecca shouted with joy, wrapped her arms around Megan's neck, and hugged her tight.

"Tomorrow, I'm going to load you into my Expedition and drive you to San Antonio. We have reservations at the Hyatt Regency. We're going to spend an uninterrupted three-day weekend in San Antonio getting to know each other, and I can promise you that you'll need your compass to find your way out of our tangled sheets," Megan said.

Rebecca cheered with delight as she hugged Megan with all her might.

"I've arranged for Madison and Shawna to take care of Tangerine, JC and Penney. Their price is outlandish, but I think you and I can pool our pennies and buy them a bag of Hershey's Kisses per pet," Megan said, as she rolled her eyes playfully. They both laughed as Megan gently traced Rebecca's eye patch. "Does that beautiful smile on your face mean yes or do you need more time to think about it?"

"Yes, yes, yes," Rebecca shouted, as Megan laughed at her pure exuberance. They held each other close as Rebecca took Megan's face in her hands. "You're truly an amazing woman, Megan Summers. I love you with all my heart and soul."

Megan smiled and kissed her gently, whispering, "This is just my way of showing you how much I love you. Besides, I had to find some way to make it up to you for being called away to the hospital last night." They both smiled.

Megan felt Rebecca slowly free the top button of her shirt and glimpse at her lacey bra as she ran her fingers beneath the collar of her shirt.

"I realized after your little stubborn, temper tantrum in the E.R. that the only way to get you to rest would be under my direct supervision. And what better place to recuperate from an eye injury than the romantic city of San Antonio."

Rebecca gave Megan her guilty little sheepish look as she kissed her softly and luxuriated in the gentle passion and warmth

♥ *TENDER HEART* ♥

in her eyes. "I haven't been to San Antonio in years," Rebecca remarked in her sweet, sultry voice.

Megan smiled and looked down shyly. "I've only been to San Antonio twice for medical conferences and both times I went alone because Holly wasn't interested in traveling at the time." Megan looked up into Rebecca's tender smile.

"It will be my pleasure to be the woman that shares the sensuality of San Antonio with you, my love," Rebecca whispered, as she tilted Megan's face up to her and kissed her gently, their lips meeting slowly as their desire ignited their passion.

Megan glided her hands along Rebecca's bare thighs and luxuriated in her lustful moans. Their kisses grew more hungry and wanton as they easily fed each other's need. Megan leaned her forehead against Rebecca's and looked down at her shapely legs barely covered by the aquamarine silk. "I love your legs, Ms. Rhodes."

Rebecca smiled and wrapped her legs securely around Megan's waist. "My legs certainly want to get to know you more intimately, Dr. Summers. In fact my entire body aches to be touched by you."

Smiling, Megan seductively placed her hands onto Rebecca's knees and slowly, tantalizingly glided them along her thighs until they disappeared beneath her wispy sundress. Rebecca gasped as she entwined her fingers into Megan's lush, shiny hair and stared deeply into her passionate eyes. Megan's thumbs glided intimately over her silky panties as Rebecca closed her eyes and pulled Megan tight against her as they both moaned softly.

Rebecca felt her breath come in rapid bursts; the electrifying heat of Megan's exploring touch consumed her. Her burning desire for this woman tore through her entire being and swelled between her thighs as she moaned softly. Rebecca ached for more as she leaned her forehead against Megan's soft cheek and trailed her hand over Megan's stomach and grazed against her erect nipple.

♥ *TENDER HEART* ♥

Megan gasped erotically as Rebecca leaned back and looked into her smoldering eyes. They stared into each other's eyes of aching lust as the doorbell intruded on their sensuous foreplay. Megan dropped her head onto Rebecca's shoulder in absolute frustration as Rebecca held her tight and ran her fingers through her thick hair.

"Once our dinner guests are gone, I promise to take you to our bed and make love to you till you don't even have the energy to find the bed sheets," Rebecca whispered in a smoky voice.

Megan gave her a stunning smile and kissed her tenderly as they turned to see Madison and Shawna walk toward them with huge smiles and bags of delicious smelling Chinese food.

Megan helped Rebecca down off the counter and watched as she hugged Madison and Shawna warmly. Megan set the bags of food on the counter as they all greeted each other with hugs and kisses. Madison and Shawna shared their heartfelt sympathy with Rebecca as she told them what had happened to her eye.

Madison put her arms around Rebecca and held her close. "How does your eye feel, Rebecca?"

"It really feels a lot better, Madison. The pain is completely gone but now this eye patch makes my eye itch like crazy. It's enough to drive a sane woman nuts."

They all laughed as they heard the doorbell chime softly just before the front door slammed. The girls all turned to see Drake, Kyle, and a very handsome man walk into the house. Drake walked up to Madison and Shawna and wrapped them in his arms. Rebecca introduced everyone and greeted the men with hugs and kisses.

Scotty stepped toward Megan and took her hands softly. Megan looked up into his intense, smiling brown eyes and was amazed at how much he looked like Tom Selleck. His dark brown, wavy hair flowed neatly as one strand strayed over his tanned forehead. His strong jaw and high cheeks appeared chiseled from stone. His beautiful teeth glowed in his tanned face as his smile embraced Megan in his charismatic warmth. Megan was impressed by his strong hands and muscular build

♥ *TENDER HEART* ♥

dressed impeccably in a forest green polo shirt and pleated khaki slacks.

"It's a pleasure to finally meet you, Megan, and hear your real name. Kyle prefers to call you Doc and Grumpy so I was starting to think you were one of the seven dwarfs."

They all burst into laughter as Megan blushed sweetly and gave Kyle a look. Megan turned back to Scotty, enthralled by his gentle masculinity and embracing warmth as she stepped into his arms and was consumed by his hug. "Kyle, where did you find this wonderful man?" Megan said tenderly.

Kyle and Scotty exchanged a warm smile as Rebecca nuzzled in beside Megan. "They owe their blessed union totally to me and my need for racy cars," Rebecca professed proudly.

Kyle and Scotty laughed as Scotty held Megan and Rebecca close in his arms. "Yes, you, little one, are totally responsible for my happiness and my headaches," Scotty said, as he rolled his eyes affectionately. They all laughed as Scotty turned to the girls and shook his head. "Five years ago Rebecca owned a Porsche and she and Kyle drove it like speed demons," Scotty said, glancing at Rebecca with a scolding glance.

Rebecca twisted in his arms and gave him a coy smile. "I'm much better now," she stated indignantly.

Scotty frowned at her and rolled his eyes. "Only because I've threatened to throw your cute little ass into jail for a night if you get one more speeding ticket. And let me tell you something else, little missy, that would not include conjugal visits with Megan."

They all burst into laughter as Rebecca gave him a terrified look and buried her face in Megan's neck. Megan held her close as Scotty looked into Megan's loving, emerald eyes and laughed.

"I was on my way to a crime scene when this Porsche came flying up behind me and raced past. I thought it had to be some kids in a stolen car. I called for backup and it took me and two other cruisers, fifteen minutes to catch up to that racing Porsche."

♥ *TENDER HEART* ♥

Rebecca laughed and leaned warmly against Scotty as he bent down and kissed her forehead. Everyone was fascinated by his story and eager for him to go on.

"I was so pissed at this point because this was such a waste of my valuable time. I stepped out of my car just as I saw the cops haul Kyle out of the driver's seat and Rebecca stepped out of the passenger side. I was livid that it was actually adults that were driving like maniacs. I stepped up to Kyle and was just about to unload on him when he grabbed my hands and went into this hysterical, sobbing act and said, "Thank you so much for saving my life, officer! This woman kidnapped me from my parking garage and forced me into her car at gunpoint. She threatened to blow my head off if I didn't do exactly what she said and kept forcing me to drive faster and faster. She said she was going to take me to a secluded cabin in the mountains and turn me into her sex slave." Everyone burst into uncontrollable laughter as Scotty smiled at his memories of Kyle's antics. "Kyle then threw himself into my arms and sobbed against my shoulder as Rebecca leaned against the side of her car and buried her face in her hands in absolute shock and disbelief." Everyone continued to laugh.

Rebecca turned to Kyle and gave him a look that could kill. "It took me twenty minutes to convince Scotty and the other cops that Kyle was kicked out of drama school and that I had no intention of turning him into my sex slave! If I could choose a sex slave it certainly wouldn't have a penis," Rebecca countered strongly.

They all burst into laughter as Kyle stuck his tongue out at Rebecca and Rebecca nuzzled closer into Megan. "In the end Scotty slapped us with a two-hundred dollar speeding ticket and gave Kyle his home phone number," Rebecca said in animated disbelief. They all laughed at this warm story.

Kyle looked lovingly at Scotty. "That was one of the greatest days of my life, getting pulled over by Scotty," Kyle said tenderly.

♥ *TENDER HEART* ♥

Rebecca scoffed at Kyle. "Yeah, you ended up with Scotty and I got the two-hundred dollar fine," Rebecca interjected fiercely.

Megan laughed and touched Scotty's arm. "That's such a beautiful story and I'm so glad you and Kyle found each other. Kyle is a very special man, even though he wears Superman boxers," Megan said. They all laughed.

"Come on, everyone, let's go into the dining room and eat. I'm starving," Rebecca said, as she guided everyone through her kitchen. "If you guys don't mind setting the table, the girls and I will get all this delicious smelling food into some bowls."

Kyle, Scotty and Drake loaded their arms with plates, cutlery, napkins and ice-cold beer as they headed into the dining room. Madison and Shawna stood at the counter and began unloading the containers from the bags. Rebecca reached into her cupboard and was about to grab a floral pottery bowl when Megan wordlessly reached up and guided her hands back down.

Rebecca looked at her with a questioning look as Megan rested her hands on Rebecca's waist and guided her to sit on the nearest kitchen stool. Their eyes locked as Megan rested her hands on Rebecca's slender thighs.

"What in the world do you think you're doing," Megan said sternly.

"I was just getting some bowls down, Megan."

"I can see that, little Miss independent. However, I would like to remind you that your personal doctor, which happens to be the woman standing before you, told you that you need to rest your injured eye and that means no reaching or heavy lifting. You have a kitchen full of friends who are here to help you, so for goodness sake, Rebecca, let us help. Let us be here for you."

Rebecca reached her hand up and gently glided the soft pad of her thumb across Megan's cheek. "I'll try. I promise, it's just that. ."

Megan leaned forward and rested her forehead against Rebecca's.

♥ *TENDER HEART* ♥

"I know, babe. You're not used to having people be here for you. Well get used to it because I'm not going anywhere."

Rebecca tilted her head slightly and grazed her lips against Megan's.

"I like the sounds of that. I also love having my personal doctor, which happens to be the woman standing before me, be here for me. That means more to me than you know, Megan, how you and everyone else are here for me." Rebecca guided Megan's face slightly closer and united their lips in a kiss of torrid desire.

Megan leaned her forehead against Rebecca's and fought to catch her breath. "Please, Rebecca, just sit on this stool and let us do the work. Just let us know where everything is and you can watch us while we work. Kind of like Snow White and the six dwarfs," Megan teased.

Rebecca burst into laughter. "That's very fitting, Meg, since Scotty was led to believe all along that you were one of the dwarfs, right grumpy?"

Megan buried her face in Rebecca's neck and nibbled on her sensitive skin as Rebecca squealed with laughter. "Be good or I'll send you to bed with no supper," Megan whispered in her ear.

Rebecca turned her head and gently held Megan's face in her hands. "As long as you promise to join me, Dr. Summers, then there is nothing else I would need."

Megan growled impatiently as she brushed her lips against Rebecca's.

"Will you guys save all that smooching for later. Some of us are starving here," Madison said.

Megan and Rebecca turned to look at Madison and began to laugh. Megan turned back to Rebecca. "You are such a distraction, Ms. Rhodes. Now stay put and let us do the work."

Megan hesitantly stepped away from Rebecca's warm thighs and reached into the open cupboard for Rebecca's bowls and handed them to Madison and Shawna.

"Where are your glasses, Rebecca?" Madison asked.

♥ TENDER HEART ♥

"The cupboard next to the fridge," Rebecca replied.

Madison opened the cupboard and reached for several tall glasses.

Rebecca watched as JC and Penney perched themselves on the window seat beneath the huge bay window overlooking her English garden.

"JC and Penney are wondering how their home could have possibly been turned into Grand Central Station without their permission," Rebecca said.

"Pricilla would not be impressed by this kind of chaos either. It must be a possessive cat thing," Madison added.

Madison filled a glass with ice water and set it on the counter beside Rebecca. She listened intently as Rebecca playfully told her how Megan had yelled at her in the emergency room.

Madison grabbed several empty glasses and turned towards Megan. "You are so mean to her, Meg. Lighten up before she trades you in for one of the other dwarfs." Megan rolled her eyes in disbelief as Madison stepped towards Shawna. "Come on, Shawna, let's get this stuff on the table."

Megan watched them leave the kitchen as she turned and gave Rebecca a scolding look. Rebecca feigned innocence and tried to reach for her glass of water with her right hand, accidentally knocking the glass over. Ice water cascaded over the counter top as Rebecca gasped and instinctively jumped off the stool.

"Oh, Oh. The one-eyed wonder has struck," Megan teased, as she quickly grabbed the roll of paper towels and knelt beside Rebecca. Megan watched Rebecca frantically mop the floor with shaking hands. She reached for Rebecca and took her by the shoulders. "Hey, sweetheart, I was just teasing. It's okay. We'll have this cleaned up in no time."

Rebecca looked up at Megan with huge tears in her eye. "I'm sorry, Megan."

Megan gently guided Rebecca to her feet and tossed the wet paper towels into the sink as Rebecca slipped into her arms.

♥ *TENDER HEART* ♥

Rebecca's tears moistened Megan's neck as she nestled her face against her.

Megan held her tight and tenderly caressed her head. "What's this all about, Rebecca? You're shaking like a leaf."

Rebecca took a small step back and reached for a tissue on the counter. "When I was a kid my father would go into a ballistic rage every time I spilled something." She wiped at her eye and looked away from Megan's concerned gaze. "I still can't stop myself from reacting to those childhood memories."

Megan reached for Rebecca's face and guided her close. "Your father is gone, Rebecca. You no longer have to fear his drunken rage." Megan guided Rebecca into her arms and hugged her tight. "The only thing you have to fear from me is a good spanking if you don't stop being such a stubborn pain in the ass."

Rebecca laughed softly against Megan's neck and leaned up to kiss her cheek. "Promises, promises."

They both laughed softly as Megan guided Rebecca back onto the stool and finished drying off the countertop and the floor. Megan tossed the wet paper towels into the trashcan, washed her hands and stepped intimately between Rebecca's thighs. "Shall we go join our family before they devour all the Chinese food on us. You know how men are," Megan said.

Rebecca slipped her hand into Megan's as they entered the boisterous dining room filled with the spicy scent of Chinese food. Drake stood and pulled out two chairs for them. "It's about time you two showed up and saved me from these crazy people."

Kyle watched Drake perform his task with undying chivalry and shook his head. "Megan, don't expect the rest of us to adopt Drake's medieval manners. Straight men haven't learned yet that holding a chair out for a lesbian still doesn't give him a hope in hell of converting her," Kyle said.

Everyone burst into laughter as Drake winked at Kyle. He blew him a kiss across the table as he slipped in beside Rebecca. "Actually, Kyle, it was you I was trying to impress," Drake said. The laughter and applause erupted around the table.

♥ *TENDER HEART* ♥

"Well, geez, lover boy, if I'd only known your intentions after all these years then you could have saved me the trouble of throwing myself into the arms of a homicide detective." Kyle said, with his lilting flair.

Rebecca shook her head at Kyle and reached to hand Megan a platter of sesame chicken. "Kyle, quit flirting with the straight boy. You're wasting your minty breath," Rebecca said.

Kyle grinned as he handed Scotty an ice-cold beer. "Scotty has always told me that it's healthy to share my fantasies."

Scotty took a deep swallow of his beer and slowly licked his lower lip as he gazed at his playful lover. "I encourage you to share your fantasies with me, not the good doctor," Scotty confirmed.

Kyle smiled impishly as he reached for Scotty's beer. "You're my greatest fantasy, Detective."

Scotty lightly cuffed the back of Kyle's head. "Start eating before I donate your body to some weird experimental research group," Scotty threatened.

Kyle gasped in animated terror as he clutched at his heart. "Now the truth comes out. You only see me as a physical being to satiate your own testosterone driven pleasures and not the spiritually complex man that works hard to achieve karmic peace and tranquility in our turbulent, emotionally driven lives."

Everyone was frozen in stunned silence as Rebecca dropped her face into her hands. "Scotty, for God's sake, stick some karmic tasty Chinese food in his testosterone driven mouth before we all completely lose our appetites!" Rebecca pleaded.

The laughter filled Rebecca's home as they all filled their plates and struggled to focus on one energetic conversation after another.

♥♥♥♥♥♥♥♥♥♥♥

Megan stood behind Rebecca on her sprawling front porch decorated with white wicker chairs and floral cushions. The porch swing swayed gently in the late evening breeze as they

♥ *TENDER HEART* ♥

waved good-bye to everyone. The taillights disappeared down the willow lined, country lane as Megan wrapped her arms around Rebecca and held her tight.

Rebecca reached up with one hand and entwined her fingers in Megan's hair and sighed happily. "I really enjoyed myself tonight, Meg. We have a very special family."

Megan smiled and nuzzled into Rebecca's neck. "We certainly do, my love."

They stood together and stared into the star-studded night as the balmy air caressed their skin.

"I love you, Meg."

Megan smiled and kissed Rebecca's soft cheek. "I love you, my Rebecca."

Rebecca turned in Megan's arms and slid her hands along Megan's waist and over her tight bottom, pulling her intimately close.

"I'm glad you don't have neighbors very close to you," Megan said shyly.

"Me too. That is one of the things I really like about the location of this house."

Megan smiled and kissed Rebecca's forehead and basked in the sensuous contact of her hands. "Are you ready to take that eye patch off, my little buccaneer?"

Rebecca's face lit up with glee. "Oh, please take this thing off, Megan. The itching is driving me nuts and I'm tired of only seeing you out of one eye," Rebecca pleaded.

Megan tilted her head back and laughed as Rebecca leaned against her shoulder.

"Let's go get your suitcase out of your Expedition and park it in the garage so I can have my personal ophthalmologist take care of my eye for me," Rebecca suggested.

Megan's smile was radiant as she held Rebecca close and gently kissed her eye patch. "And what sort of payment will I receive for services rendered?" Megan asked, seductively.

Rebecca gave Megan a playful, alluring smile and slowly, tauntingly, undid the next two buttons on Megan's shirt. She

♥ *TENDER HEART* ♥

lightly traced the exposed edges of Megan's bra with her fingertip and stared into her moist, emerald eyes. "Come into my bedroom, beautiful lady, and I'll be happy to repay you for all services rendered. If you're good, I might even leave you a tip," Rebecca said, mischievously.

Megan burst into laughter and reached into her pocket for her keys. "Let's go then. I plan on earning that tip and I might even have to hang a tip jar beside my stethoscope." They both burst into laughter and headed toward the driveway hand in hand.

♥♥♥♥♥♥♥♥♥♥

Megan set her suitcase down in Rebecca's bedroom and absorbed the feminine, inviting ambiance. Her king size, oak, four poster bed was displayed elegantly in the center of the room and covered by a goose down duvet in a gold, floral brocade print and matching sheets. Megan's toes sank into the plush gold carpeting as she admired the tan saddlebag couches facing the white marble fireplace. Megan was in awe of the floor to ceiling windows dressed fashionably with heavy cream, paisley print drapes and blinds. She looked around this exquisite room and felt like she had found her way home.

Rebecca entered the room quietly and was moved by the look of profound happiness in Megan's eyes and reached up to caress her cheek. "Welcome to our bedroom," she whispered.

Tears glistened in Megan's eyes as she melted into Rebecca's arms and hugged her tight. Rebecca held her close, wiping away Megan's tears and kissing her with gentle, sensuous arousal. She leaned her forehead against Megan's and gently traced her moist lower lip with her fingertip. She closed her eyes and released a gasping breath as Megan took her finger into her mouth and caressed it with her tongue. Rebecca slowly opened her eye of seductive passion as Megan gently released her fingertip.

"Where's your tip jar because I'd better start tipping you now," Rebecca breathed. They both laughed softly as Rebecca

♥ TENDER HEART ♥

slowly, tenderly pulled Megan's dress shirt out from her jeans. She slowly released the last four buttons and stared into her radiant green eyes. "I prefer that my personal ophthalmologist be wearing a lot less clothing when she takes care of my eye, so if you would be so kind as to slip into something more comfortable I would gladly meet you in my bathroom," Rebecca said, seductively.

Megan smiled blissfully and held Rebecca's glowing face in her hands. She leaned intimately close to Rebecca's lips and whispered, "You're a bossy little thing, Ms. Rhodes."

Rebecca smiled sweetly and brushed her lips against Megan's, moist, slightly parted lips. Their tongues joined in a slow, sensuous dance. Rebecca glided her hand inside Megan's open shirt and lightly trailed her fingers across her slender belly. Megan's gentle gasp burned between Rebecca's thighs as she glided her hand slowly upward and brushed her thumb over Megan's erect nipple. Megan released a throaty moan as Rebecca slowly slipped away and walked towards her bathroom.

Megan watched her in stunned disbelief, dropped back into Rebecca's couch, and buried her face in her hands, releasing a frustrated groan.

Rebecca poked her head out of her bathroom and giggled uncontrollably at Megan's frustration. "You'd better get undressed, Dr. Summers, or I'm going to have to hire another, more willing doctor to meet my many needs."

Megan raised her head and bounded off the couch toward the bathroom just as Rebecca squealed and slammed the bathroom door closed, hiding for dear life.

Megan slowly opened the door and stepped into Rebecca's spacious bathroom suite. Floor to ceiling mirrors covered one wall and enhanced the size of the room. A large glassed-in, double shower stall stood enclosed in glass blocks. The far corner of the room invited you to climb four steps and slip into a jade green whirlpool tub. This unique bathroom amazed Megan as she turned and easily found Rebecca cowering behind the door and hiding her face behind her hands. Rebecca gasped as

♥ *TENDER HEART* ♥

Megan wordlessly reached for her and guided her to sit on the white marble bathroom vanity; she stood between her parted thighs.

Rebecca watched her playful smile with animated anticipation, knowing that she was going to pay for her sexual teasing. The burning passion in Megan's eyes tingled along Rebecca's thighs.

Megan took Rebecca's face in her hands and kissed her with slow, moist, gentle kisses. Rebecca glided her hands onto Megan's waist and slid herself intimately against her hips. Megan gently pressed herself between Rebecca's thighs and heard her sweet, erotic sounds. She leaned her lips back from Rebecca's and held her face still as she felt her press against her in urgent, wanton need. Rebecca stared at Megan's lips and ached to taste her tongue as Megan trailed her finger across Rebecca's warm lips, down her throat and slowly, teasingly between her breasts. Her fingers trailed over Rebecca's belly and gently floated beneath her elegant sundress. Megan's thumbs resumed their path over her silky panties and dipped beneath the elastic waistband. Rebecca's gentle gasp escaped from her lips as she closed her eyes and leaned back against the mirror in delightful ecstasy.

Megan smiled sheepishly and quietly walked out of the bathroom. Rebecca opened her eye and saw Megan's triumphant smile as she closed the bathroom door behind her. "Touché, Dr. Summers! Touché!"

♥♥♥♥♥♥♥♥♥♥

Megan closed her suitcase and smiled as she caught her reflection in a floor length mirror. Her thigh length, jade green, cotton velour robe fit her beautifully and accentuated her legs and sensuality. She felt consumed by excitement as she set the suitcase on the floor, gathered Rebecca's eye drops and headed towards the bathroom. She stopped suddenly and laughed to herself as she saw her stethoscope dangling from Rebecca's

♥ *TENDER HEART* ♥

bedpost. She smiled as she thought of where their lives had taken them since Rebecca made that comment in the E.R.

Megan stopped in the doorway of the bathroom and leaned against the doorframe as she fully enjoyed the sight before her. Rebecca was sitting on the same spot on the vanity wearing a dazzling, gold colored, satin jacquard robe. She was leaning back against the mirror with her eye peacefully closed, her hands resting at her sides. The robe rested loosely above her knees and Megan admired her shapely, tanned legs. A gold satin belt gathered the robe at her slender waist. Megan's eyes were riveted to the gentle curve of Rebecca's breast beneath the slightly parted satin.

"That's a beautiful look in your eyes, Dr. Summers."

Megan smiled sweetly and stepped toward this vision of loveliness. "It only reflects the incredibly beautiful woman that I'm looking at." Megan set the eye drops down on the counter as Rebecca sat up and ran the palms of her hands along the collar of Megan's rich robe. Megan rested her hands on Rebecca's thighs and smiled.

"This robe is absolutely stunning on you, Megan. It accentuates your eyes and finally gives me a glimpse of your beautiful legs."

Megan ran her hands along Rebecca's thighs and just under her satin robe. "You look ravishingly beautiful in this gold satin, my love. It brings out the brilliant gold color of your eyes." Megan leaned toward Rebecca and stepped between her thighs, and watched the satin robe glide higher. Rebecca reached toward Megan's face and gently guided her closer as she met her lips with a gentle, yearning kiss. Megan leaned back and gave Rebecca a radiant smile as she carefully removed her eye patch and meticulously instilled more drops.

Rebecca leaned back against the mirror and basked in the soothing sensation of the eye drops. Megan took a warm, wet, washcloth and gently wiped her eye, trying to concentrate on her task and not on Rebecca's sensuous breasts.

♥ *TENDER HEART* ♥

Rebecca slowly opened both eyes and shouted with glee. "I can see again."

Megan took her in her arms and hugged her tight to share in her excitement.

"Thank you for taking such good care of me and my eye, Dr. Summers." Megan smiled and kissed Rebecca's cheek softly.

"You're very welcome, my love. I hope you realize that I expect payment immediately after each treatment," Megan teased.

Rebecca gave her a sensuous look as she reached along the wall and turned off the light, creating a soft, romantic glow with the illumination of several nightlights. Rebecca reached for the plush collar of Megan's robe and pulled her closer. "It would be my absolute pleasure to repay you for your love and kindness."

Megan's eyes were filled with desire as she slowly enjoyed the sight of the stunning woman before her. She gently glided her fingers along Rebecca's tanned legs and toward her waist, easing the satin tie from its bow and watching as the robe gently parted.

Rebecca, mesmerized by the sensuous wonder in Megan's eyes, slipped off the counter and stood before her.

Megan was awestruck by Rebecca's beautiful body as she slipped her hands beneath the parted robe and felt her silky smooth skin. Rebecca basked in her incredible, feathery touch as she reached for the belt on Megan's robe, easily dropping it to the ground.

Megan leaned toward Rebecca's full, sensuous lips and gently ran her tongue along her lower lip. Rebecca gasped with arousal as she slipped her hands beneath the collar of Megan's robe and glided it over her shoulders, watching it fall to their feet. Rebecca openly admired Megan's beautiful breasts and slender waist as she felt her robe slide down her arms and join Megan's on the floor. They floated in each other's intense eyes as Megan leaned toward Rebecca and devoured her lips with burning passion. Erotic gasps escaped from their throats as their

♥ *TENDER HEART* ♥

bodies connected and their fingers freely explored each other's skin for the first time.

Rebecca leaned her forehead against Megan's cheek and struggled to catch her breath as she held her close. Megan ran her hands softly along Rebecca's back and smiled at their intimate reflection in the mirror. Rebecca looked up into Megan's glimmering emerald eyes and took her by the hand to her bed, guiding her beneath the cool, cotton sheets.

Rebecca eased herself on top of Megan and gently brushed away a stray strand of hair. "You are so beautiful, Megan Summers." Megan's smile exploded in Rebecca's heart.

"I love you so much, Rebecca Rhodes."

Rebecca leaned toward Megan's yearning lips and whispered, "I love you, my Meg." Their lips met in a rapturous kiss as their tongues teased and escalated their desire. Megan moaned softly as she separated her legs and eased Rebecca to rest intimately against her. Rebecca pressed herself firmly against Megan, luxuriating in her sensuous sounds of pleasure as they rhythmically swayed and thrust against each other's flowing passion. Rebecca kissed Megan softly, tenderly, with warm moist kisses along her cheek and neck. Megan moaned and writhed beneath her as she gracefully glided her hands freely along Rebecca's back and shapely hips. Her hands found the delicate curves of her shapely ass and lingered through her intimate contours.

Rebecca gasped and exhaled deeply with each feathery caress as she looked deeply into Megan's eyes and kissed her lips with desire she'd never known before. Rebecca abruptly leaned away and smiled impishly as she heard Megan's aching groan of disapproval, then smoothly lowered herself to her lover's beautiful, firm breasts. She gently blew a breath of warm air across Megan's erect nipple before taking it deeply in her mouth. She bathed it with her warm tongue as Megan moaned and arched her neck. Rebecca caressed her nipple with smooth, long strokes, feeling its growing hardness against her tongue. Megan moaned as she ran her fingers through Rebecca's lush hair,

♥ *TENDER HEART* ♥

basking in the thrilling sensations consuming her body. Rebecca savored Megan's uninhibited pleasure as she left each nipple hot, hard, and wet. She eagerly moved lower to cover Megan's slender belly with warm, wet kisses as she lightly brushed her breasts against Megan's dark mound of hair and felt her own nipples tingle. Megan began to sway beneath her with aching anticipation as Rebecca moved lower between her legs and inhaled her beautiful womanly scent. Rebecca kissed Megan's dark mound and breathed deeply as her scent permeated into her every cell. Rebecca rested her cheek against the inside of Megan's thigh and glided her hands beneath her legs. "God, baby. You're so beautiful," Rebecca groaned breathlessly as she ached to taste this incredible woman.

Megan ran her fingers through Rebecca's hair and thrived on their almost unbearable closeness. "You feel so wonderful, my darling," Megan said in a thick, passionate voice.

Rebecca nuzzled her cheek against Megan's soft mound of hair and looked up into her rapturous smile. "Is this where you ache for me, Meg?"

Megan arched her neck and answered in a passionate, throaty voice, "God, yes!"

Rebecca smiled and ran her tongue lightly along the inside of Megan's thigh. "Well then, I do believe I promised to kiss it better for you," she whispered. Rebecca leaned closer and glided her fingers into the nest of dark curls. Her fingers trailed between her glistening folds and deeply into her pool of wetness as she watched her arch her hips and moan with ecstasy. Rebecca was consumed with her passion and desire for this woman as she traced her wet fingers along the inside of her thighs. She leaned closer as she glided her tongue along Megan's sensitive tissue and tasted her for the first time.

Megan arched her hips and emitted a deep, throaty moan as Rebecca rhythmically caressed her with her tongue. They swayed and thrust to their own intimate sounds, both gasping with undeniable pleasure. Rebecca luxuriated in Megan's rich wetness and sweet taste as her fingers glided between her

♥ *TENDER HEART* ♥

thrusting folds and discovered her inner depths. Megan gasped and purred her skilled lover's name as Rebecca's tongue danced intimately with Megan's erect tissue. Megan exhaled a deep, groaning breath and suddenly stopped thrusting her hips as her quivering thighs tightened around Rebecca's shoulders.

"Oh my God, Rebecca," Megan said, in a deep rasping voice. Heady seconds passed as Rebecca slowed her pace and felt Megan's explosive shudder beneath her tongue as wave after wave of undulating spasms caressed her fingers. Megan shouted Rebecca's name and tensed against the overwhelming onslaught of hypersensitive orgasms cascading throughout her entire being. Megan groaned one final time, holding Rebecca's head firmly in her hands as she collapsed listlessly back onto the bed with rapid, irregular breathing. Rebecca smiled as she brushed her wet chin against Megan's glistening mound and eased herself to lie on top of her.

Rebecca reached for a tissue to wipe her damp chin. Megan gently eased the tissue from her hand and held her face tenderly as she dried her chin. Rebecca was deeply moved by Megan's loving tenderness and caressed her beautiful, flushed face.

"Where's my compass? I definitely need a compass to find my way back to earth," Megan said raggedly.

Rebecca laughed softly and kissed her warm lips. "I'm here, baby. I am your compass," Rebecca whispered.

Gentle tears collected in Megan's eyes as Rebecca leaned down to her and kissed her with passionate tenderness.

Megan lay with her eyes closed as Rebecca's fingers lingered along her chin and throat and down to her shapely, firm breasts. She slowly opened her eyes and looked deeply into Rebecca's beautiful face. They were both overcome by the strength of their love. Rebecca looked into Megan's dreamy eyes and leaned toward her, kissing her with gentle, seductive passion as Megan tasted herself on Rebecca's tongue and kissed her with astounding desire.

"You're an incredible lover, Rebecca Rhodes."

♥ TENDER HEART ♥

Rebecca smiled deeply and trailed her finger along Megan's full lower lip. "You're wonderful to love, Megan Summers."

Megan watched a playful smile curl Rebecca's lips as her fingers made tiny circles on Megan's chest.

"You're the most delicious creature I've ever tasted," Rebecca purred.

Megan laughed and rolled Rebecca onto her back, carefully easing herself on top of her. She separated Rebecca's thighs with her knee and leaned intimately against her, aching to feel her wet passion. Rebecca moaned softly as she basked in Megan's gentle, swaying weight on her. She rested her hands on Megan's tight bottom and pulled her toward her as her fingers trailed over her soft, warm skin.

Megan looked deeply into Rebecca's loving eyes and met her lips softly, teasingly, moving back slightly and causing Rebecca to raise her head and chase the lips she desperately craved. Rebecca fell back onto the pillow and closed her eyes as a burning passion flared in her soul like never before. She arched her hips and pressed herself tightly against Megan's dark curls as she felt the flow of her own wetness. Megan softly kissed her neck and throat as she luxuriated in her wondrous, erotic sounds.

Rebecca glided her fingertips along Megan's back and stopped at her shallow curve, pulling her tightly against her and moving lower to caress her shapely, sexy bottom. Rebecca arched her neck with a gasping moan as Megan took her nipple in her mouth and taunted it with her warm, wet tongue, leaving it erect and aching for her. Rebecca moaned and ran her fingers through Megan's beautiful hair and arched her back, easing her breast deeper into Megan's mouth. "Oh, God! Yes, Megan. You feel so wonderful."

Megan smiled and leaned toward Rebecca's lips. "You're wonderful, my love, and you have such a beautiful body." Megan gently brushed her lips against Rebecca's as Rebecca entwined her fingers in Megan's hair, resting her hands on the back of her head and pulling her closer as she probed her deeply with her kisses. Megan fed Rebecca's insatiable, burning hunger

♥ *TENDER HEART* ♥

as she glided her hand lightly across Rebecca's hard, wet nipples, increasing her gasping breaths with each feathery touch. She trailed one finger lightly between Rebecca's breasts and over her belly, gently tracing the outline of her puckered belly button. Rebecca arched her hips higher and groaned impatiently as Megan taunted her with gentle, elusive caresses. Megan took Rebecca's tiny earlobe between her teeth and teased it with her tongue as she smiled at Rebecca's burning desire.

"Patience, my precious darling, patience," Megan breathed.

Rebecca swiftly glided her hands along Megan's ribs and began tickling her mercilessly. Megan burst into joyous laughter as she quickly grabbed Rebecca's hands and pinned them above her head. They both giggled with playful excitement as Megan held both Rebecca's hands in her one hand and stared deeply into her sensuous eyes. She slowly glided her fingertips along Rebecca's outstretched arm and down her ticklish ribs. She retraced her pattern around her belly button and delighted in Rebecca's heavenly sigh. Megan gently opened her hand flat and felt Rebecca's soft mound of curls against the palm of her hand. She sighed deeply as she rested her forehead against Rebecca's. They stared into each other's passionate eyes.

Rebecca eagerly separated her legs further and gasped softly as Megan's fingers glided along the inside of her thighs. Rebecca freed her own hands and floated her fingertips along Megan's smooth back and across her tight ass as she ached for her lover's touch. Megan was a willing captive of the uninhibited lust in her eyes as she lightly caressed the inside of Rebecca's thighs, heightening her explosive, burning desire. Rebecca never wavered from Megan's sensual green eyes as she entwined their fingers on her own thigh. Megan gave her a breathtaking smile as she slid their hands up along her thigh and lightly across Rebecca's wetness. Rebecca released an erotic moan as Megan slowly released her hand and ran her fingers through her sexy mound of hair and finally into her unbelievable pool of wetness. Rebecca closed her eyes and held Megan tight as sensations of pleasure showered her soul.

♥ *TENDER HEART* ♥

Megan moaned with joy as she slowly, lightly caressed Rebecca into an intense, erotic rhythm. Megan basked in her extraordinary responsiveness as she gently entered and explored her. Rebecca gasped with intense pleasure and arched her hips to guide Megan in deeper.

"Oh God, yes, Megan! You are so incredible." Megan kissed her softly and took her lower lip into her mouth as she slipped her fingers toward Rebecca's greatest sensitivity and lightly swirled her in her own wetness. Rebecca began breathing rapidly against Megan's cheek, rocking her hips faster and digging her fingertips into Megan's back. Megan was mesmerized watching her as Rebecca suddenly stopped rocking and buried her face in Megan's neck.

"Oh God, Megan, yes," Rebecca screamed, as a burst of wetness bathed Megan's fingers and engulfed her in continuous, undulating spasms.

Megan carefully eased her fingers from within Rebecca and gently lay her back down on their pillow, resting easily between her thighs. Megan leaned closer and kissed the tears on Rebecca's cheeks as Rebecca's labored breathing eased slowly and she opened her eyes. She smiled at the deep passion in those beautiful green eyes and reached up to caress Megan's cheek. Megan used her thumb to brush away Rebecca's tears and leaned closer, kissing her tenderly. Rebecca reached up and held Megan's beautiful face in her hands.

"That was the most unbelievable experience of my life. You took me to such explosive heights, my love." Megan smiled beautifully and brushed a stray strand of hair away from Rebecca's eyes.

"I love you so much, Rebecca, and I want to make love to you for the rest of my life." Rebecca's smile caressed Megan's heart as she tenderly guided her face closer and kissed her deeply.

"I love you so much, Meg. You are my soul mate and my tender heart."

♥ *TENDER HEART* ♥

Megan's eyes filled with tears as she leaned toward Rebecca and claimed the lips that have rekindled the flame in her heart.

Rebecca easily rolled Megan onto her back and straddled her thigh, leaning toward her neck and arousing her with a trail of wet, soft kisses.

Megan arched her neck and writhed in moaning ecstasy. "God, Rebecca. I love to feel your wetness against my thigh."

Rebecca gave her a beautiful seductive smile and pressed herself firmly against her thigh. "You make me so wet, Dr. Megan Summers." They both burst into smiles as Rebecca basked in Megan's gentle, passionate sounds as she leaned toward her lips and kissed her with incredible, burning desire. Rebecca's love for this woman consumed her as her hand traced its way to Megan's sensuous center and gently sent her on another unbelievable, explosive journey.

Rebecca lay peacefully satiated on Megan's chest as her finger made light, feathery circles over Megan's warm breast. Megan smiled and held her close in her arms as her fingers traced a jagged scar behind her right shoulder.

"How did you get this nasty scar, sweetheart?" Megan asked.

Rebecca nuzzled deeper into Megan's arms and tilted her face up. "When I was ten I left my brand new bike on our driveway. My father was so drunk that he never saw it and ran over it with his car. He flew into one of his usual rages and picked up what was left of my bike and threw it at me. I did my best to get out of the way, but something caught my shoulder blade and tore the flesh. I took off and hid in the woods for hours and tried to stop the bleeding myself. I came home when it was dark because I knew my father would have passed out by then. My mother was frantic with worry and had spent hours looking for me. She did her best to patch me up because we couldn't go to the hospital and explain what my father had done to me." Rebecca stopped to see the tears stream down Megan's cheeks and leaned up to hug her tight.

"I'm so sorry he hurt you like that, darling."

♥ TENDER HEART ♥

Rebecca smiled and dried Megan's tears. "He's long gone from my life, sweetheart. Unfortunately, the scars and memories remain."

Megan held Rebecca in her arms and covered the scar with her hand, wishing to erase all of Rebecca's painful childhood.

Rebecca leaned up on her elbow and gently caressed Megan's damp cheek. "The happiness you've brought into my life, Megan, overshadows all the pain of my childhood." Megan's smile was radiant as Rebecca looked down at her sensuous body and their intimately entwined legs. "I've experienced more intense pleasure and happiness with you in three days than I did in ten years of marriage."

Megan laughed softly and traced Rebecca's moist lower lip. "Are you comparing me to a man, young lady?" Megan scolded playfully.

Rebecca burst into laughter and slowly trailed her eyes over Megan's irresistible body. "You, my dear tender heart, are every inch a woman, and I could never mistake you for anything else," Rebecca said.

Megan laughed and traced her finger teasingly around Rebecca's soft nipple. "I bet things would have been different if you'd bought your husband Superman boxers and turned him into a 'man of steel,'" Megan said, laughing at the grimacing expression on Rebecca's face.

Rebecca raised herself over Megan and leaned close enough to feel her breath. "I don't want a 'man of steel,' my beautiful Meg. I want you. I want your incredible love and your insatiable passion."

Megan's eyes were brimming with love as she reached up and took Rebecca's face in her hands.

"I'm yours, Rebecca. Now and always." Rebecca's eyes filled with tears as she lowered herself to kiss the woman who owned her soul.

♥ *TENDER HEART* ♥
CHAPTER SEVEN

Rebecca and Megan spent their first day in San Antonio walking among the shops, talking, laughing, and exploring this romantic city in perfect harmony.

Rebecca twirled slowly in awe and rested her sunglasses on the top of her head as she took in the surroundings at the entrance to Sea World. Megan paid for two tickets and guided the overwhelmed Rebecca in through the front gates. Megan handed in their tickets and accepted the guide map of the park. She followed Rebecca through the turnstile and guided her away from the crowd. She gently reached forward and slipped Rebecca's glasses back on her face. "I'd like you to keep your sunglasses on whenever we're outside, okay, darling? It'll help protect your injured eye. I know you said it feels one-hundred percent better but I'd still like us to protect it as much as we can."

Rebecca tilted her head sweetly and reached forward to straighten the collar of Megan's white, sleeveless cotton top. "You're something else you know that, Dr. Summers? You're just too good to be true."

Megan gave her a sweet smile as she slowly unfolded the map.

"You mean to tell me that this place is so big that we need a map to find our way around?" Rebecca asked innocently.

Megan looked at her over the edge of the map and slowly leaned towards her, marveling in the vision of Rebecca in her slim fitting, red sundress. "You, my darling, with the lost childhood, have no idea. We could spend the entire day here and still not see everything." Megan quickly referred back to the map at the list of show times as Rebecca stared around them in disbelief. Megan found the information she wanted and folded the map into the pocket of her black pleated shorts. "Come with me, sweetheart. There's someone I want you to meet," Megan

♥ TENDER HEART ♥

said, as she rested her hand on Rebecca's slender waist and guided her forward.

♥♥♥♥♥♥♥♥♥♥

"Now I need a volunteer from the audience. Who's going to be the brave soul to come out on our stage and be my assistant," the announcer said.

Megan playfully raised Rebecca's hand.

"The pretty lady up in the green section with the red sundress and sunglasses. Why don't you come down here and meet Shamu up close and personal."

Megan burst into applause and laughter when she realized that Rebecca had been chosen. Rebecca looked at her in shock.

"Megan. What have you volunteered me for?" Rebecca said suspiciously.

Megan guided Rebecca to her feet. "This is going to be an experience of a lifetime for you, brave little soldier. Now get going, Shamu awaits you."

Rebecca gave Megan one final untrusting look before she headed out the aisle and down the metal steps. Everyone applauded her bravado as she made her way to center stage and was introduced to the crowd.

"Well, welcome to Sea World, Rebecca. You certainly are in for a treat this morning," said the announcer.

It was his turn to get Rebecca's suspicious stare. "This is my first time ever at Sea World so I have no idea what you need me to be your assistant for," Rebecca said carefully.

The entire crowd broke into applause. Megan could hardly contain her laughter as she watched a terrified Rebecca stand at the edge of the killer whale stage area, keeping one eye on Shamu, floating gracefully before her.

"Well, Rebecca, Shamu would like to give you a kiss."

Rebecca quickly took one terrified step back. "Oh, no! Actually my preference doesn't lean towards killer whales."

♥ *TENDER HEART* ♥

The entire crowd burst into laughter as the announcer carefully took Rebecca's arm and held her still as he explained exactly how simple and sweet the whole experience would be. He guided a reluctant Rebecca into position and readied Shamu and the crowd for the big moment.

Megan couldn't help but smile as she watched Rebecca give her a small feeble smile just before she wrapped her arms around herself and closed her eyes tight. Megan and the entire crowd gasped as they watched the massive gentle whale ease itself slowly out of the tank and brush it's huge pink tongue against the side of Rebecca's face. The applause was thunderous as everyone watched Rebecca slowly open her eyes and reach forward to touch the gentle giant. Her expression was filled with awe and wonder as she looked up into the crowd to find Megan beaming at her and clicking madly with her camera.

After the show Megan guided a stunned Rebecca through the crowd and towards the ice cream stand. "Did you see it, Meg? Did you see it? He came right out of the water and planted a juicy wet one right on my cheek!" Rebecca beamed.

"That was amazing, Rebecca. I have never known anyone who received a kiss from Shamu, you lucky girl you. His big old pink tongue just about swallowed you up," Megan teased.

Rebecca hadn't stopped smiling as she handed Megan their vanilla cones and paid for the ice cream. She took a lick to prevent the ice cream from dripping on her hand as she followed Megan through the crowd. "Actually, Meg, Shamu's tongue doesn't hold a candle to what yours does to me." Rebecca continued to lick at the droplets of melting ice cream as Megan watched her in wonderment.

"And do you have any idea what watching your tongue right now is doing to me?" Megan said, softly.

Rebecca's eyes glowed with mischief as she slowly licked the ice cream off her lower lip. "I hope melting you the same way your ice cream is melting all over your hand."

♥ *TENDER HEART* ♥

Megan quickly looked down at the disappearing cone and took several quick licks. "Ah, now look what you've done. You're so damn distracting, Ms. Rhodes."

Rebecca laughed with delight as she handed Megan several napkins. "Come on, Dr. Summers. Let's go see all the other shows before I decide that the only show I want to see is you laying naked between our sheets."

Megan leaned intimately close and discreetly licked the edge of Rebecca's ice cream. "If you ask me nicely I might even volunteer to be your assistant on center stage," Megan purred.

Rebecca sighed heavily as she touched the soft pad of her thumb to the drop of ice cream on Megan's wet lower lip. "You, Megan Summers, will forever be my partner on center stage."

Megan smiled deliriously as she gently kissed Rebecca's thumb. "Come on, my little seductress, before the next show becomes our hotel room," Megan said impatiently, as she guided Rebecca towards the sea lion exhibit.

Rebecca talked non-stop about the ballet antics of the sea lions as they walked past a child enjoying a huge blue cotton candy. Rebecca stopped in mid sentence and turned back to watch the child pluck at the sugary treat and stuff it in her mouth with delight.

Megan smiled as she reached forward and brushed her fingertips across Rebecca's sun kissed cheek. "Have you ever had cotton candy, babe?"

Rebecca shook her head, no, as Megan gently tucked a loose strand of hair behind her ear. She rested her hand at her elbow and guided Rebecca to the nearest cotton candy cart. Megan bought her a big puffy, swirling, paper cone of pink, wispy sugar and watched Rebecca stare at it in wonder.

"I'll show you how to eat it, babe. You just pinch a bunch between your fingers and pull," Megan said, as Rebecca watched her ease the wispy candy in her mouth.

Rebecca dug her fingers in and pulled out a long strand and eased in into her mouth, smiling with glee. "That is pure sugar once it hits your tongue." Rebecca declared.

♥ *TENDER HEART* ♥

"So are you, babe. So are you," Megan said, as she guided a beaming Rebecca towards the stingray pool.

They spent the entire day visiting all of the displays and seeing each of the shows as they shared in the beauty of the experience.

♥♥♥♥♥♥♥♥♥♥

Rebecca slowly raised her head from its resting place on Megan's shoulder as the early morning sun forced its way through the blinds. She marveled at the way Megan's long, midnight black eyelashes rested against her tanned face. Her high cheekbones curved gracefully downward to her strong jaw. Megan's rosy lips were swollen from their night of endless passion as they rested slightly open in peaceful slumber. Rebecca followed the lines of her well-defined shoulders and over her curvaceous breasts. Her eyes lingered along Megan's flat tummy to where the tangled sheets rested below her belly button. Rebecca slowly reached for the sheet and tugged them free of her own legs as she slowly pulled the sheet up to Megan's shoulders.

Megan stirred and slowly opened her sleepy eyes. Rebecca smiled as she brushed a stray strand of hair away from Megan's eyes. "Good morning, my tender heart," Rebecca whispered.

Megan arched her back and stretched her arms above her head before pulling Rebecca back into her arms. "Good morning, sweetheart. What time is it?'

Rebecca raised her head off of Megan's chest and peered at the bedside clock. "Eight a.m.," Rebecca said, as she leaned herself up on her elbow. She slowly trailed her finger along Megan's sexy lower lip. "How are you, darling?" Rebecca said.

Megan smiled deeply as she ran her fingers through Rebecca's disheveled hair. "I'm having a hard time believing that someone as wonderful as you can be real."

Rebecca leaned closer and kissed her with gentle tenderness. She leaned back slightly and eased the sheet below Megan's

♥ *TENDER HEART* ♥

breasts as her thumb glided around her soft nipple. "I woke up this morning and just had to stare at you for a few minutes to make sure that you and this weekend have not been a figment of my imagination." Rebecca's thumb traced the lower curve of Megan's breast as she paused to gather her thoughts. "You're the best thing that's ever happened to me, Megan. I'm terrified that I'm going to lose you like I've lost everything else that I've cherished."

Megan reached up and cupped Rebecca's face in her hands. "You're not going to lose me, Rebecca. Everything about you and us feels so right. I vow to you on this ungodly early Saturday morning to be your wife, through sickness and health, till death do us part."

Rebecca smiled as she wiped at the tears on her cheek. "Promise to stick with me even when I'm a stubborn pain in the ass?"

Megan easily rolled Rebecca onto her back and nestled herself between her parted thighs. She entwined their hands together and pinned them above Rebecca's head. "I promise to be your wife regardless of your stubborn streak, my girl with the sexy ass." Megan leaned down and kissed Rebecca's sweet, smiling lips. "Do you promise to be my wife through thick and thin regardless of my trivial temper tantrums?" Megan said, as she nibbled on Rebecca's lower lip.

"I'd hardly call your temper tantrum in the E.R. trivial, Dr. Summers, however, I vow to be your wife from this day forth regardless of your imperfections."

Megan leaned back and stared at Rebecca in shock. "What imperfections?"

Rebecca burst into laughter as she rolled Megan onto her back and eased herself lower. She slowly took Megan's nipple in her mouth and caressed it with her warm tongue as it peaked instantly in her mouth. Megan arched her neck and moaned softly. Rebecca sucked it deeply into her mouth and slowly released it as she slipped to the edge of the bed. Megan quickly opened her eyes and turned to stare at her. Rebecca leaned down

♥ *TENDER HEART* ♥

and kissed the tip of her tiny nose. "I have to pee. And while I'm doing that I'd like you to think long and hard about how you are going to work on those imperfections," Rebecca stated.

Megan groaned in disbelief and lunged for Rebecca. Rebecca squealed and quickly dodged Megan's arms as she headed to the bathroom in their presidential suite. Megan grabbed the nearest pillow and threw it right at her just catching her in the bottom as she turned to get away. Rebecca grabbed the pillow off the floor and tossed it right back at Megan as she followed its path and dove into Megan's arms. They both rolled and entwined in the king size, oak canopy bed as their laughter filled the room.

Megan guided Rebecca on top of her and held her tight in her arms. Their lips met slowly, softly as Rebecca's moan echoed in her throat. Megan traced her lower lip with her tongue and guided it between her lips as Rebecca opened her mouth and allowed Megan into her sweet cavern. Megan glided her hands softly over Rebecca's back and bottom as their tongues feverishly clashed and entwined. Megan swiftly rolled Rebecca onto her back and eased herself lower. She took Rebecca's erect nipple in her mouth and tugged on it gently with her teeth before bathing it with her tongue. Rebecca arched her back and buried her breast deeper in Megan's mouth as she groaned in ecstasy. Megan allowed Rebecca's aching nipple to slip from between her lips as she eased herself off Rebecca and onto the side of the bed. She took one long, sensual admiring look at Rebecca's gorgeous body before rising to her feet.

"I have to pee. When you feel you can live with my imperfections then maybe you can join me in the shower," Megan stated, as she headed towards the bathroom with a deliberately sexy swing of her hips.

Rebecca watched her in disbelief as she disappeared into the bathroom. She flopped onto her tummy and buried her face in the dislodged sheets as she screamed with frustration. Rebecca heard the toilet flush and quickly got to her feet. The shower water came on as Rebecca stepped towards the Queen Anne

♥ *TENDER HEART* ♥

chair and reached for her gold satin jacquard robe and secured the tie at her waist. She stepped around the small circular mahogany table and headed into the bathroom. She stopped in the doorway and peered through the frosted glass framing the large shower as she watched the silhouette of Megan's sensual body. She moved with the grace of a dancer as she stood beneath the steaming shower and finger combed the water through her hair. Rebecca was mesmerized watching this graceful display as she realized her bladder was about to burst.

Rebecca washed her hands at the double sink with inlaid gold faucets. She reached for the plush white hand towel embossed with the hotels emblem and turned to watch Megan lather shampoo in her hair. She folded the hand towel neatly on the rack and headed for the shower door. She tugged the frosted double door open and stood with her hands on her hips.

Megan rinsed the last bit of shampoo from her hair as she stood watching Rebecca glare at her. She brushed the droplets of water from her eyes and stepped out from under the flow of water.

"Don't you ever leave me wanting you like that again, Dr. Summers, and you know that there is not one imperfect thing about you, and that makes it harder for me to believe that you're real."

Megan silently stepped before Rebecca and firmly tugged on the tie at her waist, throwing it onto the bathroom floor. She slid her wet hands beneath her collar and eased the robe over her shoulders and unceremoniously tossed it back over Rebecca's head. She slid her hands into Rebecca's hair and held her head firmly in her hands, crushing her lips to Rebecca's.

They both gasped with burning need and insatiable desire as Rebecca pushed Megan back into the shower and pinned her back against the tiled wall. Rebecca's hands molded to Megan's breasts as her nipples strained against her palms. Rebecca knelt lower and took a straining nipple in her mouth and caressed it to a rock hard peak. Megan arched her head against the cool tile and gasped with ecstasy as Rebecca's hands slid over her belly

♥ *TENDER HEART* ♥

and hips, pulling her intimately against her. Megan closed her eyes and held onto Rebecca's shoulders for support as Rebecca dropped to her knees, gently separated Megan's thighs and buried her tongue in her warm wetness. Megan arched her back and screamed her lovers name as Rebecca's tongue found Megan's erect center and plunged her into an abyss of euphoric sensations. Rebecca slid her hands onto Megan's bottom and caressed her intimately as she swirled her tongue rhythmically around and around.

Megan squeezed Rebecca's shoulders and thrust against her one final time as a kaleidoscope of sensations and shimmering lights exploded from the tip of Rebecca's tongue right through the top of Megan's head.

Megan leaned back heavily against the tiled wall and gasped for air as Rebecca kissed her way back up to Megan's lips.

"That was amazing," Megan gasped.

"It would have been equally amazing in bed if you allowed me the opportunity to show you instead of teasing and taunting me like that, then taking off," Rebecca stated.

Megan growled deep in her throat and twirled Rebecca around, positioning her face first against the wall of frosted glass. "If I do remember correctly, my little tease, you were the one that woke up my breasts with that amazing tongue of yours and then had the gall to announce that your bladder was a bigger priority than my pleasure. I, on the other hand, always finish what I start," Megan challenged.

Rebecca laughed knowingly as she bent over slightly and pressed her bottom firmly against Megan's damp, dark mound. Megan wrapped her arms around Rebecca's slender waist and eased her thighs apart as she pressed herself intimately close. Rebecca sighed delightfully as she closed her eyes and rested her forehead against the cool decorative glass.

Megan pressed her breasts against Rebecca's back and kissed her way across her shoulders. "I need to show you how real I am and how real we are. I need you to believe that what we have is precious and that we will fight to keep it alive. Forever,

♥ *TENDER HEART* ♥

Rebecca. That's what I want from you. That's what I want to give you. Imperfections and all. I want to give myself completely to you and only you."

Rebecca turned around with big tears in her eyes and melted into Megan's arms.

"That's all I could ever ask for from you, Meg, is you. You are what I have always dreamed of in a partner and lover. You are my forever girl, imperfections and all."

Megan growled playfully and nibbled on Rebecca's earlobe. Rebecca squealed and tried to duck her head away as Megan turned her around and faced her against the frosted glass.

Rebecca turned her head slightly to watch Megan as she felt her warm moist tongue trail along her spine with delightful arousal. "Since you're a woman of your word, Dr. Summers, I would really like to see you finish what you started in our bed," Rebecca challenged.

Megan stood tall and pressed her breasts firmly against Rebecca's back as she nibbled gently at her shoulder. "This is something I hope we never finish, my darling Rebecca." Rebecca closed her eyes and leaned her cheek against the wet, cold glass as Megan's hands slid down her sides and over her hips. Her fingertips glided over the inside of her thighs and gently eased her legs apart. Rebecca gyrated her bottom slowly against Megan's dark mound and moaned with pleasure. Megan eased her fingertips along the insides of Rebecca's thighs and entwined into her dark, moist mound. Her fingers trailed into her wet, velvety folds and thrust deep inside her. Rebecca gasped and rocked against Megan's fingers as a swell of intense need and desire burned in her belly. Megan's other hand found Rebecca's wet erect center and caressed her lightly over and over. Rebecca's moans of ecstasy vibrated off the glass wall as she thrust harder and faster against Megan's hands. The intense pleasure filled Rebecca's chest as her nipples tingled against the cold glass wall. Rebecca suddenly stopped thrusting as intense undulating spasms exploded between her thighs and showered her with a spray of pure erotic pleasure.

♥ *TENDER HEART* ♥

Megan held Rebecca tight against her as she watched her struggle to catch her breath. "That is just an example of how real we are," Megan whispered in her ear.

Rebecca turned and melted into Megan's arms, hugging her with all the love in her heart.

♥♥♥♥♥♥♥♥♥♥

They spent the rest of their morning exploring the historic Alamo and absorbing the rich history surrounding San Antonio.

They spent their afternoon at the Imax Theatre watching movies on the Serengeti Plain of Africa and the world's undersea beauty.

Megan reached her hand out to Rebecca as she helped her step onto the flat-bottom boat on the River Walk. They settled onto the cushioned seats at the front of the boat and stared in awe at their surroundings. The rest of the passengers boarded and took their seats as the captain welcomed everyone and began their one-hour tour with the history of the romantic San Antonio River Walk.

Megan helped Rebecca disembark from the flat bottom boat and guided her by the elbow towards their favorite Mexican restaurant on the bank of the River Walk.

They both sat back in their chairs and sipped their margaritas in silence. Megan reached over and brushed the soft pad of her thumb across Rebecca's chin and guided her eyes back to her. "What's wrong, sweetheart?" Megan said.

Rebecca sadly looked down at her drink and rubbed her fingertip along the salt encrusted edge of her glass. "I'm just sad to see this weekend come to an end," Rebecca shared.

Megan cupped her chin in her hand and raised her eyes to meet hers. "This is only the beginning, my sweet Rebecca. I promise you that we will share many wonderful weekends like this in places you've never even dreamed of."

Rebecca took Megan's hand in hers and squeezed it tight. "I'm going to hold you to that promise, Dr. Summers. But I'm

♥ *TENDER HEART* ♥

going to tell you right now, you're going to have a tough time topping this weekend," Rebecca said.

Megan slowly brought Rebecca's hands to her lips and kissed them gently. "I look forward to trying," Megan said, as she discreetly reached over and kissed Rebecca's cheek as she watched a brilliant smile spread across her beautiful face.

Their dessert dishes were being cleared away as Megan paid their bill and thanked the waitress. Rebecca rested her hand on Megan's arm as they descended the steps to the edge of the River Walk. They strolled along the historic River Walk in peaceful silence and enjoyed the beautiful balmy night air and each other's loving company.

Megan looked over at Rebecca's beautiful expression and smiled. "What are you thinking, sweetheart?"

Rebecca smiled and nuzzled closer to Megan. She took a deep breath and looked into the emerald eyes that melt her soul. "I'm thinking that I don't want this fairytale weekend to end. I'm also feeling so blessed to have you and your incredible love, and I can't imagine a minute without you."

Megan stopped at a secluded bench and guided Rebecca to sit beside her.

Rebecca leaned toward Megan's lips and kissed her softly. "I love you so much, Megan, and this has been an incredible three days."

Megan's smile illuminated her face as she hugged Rebecca against her. "I love you with all my heart, Rebecca, and you have given me the most beautiful memories of San Antonio."

Rebecca smiled and cuddled into her arms and entwined her fingers in Megan's hand.

"Did I tell you that Tangerine called?" Rebecca revealed quietly.

Megan burst into laughter and shook her head. "She did. What an intelligent lesbian goldfish we have. What did she say?"

Rebecca smiled playfully and gently caressed Megan's strong, feminine hand. "She said to tell you that JC and Penney came to visit her and they have all become special friends,"

♥ *TENDER HEART* ♥

Rebecca stated with glee. Megan laughed at Rebecca's endearing charm as she held her close. "So much so, that they decided they would all like to live together in the same house," Rebecca announced excitedly.

Megan gave Rebecca a beautiful smile and kissed her forehead. "What a wonderful idea. Why didn't we think of that? What do you think of all of us living together, sweetheart?"

Rebecca felt as if she would burst with incredible happiness. "I would love to live with you, Meg, and share our lives completely," Rebecca said, while squeezing Megan's hand with incredible exuberance.

Megan smiled and gently touched Rebecca's glowing face. "My heart and my life belong to you, Rebecca Rhodes. I would love to unite our lives together in every possible way." Megan paused and looked away.

Rebecca could see the cloud of sadness darken her emerald eyes. Rebecca tenderly touched Megan's chin and guided her eyes toward her. "What do you think about us both selling our homes and our painful memories and starting fresh together?" Rebecca said softly.

A glowing smile lit up Megan's emotional eyes. "I would love that with you, Rebecca."

Rebecca smiled and kissed Megan softly, tenderly, teasing her with her tongue and escalating their wanton desire into a kiss of burning passion. Rebecca leaned against Megan's shoulder and playfully toyed with the buttons on her beautiful cream blouse. "I bought a gorgeous house two months ago that my company has been renovating for resale. I would love for you to see it, Megan. It has the most beautiful rock garden and pool in the backyard and could easily accommodate a goldfish pond."

Megan gave her an enthusiastic smile. "Sounds wonderful. When can we go see it?"

Rebecca laughed sweetly at Megan's enthusiasm. "Tomorrow, on the way home, if you like, sweetheart."

Megan clapped her hands with delight as Rebecca marveled at her pure joy.

♥ *TENDER HEART* ♥

"I told Tangerine, JC, and Penney to go check it out and they told me they already picked out their bedrooms," Rebecca said.

Megan burst into laughter and looked into Rebecca's eyes. She leaned toward her and tenderly kissed her lips, then felt Rebecca's tongue seductively probing her. Megan sighed with sexual desire as Rebecca took her hand and guided her back onto the River Walk and along the path to their hotel.

They had barely gotten in the door of their room when Rebecca stopped Megan from turning on the lights and playfully pressed her up against the door. Their lips met in a kiss of dire need and heated passion as they excitedly removed each other's clothes and let them lie where they had fallen.

Rebecca took Megan by her strong shoulders and guided her to sit on the plush, inviting couch. She reached out and slipped her hands into Megan's as she gracefully straddled her thighs. Rebecca leaned back, in awe of the faint shadows of moonlight filtering in through the blinds; the light cast a glow across Megan's beautiful, full breasts.

Megan glided her hands along Rebecca's shapely bottom and pulled her intimately against her, luxuriating in her beautiful feminine scent. Megan tilted her face up to Rebecca and met her lips in a frenzied kiss as they devoured each other. Rebecca connected intimately with Megan's soft mound of hair and rhythmically swayed against her as an urgent, tingling sensation built between them. Megan floated her fingers along Rebecca's spine and down to her gyrating bottom as she luxuriated in her escalating passion.

Rebecca tilted her head back and moaned softly as Megan leaned toward her and gently took her nipple in her mouth. Rebecca's moans fanned their fiery passion as she ran her hands through Megan's hair, gently guiding her closer and her nipple deeper. Megan rested her hands on Rebecca's bottom as she felt her rock harder and faster. She slowly released her taut nipple as Rebecca took her other nipple between her fingers and guided it to Megan's waiting mouth. Megan smiled seductively as she took Rebecca's offering and sucked deeply on her fingers and nipple.

♥ *TENDER HEART* ♥

Rebecca closed her eyes and groaned with ecstasy as she felt Megan consume her with her flickering tongue. Rebecca suddenly held her breath and hung on to Megan tighter; a deep groan escaped from her throat as an explosive wave of ecstasy cascaded throughout her entire being. She fell limply into Megan's strong arms as intense, rhythmic spasms erupted between her thighs.

Megan held her close and kissed her rosy cheeks as she allowed Rebecca to catch her breath. Rebecca rested her head on Megan's shoulder and sighed with complete contentment. Megan gave her a loving smile as she gently brushed away a stray strand of hair from her eyes. "How would you like to join me in a warm, soothing bubble bath, sweetheart," Megan whispered.

Rebecca smiled and teased Megan's ear with her tongue. "I would love to, darling. However, I'm not sure that my legs are functional yet."

Megan tilted her neck back to allow more room for Rebecca's wandering lips. "Umm. You keep kissing me like that and we'll both be unable to walk in a minute. How about I help you into that bubble bath and we'll continue this discussion there," Megan said hoarsely.

"Sounds wonderful to me," Rebecca said, as she eased herself slowly off of Megan's lap. She helped Megan to her feet and led the way to the sunken alabaster whirlpool tub.

After their leisurely bath, Rebecca placed her eye drops in her eye. She turned the lights out in their bathroom and allowed her eyes to adjust to the dim lighting in their breathtaking presidential suite. She caught a glimpse of a silver reflection at her feet and bent down, laughing as she picked up a Hershey's Kiss. She looked farther along the plush carpeting and saw a trail of Hershey's Kisses. Rebecca picked up each foil wrapped chocolate until she came upon a note. She held the note up and smiled as she read:

You're one kiss closer.

Rebecca's face glowed with pure joy as she peeked around the corner at their king size canopy bed and her lips curled into a

♥ *TENDER HEART* ♥

lustful smile. She stepped to the edge of the bed and slipped out of her gold satin robe, easing herself between Megan's legs and happily nibbling on the Hershey's Kiss resting on Megan's belly.

Megan lay with her hands above her head and giggled with pure pleasure as Rebecca took the sweet treat into her mouth. She eased herself above Megan and smiled into her beautiful, bright green eyes. She leaned toward her lips and kissed her gently, seductively slipping the chocolate onto Megan's eager tongue. Rebecca slipped the melting chocolate back into her own mouth and drifted lower to Megan's taunt nipple. Megan moaned with smoldering passion as she watched Rebecca take her sensitive nipple in her mouth and coat it with the melting chocolate. Their eyes met with undeniable rapture as Rebecca's tongue traced lazy circles around Megan's aching nipple.

Megan struggled to keep her eyes open as she slid her hand over her own breast and slowly floated the soft pad of her thumb across Rebecca's chocolate smeared lips. Rebecca took Megan's nipple deep in her mouth and bathed it with her warm tongue as she watched Megan seductively lick the chocolate from her own thumb.

Rebecca moaned with simmering lust as she slid her hand along the inside of Megan's thigh and parted her legs. She shifted to Megan's other nipple and tugged it playfully with her teeth. She cradled the rigid, pink nipple in her tongue and caressed it rhythmically as her fingertips traced a slow, taunting path from Megan's knees to her dark mound.

Megan moaned with urgency and arched her hips towards Rebecca's wandering hand. She took Rebecca's beaming face in her hands and arched her neck in need.

"God, Rebecca, please touch me."

Rebecca took Megan's nipple in her mouth with aching hunger as she glided her fingertips through her dark, curly mound and deep into her wet center.

Megan arched her hips and drove Rebecca's fingers deeper as she emitted a deep guttural cry of joy. Megan sheathed Rebecca's driving fingers as she thrust to her hungry pace.

♥ *TENDER HEART* ♥

Megan arched her back to force her breast deeper into Rebecca's hot, caressing mouth as she felt a pulsating tension build tighter and tighter with each voracious stroke. Rebecca's thumb glided through Megan's glistening folds and found her erect, sensitive tissue. Megan uttered a hoarse cry and struggled to breathe as Rebecca's thumb continuously circled over her wet, burning center. Megan labored to catch her next breath as she wove her fingers into Rebecca's thick hair. She clenched her teeth tight and thrust one final time. Her hips tensed and arched high as an explosive quiver began beneath Rebecca's caressing thumb.

"Oh God, Rebecca, I'm coming!" Megan hissed, as a wave of cascading spasms gripped every nerve in her body like a tightly coiled spring, exploding like a raging volcano of blissful ecstasy.

Megan weakly gathered Rebecca into her arms and held her close as her breathing gradually returned to normal. Rebecca kissed the bounding pulse in Megan's neck and sighed with pure contentment. She carefully, slowly removed her fingers from deep within Megan's pulsating center as Megan winced from the sensitivity of the movement. Rebecca eased her wet fingers through Megan's glistening mound and across her flat belly. She rested her hand on Megan's firm breast and gently skimmed her thumb over her taunt, rosy nipple.

"Have you made it back to earth yet?" Rebecca whispered.

"Not quite. I'm still circling somewhere around Pluto," Megan said in a gravely voice.

Rebecca smiled and looked up into Megan's clouded eyes. "That was so beautiful," Rebecca said.

Megan entwined her fingers in Rebecca's hair and gazed into her moist eyes. "That, my darling girl, was one of the most incredible orgasms I've ever had."

Megan rolled a beaming Rebecca onto her back and kissed her tenderly. "I would like to try and send you on a similar journey if I may, Madame."

Rebecca took Megan's face in her hands and glided her moist tongue over her full lower lip. "I expect you will have no

♥ *TENDER HEART* ♥

trouble sending me on that same journey, my exquisite lover. No one has ever fulfilled my passion and desire as you, my Megan."

Megan leaned closer and softly brushed her lips against Rebecca's. Rebecca closed her eyes and parted her lips as Megan touched her tongue to Rebecca's and kissed her with a hunger that ignited them both. They moaned and gasped as their tongues struggled to devour and consume.

Megan took Rebecca's lower lip into her mouth and sucked it gently as Rebecca arched and purred beneath her. She urgently moved lower and left a trail of moist kisses along Rebecca's neck and chest before stroking her firm nipple with her tongue and lips. Rebecca swayed beneath her and parted her thighs to invite Megan closer. Megan left her nipples wet and tingling as she led a trail of soft, suckling kisses to her belly. Megan placed her hands on Rebecca's hips and gently rolled her onto her stomach. Rebecca reached for a pillow and placed it beneath her breasts as Megan smiled mischievously and eased herself between Rebecca's parted thighs. Megan glided her hand over Rebecca's shapely ass and up her back, kneading her glistening muscles. Rebecca's eyes drifted closed as she moaned with delight.

"You, little lady, have a gorgeous ass," Megan whispered, as she brushed Rebecca's hair off her shoulder and placed soft, wet kisses along the nape of her neck and slowly down her spine. Rebecca arched her bottom and pressed herself firmly against Megan's lap.

"Is there something you want, my little lover?" Megan whispered into Rebecca's ear, as she outlined it with the tip of her tongue.

Rebecca tipped her head slightly and looked into Megan's dreamy eyes. "You and your touch are all I want, my Megan." Rebecca placed her hand over Megan's and slowly, bewitchingly, guided it back down over her bottom and between her moist thighs. Megan's eyes drifted closed as she moaned and buried her fingers into Rebecca's velvety, wet folds. Rebecca groaned heavily into her pillow and clutched the corners tightly as Megan's fingertips found her peaked tissue. Rebecca arched higher and thrust harder as a spiraling force of tension and ecstasy flowed beneath Megan's caressing fingertips. Megan sighed with ecstasy as she leaned her forehead against Rebecca's back and glided her hand over her undulating bottom.

"Oh God, Megan," Rebecca cried into her pillow as she thrust one final time. "Oh God, Megan, yes," Rebecca screamed, as an explosive wave of euphoria mushroomed beyond Megan's touch and consumed Rebecca entirely.

Rebecca lay spent as Megan lay beside her and gently trailed her fingertips along Rebecca's spine. "Sweetheart," Megan said.

"Umm," Rebecca barely uttered.

"I think I'll invite Mr. Hershey to bed with us every night," Megan stated.

Rebecca barely opened one sleepy eye and burst into satiated laughter.

♥ *TENDER HEART* ♥

♥ *TENDER HEART* ♥
CHAPTER EIGHT

Megan quickly donned her gown and gloves and stepped into the trauma room. She watched as Drake swiftly intubated the female trauma patient. He removed the stylet from the endotracheal tube and attached it to a flow of oxygen. The respiratory therapist listened for breath sounds and took over.

Megan stepped towards the view box and began reviewing the patients x-rays and CAT scan. She turned to see Drake scrub his hands at the sink beside her.

"Good morning, beautiful," Drake said.

Megan gave him her magnificent smile. "Good morning, Dr. Darrow."

Drake took one step back and reached for several paper towels. "If that smile on your face is any indication of your weekend then I'm totally jealous," Drake said in admiration.

Megan looked away shyly and smiled. "It was the most incredible three days of my life, Drake. And on the way home Rebecca showed me a stunning house that we are going to move into in three weeks."

Drake laughed softly and leaned closer to Megan. "You lesbians are something else. You certainly don't believe in wasting time."

Megan blushed and looked into Drake's warm blue eyes. "I love her very much, Drake. Everything about her feels so right."

Drake tossed his wet paper towels in the nearest trashcan and rested his arm around her shoulders. "Seeing you and Rebecca so happy together means the world to me, Meg. I wish you both a lifetime of love and happiness."

Megan smiled beautifully and kissed his cheek. "Thanks, Drake. I've never felt this deep sense of connection and love with anyone like I do with Rebecca. We owe it all to you and your wonderful timing of signing your house papers."

♥ *TENDER HEART* ♥

Drake's smile danced across his eyes as he hugged Megan tight. "I think I'll remind you and Rebecca of that for many years to come." Megan laughed sweetly.

Drake directed her attention to the view box as Dean gowned and stepped into the trauma room. Drake waited for him to join them and explained the trauma patient's history. "Thirty-two-year-old belted female lost control of her minivan and rolled it several times down a ten-foot embankment. The roof of her van crushed in like a tin can on top of her. She presents with a closed head injury, looks like an epidural hematoma on her CAT scan, facial smash, bilateral pneumothorax, multiple fractured ribs, fractured pelvis, fractured right femur and a lacerated liver." Drake watched Dean intently assess the x-rays as Megan focused on the CAT scan of the patient's head.

"I want to take her to the O.R. and repair her lacerated liver if you both want to join me and drain that nasty blood clot on her brain."

Megan snapped the CAT scan off the view box and handed it to her senior resident. "What do you think of Drake's assessment, Dean?"

Dean held the scan up to the light and squinted as he assessed the injuries. "Good call, Drake, definitely an epidural hematoma. We'd better move on this quick. I checked on the patients in the NICU, Megan, so we're free to go to the O.R. as soon as a room is ready," Dean said.

Megan gave him a pleased smile and placed one hand on each gentleman's arm. "I love being surrounded by brilliant men. It gives me a reason to believe there is actually a purpose for men in my life," Megan quipped.

Dean and Drake groaned at her sarcasm as she quickly walked out of the trauma room, dodging the several rolls of gauze that bounced off the swinging doors, narrowly missing her head.

♥♥♥♥♥♥♥♥♥♥♥

♥ *TENDER HEART* ♥

Megan changed out of her O.R. scrubs and back into her tweed pleated trousers and matching velvet shirt. She slipped into her crisp white lab coat and headed toward the Neurosurgical Intensive Care Unit to check on the trauma patient she had just finished operating on.

Megan carefully reviewed the patient's lab results with Dean, going over what she wanted done. Her pager chimed at her waist. She automatically unclipped it from her belt and read the message.

Hello Sweetheart,

Please call me on my cell phone.

I love you. Always.
R.

Megan had spoken to Rebecca just before going into the O.R. and knew that she was driving across town to meet with a client. Megan felt concerned as she picked up the nearest phone in the nurse's station and dialed Rebecca's number.

Megan barely heard the phone ring before Rebecca's voice said, "Hello, my tender heart." Her voice instantly caressed Megan's soul and put a glowing smile on her beautiful face.

"Hello, my lover. Are you okay, sweetheart? Your message sounded urgent."

"I'm okay, sweetheart, but my sister's not. I just got a phone call from my aunt and uncle. Lindsay's school just notified them that she fell on the playground and hit her head on the bottom of the slide. Apparently she has a nasty gash and is bleeding badly."

Megan felt deeply concerned and heard Rebecca's gentle sniffle.

"They called an ambulance and are bringing her to your E.R. My aunt and uncle are on their way. Kyle is staying to take care of things with our client and I'm at least thirty minutes away,

155

♥ *TENDER HEART* ♥

especially in this damn afternoon traffic," Rebecca snapped irritably.

Megan rubbed her forehead and took a deep breath. "Try not to worry, sweetheart. I'll go down to the E.R. and meet Lindsay as she arrives. I promise to take care of her. I want you to promise me that you're going to drive safely and within the speed limit in that silver bullet of yours. I don't think Scotty was kidding when he threatened to throw your cute little ass in jail for a night if you got another speeding ticket." Megan could hear Rebecca giggling through her tears as her heart constricted for this special woman. "I can't survive a night without your sexy, warm body next to mine, Ms. Rhodes, so promise me you'll drive carefully." Megan heard her take a deep breath as her heart ached to hold her.

"I promise to drive carefully, Meg, because I don't ever plan on spending a night without you."

Megan smiled and hugged the phone close. "That's my girl. Don't feel sad, baby. I promise to take care of Lindsay till you get here."

"She's going to be so scared, Meg. It's all going to be so overwhelming for her."

Megan smiled at Rebecca's deep love for her Down's syndrome sister. "I will do my best to make her feel comfortable, sweetheart. I promise to be much better behaved than when you and I first met."

Rebecca laughed at Megan's sense of humor. "Your emotional display instantly drew me to you, Dr. Summers. Lindsay will probably take just as long to fall in love with you as I did."

Megan smiled and wished she could hold Rebecca in her arms. "See, baby, so don't worry. Just get here safely because I have plans for you for the rest of your life."

"I love you, Meg."

Megan smiled and looked down shyly. "I love you, my Rebecca. See you soon, lover." They both said good-bye as Dean and Megan quickly headed down to the E.R.

♥ TENDER HEART ♥

♥♥♥♥♥♥♥♥♥♥

Megan stood with Dean and Drake as they watched Lindsay's stretcher being unloaded from the back of the ambulance. Megan smiled as she saw a beautiful young woman sitting cross-legged on the stretcher with a big bandage on her head, crocodile tears in her golden eyes and a lollipop sticking out of her mouth.

The stretcher rolled toward them as Lindsay spotted Drake and shouted his name. Drake smiled and leaned toward her, kissing the tip of her tiny nose. "Hello, sunshine. Looks like you fell down and bonged your precious head," Drake said, as he wiped away Lindsay's tears.

"I did, Drake, and you should have seen all the blood. It was scary!"

Drake squeezed her hand tight. "I bet it was. Why don't we get you inside and have a good look at your ouchy. Before we do that I want you to meet Dr. Megan Summers and Dr. Dean Smith. Megan is a friend of Rebecca's and she is the doctor who looks after young women that tumble into slides head first."

Lindsay looked up at Megan with a trusting smile and slipped her hand into Megan's.

"Hello, Lindsay. Let's go look at your head," Megan said, as they wheeled her into an empty observation room.

The men helped to settle Lindsay in the observation room then left. Sharon, the E.R. nurse, took Lindsay's vital signs and Megan helped her get more comfortable on the stretcher. Megan took Lindsay's lollipop, set it in a cup, and helped her to remove her bloody sweatshirt. She guided Lindsay's arms into a hospital gown.

"I know these gowns are not the most comfortable, Lindsay, so I want you to pretend that you're a fairy princess slipping into her Ball gown."

"Oh, that would be such fun! And could I pretend that the dressing on my head is my royal crown, Dr. Megan?"

♥ *TENDER HEART* ♥

They both laughed and created an imaginary story as Megan instantly succumbed to Lindsay's uninhibited love and charm.

Lindsay continued to sit cross-legged on the stretcher as Megan sat at her feet.

"Tell me what happened to your head, Lindsay."

"Some of the boys in my class were flying a kite in the playground. It was such a pretty purple and yellow color with a long yellow tail. I was watching it spin and spin when it suddenly crashed to the ground. We all started running to see if it was okay and before I knew what happened I had tripped and fell into the slide. My friends told me to sit still while they ran for the teacher. Blood started running down my face and it really hurt but I tried really hard not to cry. Rebecca would have been really proud of me."

Megan was amazed by her articulate story as she reached out and squeezed Lindsay's chubby hands. "I'm sure she will be. We're all very proud of you, Lindsay. Now tell me, does your head still hurt?"

"Not like it did, Dr. Megan, but I do have a little headache."

Megan leaned closer and casually assessed Lindsay's eyes and face as she asked her more questions about her school. Lindsay happily held her hand and told her all about her teachers, her friends, and the class pet, Oscar the gerbil.

Sharon handed Megan a warm, wet, washcloth and towel. She thanked her and proceeded to wipe the blood off Lindsay's beautiful, chubby face. They sat close together as Lindsay looked up at Megan with huge, frightened eyes. "Dr. Megan, can I ask you a question?"

Megan smiled warmly into Lindsay's emotional, moist eyes. "You can ask me anything, Lindsay. What is your question?"

Lindsay swallowed hard and entwined her own pudgy hands tightly together in her lap. "Are you a real doctor, Dr. Megan? You know, the kind that gives kids needles?"

Megan smiled beautifully and held Lindsay's face still with one hand. "Yes, Lindsay, I'm a real doctor and I promise not to give you a needle, as long as you promise to be a good girl."

♥ *TENDER HEART* ♥

Lindsay gave her a radiant smile and hugged Megan tight. "I promise to be a good girl, Dr. Megan. Honest I do!"

Megan was overcome by the openness and warmth of this precious Down's syndrome child as she finished cleaning Lindsay's face and smiled at the beautiful golden eyes that were so familiar. She set the bloody washcloth aside and stepped to the sink to wash her hands. She slipped into a pair of gloves and sat back down in front of Lindsay. "The first thing I need to do, Lindsay, is give you another hug."

Lindsay beamed with joy as she reached for Megan and hugged her tight.

Megan leaned back and slipped off the stretcher. "Now, I need to look at the cut on your head. Would that be okay?"

Lindsay nodded her head slowly and gave Megan her permission. Megan stood beside Lindsay's stretcher and began peeling the layers of gauze away.

"Rebecca called me when she first found out you were hurt. She should be here shortly, as well as your Mom and Dad." Lindsay's face lit up like a child's on Christmas Eve.

"Rebecca is a special lady. She's a very special friend of mine. Did you know that we met right here in this emergency room?"

"Really, Dr. Megan?" Megan continued removing the blood soaked gauze while she recounted the story of how they had met. Lindsay loved her story.

"Did you know that Becky bought me a puppy for my birthday last month, Dr. Megan?"

"No, I didn't. What did you name your birthday puppy?"

"Rebecca wanted me to name her 'Chewy' because she chewed up my new sneakers." Lindsay rolled her eyes as Megan laughed. "I named her Pippi, after my favorite book, Pippi Longstocking."

Megan laughed and finished removing all the gauze to expose the two-inch gash on the right side of Lindsay's head. "I think that's a wonderful name for your new puppy, Lindsay. I used to love reading all the adventures of Pippi Longstocking."

♥ *TENDER HEART* ♥

Lindsay gave Megan a loving smile as Megan guided her to lie back down on the stretcher. Dean and Drake walked back into the room and Megan watched as Lindsay innocently flirted with the boys while she irrigated and sutured her laceration and applied a clean dressing.

Drake and Megan were standing at the nurse's station as Rebecca hurried through the automatic doors and instantly melted into Megan's arms. Megan wiped away her tears, and kissed her forehead. She explained what had happened since Lindsay's arrival and tried her best to comfort her.

"She's going to be just fine, sweetheart. Lindsay is such an amazing young lady. She must get that from you."

Rebecca smiled and dried her eyes. "Where is she, Megan? Can I see her?"

Megan held her close. "I've sent her for skull x-rays just to make sure everything is okay. I offered to go with her but she said that she wanted Dean to go with her and hold her hand. Rebecca laughed as Megan added playfully, "She's such a little flirt. She must have gotten that from you as well, my love." They all laughed warmly as Megan guided Rebecca toward Lindsay's observation room.

Lindsay was coming down the hall with Dean at her side. As soon as Lindsay saw Rebecca, she sat bolt upright on the stretcher and reached her arms out with bubbling excitement, shouting, "Becky!"

Rebecca rushed to her side and pulled her into her arms, hugging her with all the love in her heart.

Lindsay leaned back and looked at Rebecca's tears. "Don't cry, Becky. I'm okay. Dr. Megan sewed me up and washed the blood off my face." Rebecca gave Megan a grateful smile as Lindsay leaned closer to Rebecca's face and whispered loudly enough for everyone in the hallway to hear, "Dr. Megan said that you and her are special friends. Is she your new lover that you

♥ *TENDER HEART* ♥

were telling me about yesterday?" They all burst into laughter as Megan buried her face in her hands.

"She sure is, sweetheart. What do you think?"

Lindsay looked up at Megan's beautiful, blushing face and gave her a huge smile. "I think you are so lucky, Becky! I would like a lover just like Dr. Megan. She is so beautiful."

Everyone burst into laughter as Megan leaned closer to Lindsay and kissed her sweet little nose. "How do you know so much about women and their lovers, young lady?" Megan said sternly.

Lindsay giggled as Rebecca looked into those vibrant green eyes and smiled.

"Who do you think taught her about the birds and the birds and the bees and the bees?" Rebecca asked.

Lindsay burst into infectious giggles and clapped her hands together. "Becky taught me all about masturbation too," Lindsay proclaimed to the world with blissful glee.

Megan could not take any more disclosures from this exuberant young woman as she turned beet red and hid her face under her lab coat. Everyone applauded Lindsay's heartwarming honesty and laughed at Megan's shy embarrassment.

Megan took a deep breath and reached for Lindsay's stretcher. "All right, Lindsay. I think you've shared just about enough of our personal lives with everyone in the E.R." Lindsay giggled into the palm of her hand as Megan guided her stretcher back into the room.

Rebecca sat at the foot of Lindsay's stretcher and listened to her recount her accident on the school playground while Megan, Drake and Dean reviewed her skull films.

Megan smiled and looked back at Lindsay playfully. "Lindsay, did you know that a goose laid two golden eggs on your head?"

Lindsay was flabbergasted as she looked at Megan. "Did not, Dr. Megan," she declared.

♥ *TENDER HEART* ♥

Megan looked back at the x-rays and tilted her head sweetly. "You're right, Lindsay. Those aren't golden eggs; they're your golden eyes."

Lindsay burst into laughter as Megan sneaked up to her and nuzzled against her. Lindsay hugged her tight. Drake gave Lindsay a clean bill of health. Then he and Dean hugged and kissed her and waved good-bye.

Megan pulled a stool up to rest beside Rebecca's shapely legs that were beautifully displayed in a gray suede skirt. Megan gave her a seductive smile and dug into the breast pocket of her lab coat. She turned to Lindsay and smiled into her glistening eyes. "I bought you a present for being such a good girl, Lindsay."

Lindsay clapped her hands with excitement and could hardly contain herself. "What is it, Dr. Megan? What did you buy me?"

Megan smiled and pulled out a brand new cherry lollipop from her pocket. Lindsay shouted with glee as Megan unwrapped the sugary treat and handed it to Lindsay.

"Thank you, Dr. Megan. Thanks a lot," Lindsay gushed.

Megan and Rebecca laughed as they watched Lindsay pop it into her mouth and smile with ecstasy. Rebecca touched her sister's face lovingly and tucked a stray strand of chestnut hair under her head dressing. "I wish you liked vegetables as much as you like lollipops," she said sternly.

Lindsay sweetly squished her face and turned to Megan. "I don't like vegetables. I like lollipops and chocolate milkshakes."

Megan laughed softly as she leaned closer to Lindsay. "I love chocolate milkshakes, too. Maybe if we're both good, Rebecca will take us out and buy us both the biggest, richest chocolate milkshake you ever tasted in your whole life," Megan suggested.

Lindsay turned to Rebecca with bubbling excitement. "Would you do that, Becky? Would you take me and Dr. Megan out for a chocolate milkshake?"

♥ *TENDER HEART* ♥

Rebecca smiled beautifully and ran her fingers through Megan's thick, shiny hair. "I'd love to, sweetheart. Consider it a date."

Megan smiled and stepped away from Lindsay's stretcher as Lindsay leaned closer to Rebecca. "I like Dr. Megan, Becky. I like her a lot."

Rebecca leaned her forehead against Lindsay's dressing and smiled into her dear sister's shining eyes. "I like her a lot too, Lindsay. I love her even more."

Megan stood with her hand on the closet handle and smiled at the two women who had touched her heart. "Lindsay, I bought you one other thing and hid it in this closet. What do you think it is?"

Lindsay squished her lips together and thought hard. "Pippi Longstocking's white horse?" Lindsay offered.

Megan burst into laughter as Rebecca looked at her with absolute shock.

"No, silly! I couldn't possibly fit Pippi's horse in here. I know that because I tried yesterday," Megan said. Lindsay burst into laughter as Rebecca looked from Megan to Lindsay, bewilderment on her face.

Megan smiled at Rebecca's expression. "I'll explain it to you later, sweetheart. Now, I need a drum roll please," Megan said dramatically.

Rebecca and Lindsay happily obliged as Megan jerked the closet door open and a bright yellow, happy-face helium balloon floated to the ceiling and over Lindsay's head. Lindsay shouted with excitement as Megan sat back down beside Rebecca and rested her hands on her knees. They both smiled lovingly and watched Lindsay stretch and reach for the string. Megan secured the balloon string to Lindsay's wrist.

Seeing the sad look in Lindsay's eyes, Rebecca reached for her and gently touched her chin. "What's wrong, Lindsay?" she asked.

Lindsay looked up at the bright, happy balloon and sighed. "Mom and Dad are going to be sad when they see what happened

♥ TENDER HEART ♥

to my head. They're always telling me not to run because I could fall and hurt myself and that's exactly what happened."

Megan reached for Lindsay's hand and squeezed it tight. "No, they're not going to be sad, Lindsay, because we're going to come up with a great story. Let's tell them that you turned into Pippi Longstocking and found out that a wicked witch was holding Rebecca and I prisoner in a castle. You landed your horse on the roof of the castle and just as we were all getting on your horse, the wicked witch started throwing flaming brooms at us and one caught you right in the head. But you were Pippi Longstocking so you were still able to get us all on your horse and ride into the sunset and get us home to safety." Megan raised her hands in triumph as Rebecca and Lindsay burst into laughter and applauded her story.

Lindsay smiled warmly at Megan and reached for her hand. "I like your story, Dr. Megan, but I think I'll tell the truth," she said.

Megan touched her cherub cheek. "You're a very wise girl, Lindsay Rhodes. Very wise indeed."

Lindsay looked toward the door and squealed with excitement as Drake guided her parents through the door. They were both in their late fifties and consumed with worry. Megan stepped back and watched Rebecca hug her uncle first. He towered above Rebecca and wrapped her tight in his arms. Megan admired his black pinstriped suit and salt and pepper wavy hair. Rebecca stepped back from her uncle and waited till her aunt released Lindsay before she turned and held Rebecca close. Rebecca was engulfed by her aunt's stocky frame as she stretched on her tiptoes to kiss her soft round cheek.

Rebecca's aunt stepped toward Lindsay with tears in her eyes and held her tight. They sat on her stretcher with her as Rebecca came to stand beside Megan. She entwined their hands together as they listened to Lindsay telling her Pippi Longstocking story with minor deviations. Megan giggled quietly and quickly covered her mouth with her hand as she saw the menacing look in Rebecca's glowing eyes.

♥ *TENDER HEART* ♥

"Lindsay! What happened to telling the truth?" Rebecca asked, glaring at her precious sister.

Lindsay looked at Rebecca's stern expression. "I liked Dr. Megan's story better," she admitted innocently. Rebecca turned to Megan and gave her a scolding look; she guided Megan closer to her aunt and uncle.

"Dr. Megan Summers, I would like you to meet my uncle Mitchell and my aunt Sarah. Mitchell and Sarah, this is my partner, Megan," Rebecca said affectionately.

"Dr. Megan is Rebecca's new lover," Lindsay added excitedly.

Megan blushed at Lindsay's blunt honesty as Rebecca's aunt touched her arm. "Thank you for everything you did for Lindsay and for Rebecca's eye, Dr. Summers. We have been dying to meet you ever since Rebecca told us about you, but this certainly isn't the setting we had in mind. We were planning on having Rebecca invite you to our home for dinner on Sunday. It looks like Lindsay's little tumble has allowed us to invite you ourselves."

"I would love to come to your home on Sunday, Mrs. Rhodes. However, I do have two requests?"

"Anything, Dr. Summers. What are they?" Rebecca's aunt said.

"One is that you please call me Megan. The second is that you serve Lindsay and I lollipops and chocolate milkshakes for dinner."

"Not on your life, Megan, not on your life," Sarah said. They all burst into laughter as Rebecca's uncle reached out and touched Rebecca's back.

"I can see that Megan might just be the right person for you, Becka. She's a real spark that one."

Rebecca slipped her hand into Megan's and squeezed tight. "I know she's the right person. She's a true tender heart my Megan."

♥ *TENDER HEART* ♥

Megan and Rebecca stood beside Rebecca's Jaguar as they waved and watched Lindsay walk away with her parents, wearing one of Megan's O.R. shirts and the happy-face balloon tied to her wrist. Rebecca leaned into Megan's arms and hugged her tight. "Thank you for everything, Meg. You were wonderful with Lindsay."

Megan smiled and hugged her tight. "See. I didn't even frighten her with my Pippi stories. She's the one that scared me with her honesty," Megan said in exasperation.

They both laughed as Rebecca kissed Megan gently, teasingly, then pulled back to run her finger slowly across Megan's lower lip.

"I loved your story about Pippi Longstocking. Lindsay will be telling that story forever.

"I'm also excited that my eye injury is behind us and you finally get to cash in your Rebecca coupon tonight. I can't wait to take you out to dinner and the symphony."

Megan held her close and stared at her beautiful lips as she brushed her tongue against Rebecca's fingertip causing her to emit her sweet, sensuous sounds. "I look forward to making our own music after the symphony," Megan whispered, as she gave her a beautiful smile and nuzzled into her neck, smelling the gentle scent of her perfume.

Rebecca hugged her tight and kissed her cheek. "You keep kissing my neck like that and I'm going to have to tie you up and take you back to that castle and turn you into my sex slave. And I can promise you there will be no Pippi around to save you," Rebecca purred into her ear.

Megan leaned back and gave her a seductively smoldering look. "That would be one of my fantasies come true," Megan breathed.

They both laughed warmly as Rebecca reached up and kissed Megan softly. "I love you so much, Meg."

Megan smiled and kissed her tenderly. "I love you, my golden-eyed lady." They kissed each other good-bye as Rebecca

♥ *TENDER HEART* ♥

slipped into her Jag and watched in her rear view mirror as her soul mate blew her a kiss.

♥♥♥♥♥♥♥♥♥♥

Megan glided the sleek Jaguar into Rebecca's spacious garage and put it into park as they continued to share their exuberant feelings of their evening at the symphony. Rebecca stepped out of the car dressed in her formfitting, black velvet dress and joined Megan. She placed her hand along the back of her beautiful, purple, silk fitted coatdress. Megan activated the car alarm and entwined her hand in Rebecca's. They smiled happily into each other's radiant eyes and slipped through the front door, oblivious to the figure silhouetted in the bushes.

Megan reset the house alarm and followed Rebecca inside. They stepped into the kitchen together. Megan reached inside the refrigerator for a bottle of white wine as Rebecca called to JC and Penney. Megan uncorked the bottle and poured them both a glass as Rebecca turned to her with a questioning look. "That's really strange. JC and Penney are usually rubbing all over our legs the moment we step into the house. Now, they're nowhere to be found."

Megan shared Rebecca's concern and took her by the hand. "Come on, sweetheart. Let's go find the pair of fur balls and see what they're up to," Megan said reassuringly.

Rebecca followed Megan around the house as they searched all of JC and Penney's favorite hiding places.

Megan got to her knees and looked under Rebecca's bed and found them huddled together on Megan and Rebecca's slippers. Megan eased them both out and handed them to Rebecca. "You two are grounded for scaring us like that. No more catnip for a week and I don't want to hear any arguments," Megan said.

Rebecca set them both down on the window seat and, still feeling ill at ease, walked around the house with Megan to ensure that all the windows and doors were locked. Convinced that everything was secure and untouched, they took their glasses

♥ *TENDER HEART* ♥

of wine into the bathroom and sank into a luxurious, relaxing bubble bath.

Megan watched Rebecca; lost in thought, tip the wine glass slightly to her lips without taking a sip. Megan gently took the wine glass from her hands and set both glasses on the edge of the coral whirlpool tub. Rebecca was jolted from her deep, troubled thoughts as Megan reached out for her and guided her into her lap. Rebecca wrapped one arm around Megan's neck and played with the bubbles floating around her breasts with her other hand. Megan tenderly tilted Rebecca's eyes to meet her own. "Is the absence of our welcoming committee at the door still bothering you, sweetheart?"

Rebecca sighed deeply and raised her hand above the water level, sending drops of water to trickle over Megan's breast. "It's just really strange, Meg. They never miss greeting us at the door. It's like they were really frightened or something. I've never seen them behave like that."

Megan glided her hands over Rebecca's shapely ass and held her tight in her lap. "They could have been spooked by a salesperson at our door when we were away. Don't let it worry you, baby. Everything in the house is in order. Please don't be frightened," Megan said reassuringly.

Rebecca frowned and gently trailed her finger across Megan's erect, aching nipple. Megan moaned with throbbing lust. She took Rebecca's face in her hands and leaned intimately close to her moist, slightly parted lips. "I would just like to make the point that Tangerine doesn't worry us like JC and Penney have this evening. She is by far our most well behaved pet. Don't you agree?"

Rebecca gave Megan a startled look and tapped her chest gently with her index finger. "Huh, goes to show you what you notice, Dr. Summers. I just want you to know that Tangerine has been swimming around her bowl with her little fins covering her eyes ever since we arrived. She also senses something is awry. She's a very perceptive little lesbian goldfish."

♥ *TENDER HEART* ♥

Megan burst into laughter as Rebecca crossed her arms across her perky breasts and gave Megan her sensuous pout. "I think I might be able to suggest something that will help take your mind off the paranoid behavior of our unruly pets," Megan purred against Rebecca's waiting lips.

"What might that be, Dr. Summers?" Rebecca breathed in a sultry voice.

Megan gently separated Rebecca's legs. She stared into her passionate eyes as she floated her hands along the insides of Rebecca's thighs. Megan tilted her head back and rested against the cool tile as Rebecca's lips burned a trail along her face and down her neck. Megan sighed with yearning hunger as she closed her eyes and skimmed her fingertips along Rebecca's spine.

Rebecca hesitantly slipped off Megan's lap and reached for the nearby thick peach bath towel and guided Megan to her feet. Megan watched her with burning interest as Rebecca draped the bath towel along the ledge of the sunken Jacuzzi. Wordlessly, she gripped Megan by the waist and sat her on the plush towel. She knelt before her in the tub and slid her wet hands along the insides of her thighs and eased her legs apart. Megan leaned back against the cool mosaic tiles and tilted her hips forward as Rebecca captured her feminine essence with her mouth.

Megan groaned with ecstasy and braced herself on tense arms. Rebecca stroked her slowly and lavishly as she felt Megan's thighs tense against her shoulders. Megan arched higher and reached for Rebecca as she rested her hand against the back of her head and pulled her in tighter to her thighs. She dropped her head back against the tiled wall and struggled to catch her next breath. "Oh, Rebecca. Yesssss!" Megan screamed as her blissful rapture exploded like a thousand fragments of uncut diamonds bouncing off the mosaic tiles.

♥♥♥♥♥♥♥♥♥♥

♥ *TENDER HEART* ♥

Megan returned their empty glasses to the kitchen and turned out the light. She returned to their bedroom and smiled as she saw Rebecca sitting on the carpet before a romantic, roaring fire dressed in an ivory satin sleep shirt.

She gave Megan a sexy, seductive smile and crooked a finger at her to join her. "Come here, my little hussy," Rebecca said.

Megan burst into laughter and crawled toward Rebecca on all fours making hungry lion sounds. She nuzzled right into Rebecca's sensitive neck and luxuriated in her precious giggles. "Please don't tell Madison that we slept together three days after we met. She'll never let me live it down," Megan said.

Rebecca held Megan's face in her hands and leaned intimately close to her sensuous lips. "I promise not to tell her that. I'm going to tell her that I was so attracted to you that it would have been two days if you hadn't been called into the hospital," Rebecca teased.

Megan gave Rebecca a playful scowl as Rebecca burst into laughter and gently eased her down among the pillows, loosening the belt of Megan's rich, velour robe. Megan looked deeply into Rebecca's tender, passionate eyes and slowly undid each button on Rebecca's satin shirt.

Their eyes never wavered as Megan glided one finger along her satiny smooth collar and down between her breasts, gently separating the shirt and exposing Rebecca's sexy body. Megan lowered herself to nuzzle into Rebecca's neck as Rebecca's gentle moans escaped from deep within.

Rebecca gracefully eased Megan's robe off her strong shoulders and watched it slide down her back to the floor. Megan reached for her robe and threw it on the couch as she laughed at the two huge sets of eyes watching them. Rebecca turned her head to see JC and Penney perched on the back of the couch intently watching the activities before the warm fire.

"Sweetheart, did you know that our cats are voyeurs?" Megan said shyly.

♥ TENDER HEART ♥

Rebecca burst into her bubbly laughter and reached for Megan, gently guiding her to lie on top of her. "They think that you might be able to teach them a thing or two, so get to the lesson, Dr. Summers. Your students and wife are waiting."

Megan growled playfully as she leaned into Rebecca's neck and basked in her gasping moans. She left a trail of warm, wet kisses along her neck to her throat and down to each breast. Megan delighted in the responsiveness of each nipple as she left them hard and wet.

Rebecca ran her fingers smoothly through Megan's thick hair, gasping at the pleasure of her kisses down her belly and across her thighs. Megan eased herself lower as Rebecca separated her thighs and encouraged Megan to explore her further. Rebecca gently swayed beneath her as Megan slipped her hand beneath Rebecca's shapely bottom and immersed her tongue into her awaiting wetness.

Rebecca arched her back and released an astonishing gasp as Megan probed her gently and inhaled her erotic, womanly scent. Rebecca rocked gently to the rhythm of Megan's tongue as they joined in a dance of passion and fire. Megan swirled her tongue and heightened Rebecca's ecstasy as her fingers entered and caressed her. Rebecca suddenly held Megan's head tight in her hands. She jerked against Megan's mouth one final time as a gentle, undulating wave of spasms pulled Megan in deeper. Rebecca's breathing became gasping and ragged as she emitted a guttural scream of explosive sexual bliss.

Megan slowly eased herself to lie beside Rebecca's completely spent body and slipped a pillow under both their heads. Megan gently brushed her fingertips across Rebecca's slender belly with a feathery touch as she watched her breathing become steadier.

Rebecca slowly opened her eyes and looked into Megan's beaming face. "That was beyond words and beyond this solar system. You're an incredible lover, Megan Summers, and why did you wait so long to find me?"

♥ *TENDER HEART* ♥

Megan laughed as Rebecca eased her onto her back and entwined their hands together, holding Megan's hands captive over her head. Megan smiled and kissed Rebecca tenderly. "I have a feeling we'll have no trouble making up for lost time," Megan said.

Rebecca smiled and kissed her with wanton desire, as she tasted their intimacy on Megan's playful tongue. Rebecca eased herself between Megan's thighs and applied gentle, rhythmic pressure as Megan closed her eyes and moaned softly.

Rebecca gently released Megan's hands and began making tiny circles on her chest with the soft pad of her index finger. Her finger teased and taunted her hard nipple as Megan moaned and writhed beneath her. The circles grew bigger and bigger on Megan's belly as Rebecca leaned against Megan's ear and tickled her with her tongue. "I bet if my journey traveled lower I would find you very, very wet, my precious Meg," Rebecca whispered in a gravelly voice.

Megan gently trailed her finger across Rebecca's chin and over her moist, full lower lip. "That's something you're just going to have to discover in your journey, my sweet Rebecca," Megan whispered achingly.

Rebecca gave her a breathtaking smile and leaned closer to her moist lips. "No, Meg. You tell me. Tell me how wet you are for me."

Megan stared at Rebecca's sensuous lips and ached to taste her tongue. "I'm so wet for you, my darling Rebecca, that you're going to need a lifejacket to stay afloat."

Rebecca sighed with pure, impatient lust as she quickly floated herself between Megan's parted legs.

Megan closed her eyes and ran her fingers deeply into Rebecca's soft, lush hair as she felt her soft, blowing breath against her wetness. Megan arched her neck and groaned impatiently. "Oh, God! Please, baby. Touch me."

Rebecca grinned wickedly as she leaned closer and elicited a moaning sigh of pure ecstasy with each stroke of her tongue. Rebecca reached up and entwined her hand in Megan's as she

♥ TENDER HEART ♥

felt their souls merge as one. Rebecca's heart burst with love for this tender woman; she felt the deep desire to please her for the rest of their lives and guided her into an explosive journey of soul-filling ecstasy.

♥ *TENDER HEART* ♥

♥ TENDER HEART ♥
CHAPTER NINE

Megan grabbed her briefcase from the passenger seat and entered the hospital through the E.R. entrance. She walked around the nurse's station and was greeted warmly by the staff.

Drake leaned against the counter and laughed as he shook his head. "Are your feet ever going to hit the ground, Dr. Summers?" he said, chuckling.

Megan beamed from ear to ear with an aura of happiness as she reached up and kissed Drake's cheek. "Never, Dr. Darrow, never! That woman is so incredible she melts my soul," Megan gushed.

Drake smiled and watched Megan head toward the elevators. "I'm sure your soul isn't all that she's melted."

Megan stopped and gave Drake a euphoric grin just before stepping into an empty elevator.

♥♥♥♥♥♥♥♥♥♥

Megan stepped out from behind the curtain and handed Sharon the completed orders on the sixteen-year-old girl she had just assessed.

"I hate to see Melissa come back in with problems with her shunt. I remember when she first came through our doors having terrible grand mal seizures when she was only fifteen. Her limbs were thrashing about so violently that it took six of us to hold her down just to protect her from hurting herself," Sharon said, sadly. "You rushed her to the O.R. and removed her temporal lobe tumor and inserted her ventriculoperitoneal shunt. She's been problem-free for a year. Now she looks so sick again."

Megan placed her hand on Sharon's shoulder. "I know. I hate to see her like this. Unfortunately, it looks like her shunt is infected. We both know that Melissa's family lives in impoverished conditions and this was bound to happen. She's such a sweet kid and I hate to have to put her through another surgery."

Sharon smiled at Megan as they walked toward the nurse's station together. "I just want you to know, Megan, that I think it's great the way you treat Melissa and her family. Her parents are very hard working people but have minimal education. You always take extra time with them to explain everything so that they can understand what's going on. You have a heart of gold, Megan."

Megan blushed and guided Sharon into the nursing station. "Try and remember that the next time I get irritable and impatient in the trauma room, okay, Sharon?"

Sharon laughed and squeezed Megan's arm. "You're a pussy cat compared to the guys around here." They both laughed and turned suddenly as they heard Drake raise his voice.

"Stop! Let me help you. Don't be so difficult," he snapped.

Megan saw a stunning, slender woman in her forties with flowing chestnut hair standing before him. The blood-soaked tea towel wrapped around her hand stood out from her crisp, red business suit.

The woman looked at Drake's name embroidered on his lab coat and took a deep, impatient breath. "Dr. Darrow, I'm just going to go back to my car to phone my office and tell them that I may be here for a while. I promise to come right back," she professed.

Drake ran his hand through his hair in frustration. "You're not stepping out of my E.R. before I see your hand. Besides, you're dripping blood all over my new shoes. I can just see it: you'll leave a trail all the way out to your car and when they find your body slumped over your steering wheel, they're going to follow your trail back to me and think that I'm the one that killed you," he said.

The elegant woman failed miserably at hiding her giggles as Drake struggled to contain the amusement in his eyes. Megan watched as Drake shoved his hands in his lab coat pockets and awkwardly shuffled his feet. Megan was filled with delight as she leaned towards Sharon.

"I better go give Drake a hand. Pardon the pun. It looks like our fearless leader has become enthralled by the feminine form in that sharp business suit."

Megan grabbed a towel from the linen cart and stepped toward the fiery confrontation. She unfolded the towel and gently wrapped it around the woman's hand.

"Thank you," the woman said as they both shared a smile.

"That should prevent Drake's fears of becoming tonight's headlines as the next hand-murderer," Megan said, as she glared at Drake disapprovingly. Megan turned to the woman and introduced both herself and Drake.

"We've tried to hire better people greeters at our doors but Wal-mart seems to have taken the cream of the crop," Megan said.

The woman burst into heartfelt laughter and introduced herself as Stephanie Cavanaugh.

Drake moved one step closer. "Mrs Cavanaugh, I'm concerned about your hand. By the looks of the blood soaked through that towel you've lost a fair amount of blood already. We have a bank of pay phones just down the hall. Why don't you call your office from there then we can have a look at your hand in assessment room one. Enough time has been wasted already," Drake explained.

Stephanie looked down at her hand then from Drake to Megan. "He's right, Mrs Cavanaugh. Your hand needs immediate attention. I'll even stick around for a few minutes to make sure he doesn't scream at you for dripping blood on your own calling card," Megan said.

"Thank you, Dr. Summers. I'll be really quick. I'd hate to do anything else to provoke his majesty's fury," Stephanie said, as she held her head high, her back straight, and walked down the hall.

"Drip blood on her calling card, provoke his majesty's fury, what the hell is wrong with women these days. A guy tries to care and he gets slammed from all sides," Drake stated, as he paced before Megan.

"What the hell is wrong with you, Drake? I have never seen you come on so strong. You're always so calm and controlled even in some pretty chaotic situations when the best of us lose it. A woman comes in with a bandaged hand and wants to make a phone call and you treat her like she has just told you she's flattened your Lexus with a tank!"

Drake sighed heavily and leaned back against the wall. He stared down the hall after Stephanie Cavanaugh for several seconds before Megan touched his cheek and guided his eyes back to her. "It's been a long time, Drake. Don't be frightened just because Stephanie stirs things in you you haven't felt in a long time."

Stephanie Cavanaugh headed back towards them as Drake pushed off from the wall. "All right, Dr. Darrow. I'm ready. But I swear if you hurt me I'll stomp on your new shoes."

Drake blinked in disbelief as he pointed into assessment room one and watched as Megan followed Stephanie into the room.

"And you tell me not to be frightened! Jesus, I should be terrified of a woman like that," Drake whispered.

Megan beamed with mischief. "I think she might just be what the doctor ordered, Drake. Never question fate," Megan breathed.

Drake shook his head and took a deep breath before entering the room.

Sharon had already set up the equipment Drake would need and guided Stephanie onto a stool. She rested her arm comfortably across a stainless steel over bed table. Drake removed his lab coat and sat directly across from her. He donned a pair of gloves as Megan straddled the stool beside Stephanie.

Stephanie couldn't help but notice the way Drake's solid chest filled his crisp baby blue dress shirt or the way the shirt tapered perfectly to his narrow waist before disappearing into his trendy, pleated khaki trousers.

♥ *TENDER HEART* ♥

"What happened to your hand, Mrs Cavanaugh?" Megan said, snapping Stephanie's attention away from Drake.

"Please, call me Stephanie. I was rinsing a glass at my sink this morning when it slipped from my hand. I tried to catch it before it shattered, but as you can see, it wasn't a clean catch. A chunk of glass is still stuck in my palm and I couldn't bring myself to pull it out so I just wrapped it up with what I could and drove straight here."

Drake carefully removed the saturated tea towel and exposed the shard of glass superficially embedded in Stephanie's palm.

"Why didn't you have someone drive you here? You could have passed out at the wheel with all this blood loss," Drake remarked carefully.

Stephanie looked over at Megan and frowned. "He's determined to give me grief over this, isn't he?"

Megan smiled and leaned closer to Stephanie's smiling eyes. "He's a man. His purpose in life is to give us all grief at every opportunity," Megan said, rolling her eyes skyward. Both women laughed together as Drake gave them a menacing look and frowned.

Drake gently probed the palm of her hand with his sterile tweezers as Stephanie shrieked and rested her good hand on Drake's arm. They both looked down at the sudden contact. Stephanie awkwardly removed her slender hand from Drake's tanned, muscular arm.

"I'm sorry," Stephanie said.

"Don't apologize. You're allowed to scream. I'm sure it hurts like hell. Don't be afraid to hold on to my arm if it helps. Just please don't dig your nails into my flesh. You've shed enough blood for the two of us today," Drake said.

Drake forced himself to look away from Stephanie's teary gray eyes and focus on his task. He picked up a clean gauge pad and returned to assessing Stephanie's injury. He dabbed at the trickling blood as Stephanie returned her hand to his arm.

♥ *TENDER HEART* ♥

Drake felt the heat of her touch penetrate his skin as his breath caught in his chest. "You didn't answer my question, Stephanie. Why didn't you have someone drive you here?"

Drake's tender blue eyes riveted Stephanie as she lingered along the sharp planes of his cheeks to the dimple nestled in his square chin. She was in awe of his rugged masculinity and tender warmth as their eyes met with startling intensity.

"I live alone, Dr. Darrow. I have two daughters who are going to university in Boston and my husband passed away two years ago. Therefore, I take care of myself."

Drake looked into her eyes and softened his tone. "I'm sorry about your husband. I'm not trying to give you a hard time. I just worry that something could have happened to you on the way here."

Stephanie was awestruck by the unusual warmth and kindness in those crystal blue eyes. "I appreciate your concern, Dr. Darrow, but I must admit I was scared and just knew I had to get here. Next time, I'll call you and ask you to ride by on your black stallion and come take care of me."

Drake couldn't help but smile into this woman's elegant face as their eyes locked in a playful exchange. "I'll only come by if you call me Robin Hood and don't mind if I bring my band of merry men," Drake said dramatically.

Stephanie and Megan burst into laughter.

"Stephanie, please call me too so I can see Drake in a pair of green tights," Megan begged. They all laughed warmly as Drake positioned his clamps carefully and pulled.

"Ouch! That hurt," Stephanie cried out.

Drake held up the chunk of jagged blood-soaked glass so everyone could see the size of it.

"Of course it hurts, Madame. I just pulled a chunk of diamond out of your hand that I plan on stealing from you and giving to the poor." Drake started to laugh until he saw the huge tears in Stephanie's beautiful gray eyes. He set the glass and his instruments down and applied gentle pressure to her hand with a pad of gauze.

♥ *TENDER HEART* ♥

Megan handed Stephanie several tissues and gently rubbed her back.

"I'm sorry, Stephanie. I'll get you something for the pain while we wait for Dr. Marissa Santiago, the plastic surgeon, to come down and suture your hand," Drake said softly.

Stephanie dried her eyes and watched Drake walk to the door. "I hope your merry plastic surgeon is not as mean as you, you big bully," Stephanie added irritably.

Drake turned in the doorway and smiled. "It wounds me deeply that you could possibly call Robin Hood mean, Mrs Cavanaugh. My intentions and my heart are always in the right place."

Both women watched Drake walk out the door as Stephanie stared after him. "I wouldn't doubt that for a minute, Dr. Darrow," she whispered.

♥♥♥♥♥♥♥♥♥♥

Megan walked into the nurse's station to return a call she received on her pager as she saw Stephanie say good-bye to Dr. Marissa Santiago. She stood with the phone to her ear as she watched Drake step toward the enchanting Mrs Stephanie Cavanaugh.

"Well, you look like you're all set. I hope your visit with us was not all as horrible as Robin Hood's treatment of your hand," Drake said shyly.

Stephanie smiled and looked down at the bulky dressing snugly wrapped around her hand. "Thanks for everything, Dr. Darrow. I appreciated all your kindness and I'm sorry for bleeding on your shoes."

Drake smiled and gently turned Stephanie's hand, taking a distracted look at her dressing. "I forgive you as long as you forgive me for causing your tears," Drake offered.

Stephanie gave him a beautiful smile and tenderly hooked her fingers in his hand. "Apology accepted."

♥ *TENDER HEART* ♥

Drake's vibrant blue eyes creased with a smile as he handed Stephanie his business card. She looked up into his eyes and carefully held the card with her one hand. She burst into a gorgeous smile as she read where Drake had written: "SHERWOOD FOREST."

"If you have any questions or problems with your hand, don't hesitate to call me here at the hospital. One of my merry men should know where to find me in this concrete jungle. And if you feel really brave and adventurous, you can come join me for one of our king's feasts as my special guest," Drake said.

Stephanie gave Drake a breathtaking smile as she slipped her business card into the breast pocket of his lab coat. "I've always fantasized about being Maid Marian for a day." She took one step back and gave Drake a wink as she waved good-bye to Megan and headed for the door.

"Wait a minute, Stephanie. Please don't tell me you're driving yourself home," Drake said.

Stephanie held her bandaged hand close to her chest and smiled. "Not at all, Dr. Darrow. I've summoned King Richard to come to my rescue." A car pulled up to the emergency room doors and a worried elderly man jumped from the drivers seat. "Good-bye, Dr. Darrow. My chariot has arrived." Stephanie waved one final time and headed into the arms of her father.

Megan finished her conversation and watched Drake stare after his Maid Marian. She set the phone down and smiled, walked around the counter and placed her hand on his broad shoulder. "Drake, go knock her socks off!"

Drake blushed and laughed as Megan kissed his cheek. "I'm going to meet the love of my life for lunch, Drake, so don't you dare page me for the next hour or I'll load my bow with the sharpest arrow and spear Robin Hood right between his sexy tights."

Drake burst into laughter as he watched Megan bounce toward the elevators with incredible exuberance.

"Give Rebecca my love, Meg."

♥ TENDER HEART ♥

Megan turned and smiled as she hit the elevator button. "I'll try and fit that in Drake, but we only have an hour so I can't make you any promises."

Drake shook his head and laughed as Megan waved and slipped into a crowded elevator.

♥♥♥♥♥♥♥♥♥♥

Megan was lost in her thoughts of their romantic lunch as she walked back through the E.R. after seeing Rebecca off in the parking lot. She inhaled the subtle fragrance of her single red rose as she brushed her nose against the silky pedals. The nurses and residents all moved quickly among the organized chaos as Sharon exited a room and walked right into Megan.

"Geez, I'm sorry, Megan," she said, as they hung onto each other.

"That's okay, Sharon. I wasn't really watching where I was going. It's just as much my fault. Have you seen Drake?"

"He headed into his office a second ago," Sharon explained.

"Thanks. I'll go see if he's still there."

Sharon watched Megan walk away and cradle the delicate rose in the palm of her hand.

"Beautiful rose, Megan. I hope the person that gave you that flower brings you much happiness," Sharon said.

"Thanks, Sharon. She certainly has done that."

Megan knocked on Drake's partially closed office door and called out his name.

"Come in, Meg. I'm in here."

Megan closed the door behind her and stepped in as she watched Drake slip a resident's evaluation form into his filing cabinet. She took his handsome face in her hands and kissed him softly. "That's from Rebecca."

Drake took the rose from Megan's hand and touched it to her lips. "And I bet this came from that same special lady."

Megan smiled brightly and nodded her head. "Speaking of special ladies, I hope that Cupid is taking care of his own heart

♥ *TENDER HEART* ♥

for a change and has sent his lovely Maid Marian flowers as a get well token from his kind heart."

Drake leaned toward Megan and kissed her softly. "A dozen, long stemmed red roses should be arriving on her desk as we speak."

Megan smiled and leaned her forehead against Drake's chin. "I'm so proud of you, Drake. You deserve a wonderful woman." Megan kissed Drake's handsome face and smiled. Drake took Megan by the shoulders and playfully guided her towards the door.

"Get out of here before you have us both misty eyed. I have too much work to do for this nonsense."

Megan stopped in the doorway and turned to face him. "Sure. I bet this nonsense is just filling you with a warm fuzzy feeling all over."

Drake tried hard not to laugh as he gently shoved Megan out the door. "Go back to work, you hopeless romantic."

Megan laughed as she headed towards her office. She was overwhelmed with joy at the glowing ember of excitement in Drake's beautiful eyes.

Megan set her rose in a crystal vase on her desk and headed down to CAT scan to meet Dean and review several of her patient's films.

♥♥♥♥♥♥♥♥♥♥♥

Dean flipped the last CAT scan onto the view box and identified two areas of concern on a sixty-year-old patient's scan. Megan analyzed the pictures before her as her pager chimed at her waist. Dean slipped the scan back into its envelope and flipped the lights on in the room. Megan reached for her pager and read the message.

    Hi Meg.
        Please call me.
                Kyle/Superman

♥ *TENDER HEART* ♥

Megan frowned and picked up the nearest phone to dial Rebecca's office number. "Hi, Superman, what's up?"

"Hi, Meg. Is Rebecca still having lunch with you?"

Megan smiled and leaned back against the counter. "I wish, Kyle. She left about twenty minutes ago for that one o'clock appointment you guys had. What's wrong, Kyle, and why aren't you with Rebecca?"

"I received a page from her an hour ago telling me that our appointment with that creep Sam Abbott was cancelled, so I've just been waiting for her to find out what happened because he never cancels our appointments."

Megan felt like she had just been kicked in the chest as she struggled to breathe deeply. "Kyle, Rebecca was with me an hour ago and she never phoned you or anyone else to cancel an appointment," Megan said.

"Kyle, where the hell is Rebecca? I don't like the sound of this and I want her found immediately," Megan snapped, as a million frantic thoughts collided into one terrifying picture.

"Megan, listen to me. I'm going to find Rebecca if it's the last thing I do! I'm going to page her and I want you to do the same. I'll call Scotty and get his help. As soon as I contact her, I'll call you and I want you to do the same if she calls you, okay?"

Megan could barely think straight as her worry consumed her.

"Kyle, find her and find her fast because I'm not going to be able to take another breath unless I know she is safe and I can see her."

Kyle grabbed his car keys out of his pocket and took a deep breath. "I know exactly how you feel, Megan. Page her, Meg, and don't give up till one of us hears from her. I'll call you as soon as I find her." They both said good-bye. Kyle bolted out of the office. Megan quickly hung up and paged Rebecca twice.

"Megan, what's wrong? You're as white as a ghost," Dean said, with overwhelming concern. He reached for her arm and eased her into a chair as Megan's pager chimed again. Megan ripped it off her belt as her heart pounded against her chest. She

♥ TENDER HEART ♥

quickly read the message and felt a strange sense of relief and confusion.

Megan:

Meet me at your truck.

Rebecca

Megan frowned and quickly rose from her chair. She stared at her pager and reread the message as if expecting it to tell her more. Dean watched her expression darken and touched her arm.

"Megan, what's wrong? What's happened to Rebecca?"

Megan clipped the pager back on her belt and headed for the door. "Something is definitely wrong, Dean. I just need to go and meet Rebecca at my vehicle and see that she's okay."

Dean stood in the doorway and watched Megan run toward the staff- parking garage.

♥♥♥♥♥♥♥♥♥♥

Megan quickly approached the front of her vehicle. She suddenly dropped the keys in her hand as she read the message scrawled in blood across her windshield. She stood in numbed disbelief and finally screamed Rebecca's name. She ran around her vehicle and the other cars screaming and searching frantically for her Rebecca.

Drake was standing in the ambulance bay watching a patient being unloaded on a stretcher when he heard Megan's blood curdling screams. He grabbed the security guard nearest him. "Page for a security emergency in the staff-parking lot now then send all the manpower you have there stat!" Drake barely finished his message as he started off in a run with three other security guards right on his heels.

Minutes later he stopped cold before Megan's vehicle and saw the message. One security guard dropped his flashlight with

♥ *TENDER HEART* ♥

a sickening thud as Drake used his cell phone to dial 911. He quickly reported what he saw and their location as Megan walked around the vehicle with tears streaming down her face. He reached out to Megan and held her tight as she collapsed in his arms. Drake screamed at the security guards to search the parking garage for any sign of Rebecca or the person who did this sick act.

Fifteen minutes later Drake stood facing Megan's vehicle, holding his cellular phone to his ear and watching her pace like a caged lion. The desk clerk at the Austin Police Department finally put him through to Scotty and Drake breathed a sigh of relief. "Scotty! It's horrible. It says:

> DOCTOR DYKE:
> LEAVE HER ALONE!
> SHE BELONGS TO ME!

"Who the hell did this, Scotty?"

"The psycho's name is Sam Abbott, among other alias's, Drake. He has always given Kyle and Rebecca the creeps so I did a thorough background check on him and much to our surprise he came up clean. He kept showing up at the real estate office trying to wine and dine Rebecca, and when she told him, 'No, get lost,' he disappeared for a couple of weeks. Then he started coming around again about the same time Megan came into Rebecca's life. Kyle was really concerned with the sudden resurgence of his visits and how this psycho would react if he knew of Megan's involvement in Rebecca's life."

"Well, by that message on Megan's windshield he must have a pretty good idea of Megan's involvement in Rebecca's life," Drake said.

"Unfortunately, I think he has caught on. Kyle was so worried about both of them that I hired a private investigator to follow this Abbott creep. He somehow managed to lift Abbott's fingerprints off a glass he used in a bar and ran them through his computers. Yesterday the results of those fingerprints came back

♥ *TENDER HEART* ♥

to us and we learned the real details of this Sam Abbott's life. He's suspected of committing violent crimes against women, but there has never been any solid evidence against him or the victims were too terrified to testify against him. This whole thing has me scared to death and I can't even imagine how Megan's feeling."

Drake watched a team of security guards surround Megan's Expedition and close off the area. "She's frantic, Scotty. I don't blame her especially after what you just told me. Find Rebecca, Scotty. For God's sake, just find her."

"I plan on it, Drake. By leaving that message on Megan's windshield it looks like Abbott wants us to find him." Scotty filled Drake in on the plan of action then asked him to put Megan on the phone.

Drake handed Megan his cellular phone as Megan handed him hers. "Keep paging her, Drake. Please keep paging!"

Megan put his phone to her ear and could barely contain herself from screaming. "What the fuck is going on, Scotty? Where's my Rebecca and who is this lunatic that has written this message across my windshield in blood?"

Tears streamed down Megan's cheeks as she ran her hand through her hair and continued to pace like an enraged beast as several police cruisers approached her vehicle. "I'm a doctor, Scotty. I know blood when I see it and that's blood all over my fucking windshield!"

"Megan, listen to me. I know you're terrified. I've sent every available police officer I have out looking for Rebecca," he said tensely.

Megan felt as if she were losing her mind as she stepped away from all the commotion around her Expedition. "Scotty, Rebecca never paged Kyle to cancel their appointment and that page I got was not from Rebecca. She never calls my vehicle a truck and she always signs off her pages with an R, never her full first name. Kyle tells me their one o'clock appointment was with that stalker, Sam Abbott, and now we can't find Rebecca. You call this terrified, Scotty? I'm beyond terror. I'm beyond panic. If

♥ TENDER HEART ♥

I knew which home Rebecca was showing this walking nightmare I would go there myself," Megan screamed.

"Megan, listen to me. I need you to stay at the hospital in case Rebecca tries to contact you. There is a cavalry of cop cars on it's way to the location where Rebecca was headed and in about fifteen minutes I'll be getting on a helicopter and heading out there myself."

Megan's anguish consumed her as she struggled to think straight. "Scotty, tell me what's going on. Why's this happening to my Rebecca?" Megan pleaded, as her voice broke.

Megan could feel her temples pounding as she attempted to digest this horrifying tale.

"Kyle has been really concerned about Abbott's presence at Rebecca's office so I immediately put him on a twenty-four hour surveillance. The guys tailing him last night watched him drive around Rebecca's neighborhood for hours, and then head back to his motel. He hadn't done anything for us to be able to pick him up, so we continued to watch him. Now the cops that were tailing him and Rebecca are all missing," Scotty explained in disbelief.

Megan felt like she was about to pass out as she squeezed the phone in her fist. "You should have warned us about this yesterday, Scotty. Now Rebecca is in grave danger and we all stand by helplessly and wait and pray that somebody gets to my Rebecca before this lunatic hurts her. God help me, Scotty, if he does hurt her, I will not rest till he rots in hell!"

"We'll find her, Meg, or I'll never forgive myself for not tailing this asshole myself.

"Listen, Megan, I'm being paged to the helipad on the roof. The police helicopter has arrived. I know this is an impossible request, but I want you to stay as calm as possible. I'm going after this guy and I'm going to bring Rebecca back to you."

"Go, Scotty. I'll be praying for that to happen."

Megan heard the dead, silent click of the phone. She held the phone white knuckled as hot tears drenched her face. She took

♥ *TENDER HEART* ♥

one step forward and smashed the phone against a concrete pillar, then dropped to her knees, screaming Rebecca's name.

♥♥♥♥♥♥♥♥♥♥

Rebecca cried with anguish as a raging Sam Abbott violently grabbed a fistful of her hair and forced her to her knees. Rebecca fought her sudden terror to understand what was happening as she clutched her purse and heard her pager wail again, praying that someone knew she was in danger. Abbott stood behind Rebecca and tightened his grip on her hair as she fought to slow down her breathing, praying that Kyle would come to help her.

Tears coursed down Rebecca's face as Abbott pressed his stubble cheek against hers and kissed her with wet, rough lips. The stench of alcohol sent Rebecca's stomach lurching as a wave of nausea splashed into her throat. She felt him press his hard body against her back as the cold steel tip of a hunting knife pierced her cheek. He leaned his foul lips into Rebecca's ear and breathed heavily.

"This master bedroom could have been ours, Rebecca," he said in a deranged, slurred whisper. He suddenly picked Rebecca up by the hair and threw her violently against the wall.

Rebecca quickly got to her feet and put her back against the wall, sliding sideways and trying to maintain any distance she could between herself and this madman. Fear gripped at her heart as she clutched her purse tightly and watched Abbott walk around the room as horrible flashbacks of her enraged father assaulted her brain. Her steadfast inner drive to maintain control and not show her father any fear enveloped her and ignited her survival instincts.

"This could have been our house, Rebecca," Abbott screamed at her from across the room. Rebecca kept sidestepping toward the closed door and tried to slip her hand into her purse. He swept his arms around the room and laughed coldly.

♥ TENDER HEART ♥

"But no! You never wanted me!" He took sudden, quick steps toward Rebecca and stood right in front of her. "You just kept saying no and pushed me away."

Rebecca felt pure panic as she heard her pager wail again and again. She silently prayed in stunned disbelief as Abbott took off his black suit jacket and threw it into the center of the room. She watched him set the hunting knife down on a window ledge and take one step back. He slipped his tie over his head and sent it toward his jacket, slowly unbuttoning his shirt with a sick sneer on his contorted, scarred face.

Rebecca felt her legs shake as she fought to maintain a clear head and to breathe slowly. Abbott slipped out of his last piece of clothing. He stood completely naked before her with his tiny flaccid penis and breathed his horrible, intoxicated breath into her face. "I couldn't understand why you didn't want me, Rebecca, when I knew that you were single." He laughed his hideous, demented laugh and ran his hands up Rebecca's arms as she stared into his psychotic eyes. "Then I learned the reason with your precious Dr. Megan Summers." His laughter echoed throughout the empty house as Rebecca struggled to formulate a plan in her head. "A lesbian. A goddamn lesbian! I would never have figured it out till I followed you two for a couple of days, beautiful Rebecca. Well, I left your precious Dr. Megan Summers a little message and when I'm done with you, I have a little surprise in store for your goddamn lesbian lover," he snarled in her face.

Rebecca's anger swelled throughout her entire being and sent a surge of adrenaline coursing through her veins. She stared into the eyes of pure evil. "You hurt my Megan and I'll make sure you live to regret it for the rest of your pathetic, sick life, you bastard!"

He lunged forward and grabbed Rebecca by the face and slammed her back against the wall several times, knocking the wind right out of her and sending her purse sailing across the floor. He finally stopped and held her up against the wall with his sweaty, naked body. "You fucking little bitch! You're really

♥ *TENDER HEART* ♥

making me angry, beautiful Rebecca. All the other women were easy to seduce into these empty houses. Not you. You were determined to give me a run for my money and that made me very, very angry, beautiful Rebecca."

Rebecca struggled to slow down her gasping breaths as she turned her face away from him. He jerked her face back and held her still with the weight of his body. "Nobody says no to me, Rebecca, and lives to repeat it. Not my parents, not my wife, not you, not anybody. I need to teach you a lesson like I taught all those other women."

Rebecca looked him right in the eye. "Bastard," she hissed and slammed her forehead into his nose.

He stumbled back two steps and screamed as blood poured from his broken nose. Rebecca ran for her purse that had come to rest below the second story bay window. She had almost made it when he grabbed her by the arm and slammed her into the wall. He fell to his knees in a daze as Rebecca fought not to lose consciousness. Blood streamed from a gash over her left eyebrow as a searing, excruciating pain enveloped her left arm. She slid along the wall and crumbled to her knees.

♥ ♥ ♥ ♥ ♥ ♥ ♥ ♥ ♥ ♥

Kyle drove like a maniac and finally screeched into the driveway alongside Rebecca's Jaguar and Abbott's pickup truck. His heart pounded against his chest as he screamed Rebecca's name and tried in vain to open the front door. He grabbed a nearby rock and smashed the ornate glass door and quickly gained access to the house. He heard Rebecca scream his name, and then suddenly, a sickening silence descended on the house.

He took the stairs three at a time and ran into the master bedroom. He stopped suddenly just inside the doorway as he recoiled in terror. Rebecca lay face down in a bleeding heap in the middle of the room as Abbott knelt above her, pinning her arms behind her back. He had sliced her blouse off her with his knife and was working on her slacks when Kyle burst into the

♥ *TENDER HEART* ♥

room. He looked at Rebecca's blood-soaked face and felt overwhelming relief as he watched her open her eyes in a daze.

"Well, Kyle, I'm impressed. It took you a lot less time to figure out what was going on than I thought it would," Abbott snarled.

Kyle tried to focus his eyes on Rebecca to will her the strength to hang on as her pager wailed again. Both Kyle and Rebecca looked towards her purse resting below the bay window.

Kyle looked back at Abbott as anger burned in his soul like never before. "Let her go or I'll kill you with my bare hands, you sick son of a bitch!" Kyle took two steps closer as Abbott dropped his knee into Rebecca's back and twisted her left arm higher, causing her to scream in agony. Kyle stopped moving as Rebecca's screams fanned his rage.

Abbott twisted the tip of his knife into Rebecca's back and gave Kyle his sick, nauseating grin. "I wouldn't take another step if I were you, big, strong, faggy Kyle. I'd be happy to slice her up into a thousand little pieces right here before your eyes if you move one step closer."

Rebecca's pager wailed in her purse again and momentarily distracted Abbott as Rebecca rolled to her right and sent him off balance. Kyle lunged forward and planted his foot dead center in Abbott's chest with a sickening thud and sent him sailing across the room. They watched him drop onto his back with a hollow thump. Kyle instantly dove on top of him and punched him in the face. Abbott raised his knife and they both struggled to control it.

Rebecca wiped the blood from her eyes and crawled towards her purse, her left arm dragging behind her in a contorted, grotesque angle. Hot, burning pain ran up and down her left arm as she used her right hand to dump the contents of her purse and grab her gun. Her mind raced a mile a minute as she quickly released the safety and tried to steady herself on her knees to get a clean shot.

♥ *TENDER HEART* ♥

Kyle rolled with Abbott towards the bay window and slammed Abbott's arm down on his own knee, trying to gain the knife. Rebecca wiped her eyes one more time with her right arm.

Rebecca screamed, "Kyle, jump out of the way!" Kyle looked at the gun in Rebecca's hand and jumped to the side as Abbott sliced down through Kyle's thigh. Kyle screamed with excruciating pain and fell onto his back as Abbott struggled to his feet and stood to face Rebecca. She pointed the gun right at him as he looked at her with cold, pure evil.

"This is going to save my lesbian lover the trouble of amputating your disgusting balls and feeding them to the neighborhood dogs," Rebecca hissed, as she steadied her hand with amazing calm and fired three times. She watched as the bullets ripped through Abbott's chest and sent him lifeless to the polished wooden floors, ending his reign of terror.

Rebecca dropped the gun and rushed to Kyle's side. Blood gushed from the gash in his thigh.

He continued to moan and looked up into Rebecca's blood-soaked face. "Nice shot, Beck. Scotty always said you could hold your own in a gun battle with Clint Eastwood."

Rebecca smiled and caressed Kyle's pale, damp face. "Hold on, Kyle. Do you hear me? I'm going to try and stop your bleeding but I need your help." Rebecca slid along the floor and grabbed Abbott's shirt and tie. She guided Kyle to help her secure the tie around his thigh like a tourniquet and used the shirt as a pressure dressing. She sat him up against the wall, and then sat in his lap, using her body as pressure over the wound.

Kyle leaned his head against Rebecca's right shoulder. She hugged him tight with her right arm and felt him weakening. They heard sirens wailing in the distance and a helicopter hovering above. Tears streamed down both their faces as Kyle leaned back against the wall and tried to focus his eyes on Rebecca. She gently wiped away his tears and struggled to catch her breath. "Don't you dare leave me, Superman. Your Lois Lane would be nothing without you. Hang on, Kyle. Do you hear me?

♥ *TENDER HEART* ♥

Hang on! Do it for Scotty and me. We need you. And who else would call Meg 'Doc Grumpy' and get away with it?"

Kyle smiled, and then reached up to weakly wipe the blood off Rebecca's cheek. "I love you so much, Beck. You don't have to worry because I'm not going anywhere. That bastard made the one fatal mistake of taking us on when I had my Superman boxers on. That sucky little hunting knife of his only put a minor tear in my cape." Kyle closed his eyes and coughed weakly as he struggled to keep talking. "Besides, you and Scotty would lead boring lives without me, and I have to stick around and make sure that Megan continues to treat you like a royal princess." Kyle gently brushed a strand of hair away from the oozing gash over Rebecca's left eye and struggled to take a deep breath. "Meg is very special, Beck. She loves you like nobody's ever loved you before."

Rebecca smiled through her blood-soaked tears as Kyle coughed one last time and collapsed back against the wall. Rebecca struggled to hold him up and screamed just as Scotty burst into the room.

♥♥♥♥♥♥♥♥♥♥

The E.R. was crowded with security, police, and concerned hospital staff. Tension and anxiety crackled in the air. Drake and Dean stood in the nurse's station as they watched Megan pace relentlessly before Madison and Shawna. Everyone in that room had said a silent prayer for Rebecca and Kyle as they watched Megan's tears course down her cheeks. Madison handed Megan a glass of ice water and watched her take a sip as she wiped away her tears. Megan handed her back the glass as the trauma call finally came in from the air ambulance crew. Everyone in the room froze with terror as Megan stepped up to the counter.

"Dr. Darrow, we have one fatality at the scene from multiple gun shot wounds to the chest and two level one trauma patients coming your way."

♥ *TENDER HEART* ♥

Megan clutched at the counter as her knuckles turned white; Madison and Shawna stood on either side of her. Nobody dared to breathe as the static cleared over the airwaves and the paramedic continued.

"The first patient is being loaded into the helicopter now with Detective Scott Timmons. Forty-year-old white male, Kyle Kennedy, deep laceration to the left thigh. Estimated blood loss at the scene is five hundred ccs. Blood pressure is eighty over forty, heart rate one hundred and forty, sinus tachycardia with no ectopy. Drowsy, pale, diaphoretic, orientated to person, place and time. The second trauma patient applied a tourniquet and pressure dressing and we put him in mast pants. Intravenous fluids are running wide open and he is now in flight."

Megan took Shawna and Madison's hands as they held each other tight and listened. "Second level one trauma patient is thirty-eight-year-old white female, Rebecca Rhodes. Open fracture of the left humerus and we have splinted her left arm. Laceration over her left eye and possible fractured ribs. Blood pressure is one hundred over fifty; heart rate is one hundred and twenty, sinus tachycardia with no ectopy. Intravenous fluids running. This feisty little lady is alert and orientated and somehow managed to save herself from being sexually assaulted and she even shot and killed her assailant."

The cheers in the E.R. were deafening. Drake looked over at the tears of joy coursing down Megan's face. "Dr. Darrow, we're loading Ms. Rhodes onto the helicopter now. She said that if Dr. Megan Summers is listening, to tell her that she could really use a Hershey's Kiss right now." Everyone in the E.R. burst into cheers and applause as Megan crumbled into Madison's arms and released tears of absolute relief.

Madison caressed her head and whispered, "She's going to be okay, Meg. Your Rebecca is going to be okay."

Madison and Shawna held Megan close. Drake stepped toward them and guided Megan into his arms. They both shared their tears of joy as Drake kissed Megan's damp cheek and leaned back. "You'd better catch your breath, Meg, so you can

♥ TENDER HEART ♥

deliver that Hershey's kiss. I hear a couple of incoming helicopters about to land."

♥♥♥♥♥♥♥♥♥♥

Megan, Drake, the trauma team, and a group of policemen shielded their eyes from the flying debris set in flight by the landing helicopter. They stood back in the receiving bay at the base of the ramp, watching, as Kyle was loaded onto a stretcher with Scotty by his side.

When the two men reached Drake and Megan, Kyle reached for her hand and Megan leaned down and kissed his forehead. "I'm so sorry I didn't stop him before he hurt her," Kyle said.

Megan leaned her face close, moved his oxygen mask and kissed his cheek. "You saved her life, Kyle. You risked your own to save hers and I don't know how I can ever thank you."

Tears streamed down both their faces as Kyle caressed her face. "Take care of her for me, Meg. Make sure she's okay."

Megan gave him a beautiful smile and kissed him softly. "I'm going to make sure you both are okay, Kyle. I promise you that. We have a team of the best vascular surgeons waiting for you in the trauma room. They specialize in Superman repairs," Megan teased.

Kyle smiled brightly as tears streamed down his cheeks.

Megan kissed him one more time and replaced the oxygen mask over his face. "Hang in there, Kyle, and I'll see you in a few minutes." Kyle squeezed her hand as Megan directed the trauma team to take Kyle to trauma room one.

Megan stepped towards Scotty's teary face and held his face in her hands, reaching on her tiptoes to kiss his damp cheek. "I can't tell you how much it meant to me when you called me and told me that you were with Rebecca and Kyle and that they were both alive."

Scotty looked down as tears streamed from his eyes and he held Megan close. "I'm so sorry we couldn't stop him sooner, Meg. He realized that he was being followed and killed both of

♥ *TENDER HEART* ♥

my police officers so he could get Rebecca alone in that house. Kyle and Rebecca fought for their lives against that sick bastard and now they're both seriously injured."

Megan held his face in her hands and raised his eyes to meet hers. "Kyle and Rebecca are going to be okay, Scotty. I'm going to make sure of that."

Scotty took a deep breath and held Megan close. "They have to be okay, Megan. I love them both so much. I can't bear to lose either one of them."

Megan hugged him tight as the second helicopter descended on the roof along with the police helicopter. Megan kissed Scotty's cheek and squeezed his hands. "Go to him, Scotty, and I'll see you shortly."

Scotty wiped at his eyes and stepped back. "Take care of Beck, Megan. Make sure she's okay."

Megan smiled as he backed away down the receiving ramp. "I will, Scotty. I promise. I won't rest till I know they're both going to be okay."

Scotty smiled just before he turned and rushed toward trauma room one.

Megan turned to see Rebecca being loaded onto a trauma stretcher. Drake held her back from running onto the roof as she saw Rebecca turn her head and their eyes instantly met. Rebecca smiled and blew her a kiss as their tears flowed endlessly.

The trauma team rolled Rebecca to Megan as everyone in that receiving bay felt tears blur their eyes. Rebecca squealed with pure happiness as Megan removed her oxygen mask and took her face in her hands and kissed her softly. Rebecca wrapped her right arm around Megan's neck and pulled her in tight as everyone watched this long awaited reunion. Megan leaned back and gently wiped Rebecca's tears away. "I can't tell you how ecstatic I am to see you, sweetheart," Megan whispered.

Rebecca pulled Megan closer and kissed her softly. "I was so scared, Meg. I thought I'd never see you again."

Megan watched Rebecca's tears flow as she gently wiped them away.

♥ *TENDER HEART* ♥

"I have never felt terror like that in my life," Rebecca gasped.

Megan held her face close and felt her tears fall onto her hands. "I'm so sorry for what that bastard did to you because of me and our relationship," Megan whispered.

Rebecca reached up and held Megan's face in her hand. "No, baby, you're not responsible in any way for what that sick bastard did to me. It wasn't anything you or I did. He's just very sick and was enraged because he couldn't possess me. He has hurt other women, Meg, and when he said he was going to hurt you that was all the incentive I needed to end his sick, pathetic life."

Megan held her face close and brushed away her tears. "I'm so grateful that you're okay, sweetheart. I'm so proud of you for ending that bastard's life. From this day forth, I'm going to dedicate my life to keeping you safe."

Rebecca gave her a beautiful smile as Megan brushed her fingers across the dressing over Rebecca's left eye. "How's Kyle, Meg? Abbott cut him really badly."

Megan smiled and caressed Rebecca's bloodstained cheek. "You saved his life, babe. It seems that the time you spent hiding from your father in the woods taught you a lot about how to stop someone from hemorrhaging to death."

Rebecca gave her a triumphant smile and turned her face to kiss the palm of Megan's hand.

"How are you feeling, sweetheart?"

"My left arm and my left side are very painful and this backboard is killing my back."

Megan leaned down and kissed her gently. "We're going to take you into the trauma room and have a good look at your injuries, sweetheart. Try and hang in there and I promise to give you something for the pain in a few minutes." Megan placed her oxygen mask back on her face and kissed her forehead. She stood tall and slipped her hand into Rebecca's and gave her a gentle wink.

"Let's go guys. Let's get Rebecca into trauma room two."

♥ *TENDER HEART* ♥

Megan sat on a metal stool at the head of Rebecca's stretcher and gently wiped away the blood on her face as the plastic surgeon, Dr. Marissa Santiago, assessed the laceration over her left eye. Megan watched Rebecca drift into a light sleep as the morphine slowly started to take effect.

Megan set the bloody washcloths aside and held Rebecca's head still as Dr. Santiago froze the area and began suturing the three-inch wound. Megan stroked her face with her thumbs as the golden eyes tried to open and focus on Megan's beautiful smile.

Drake stepped in behind Megan and rested his hands on her shoulders and smiled down at Rebecca.

"Hi, beautiful. How's your pain?"

"It's not too bad, Drake. The morphine really helped but it makes me feel really groggy. I want to be awake to know what's happening around me."

They all smiled as Dr. Santiago leaned closer to her face. "Rebecca, I wish you weren't so loved because you really make it hard for me to complete my task here."

They all smiled as Rebecca turned toward the elegant doctor and mumbled through her oxygen mask, "I've been blessed with an incredible family, Dr. Santiago." They all smiled as they watched Rebecca struggle to keep her eyes open. She finally drifted off into a light sleep.

Drake leaned closer to Megan. "What are the extent of her injuries?"

Megan looked over at Rebecca's left arm packed in ice then turned to Drake. "She has a spiral, comminuted fracture of her left humerus, three fractured ribs on the left side and this laceration over her left eye. A knife puncture wound to her right cheek and upper back, multiple bruises and scrapes and superficial cuts up and down her back from when that bastard sliced off her blouse." Megan's tears fell onto her cheeks as she caressed Rebecca's hair and watched her sleep.

Dr. Santiago finished suturing Rebecca's laceration as Drake kneeled before Megan and guided her face back to his. He gently

♥ *TENDER HEART* ♥

brushed away her tears as Megan reached for a tissue in her lab coat pocket. "Her childhood was a living nightmare and now this has to happen to her. She doesn't deserve any of this shit, Drake. She's been fighting men off her entire life."

Drake rested his hands on Megan's knees and watched her dry her eyes. "Now all of those men are gone, Meg, and she has found the most amazing woman that she could ever ask for."

Megan smiled and took a deep breath. "No one will ever hurt her again, Drake. I'm going to make sure of that."

Drake smiled and playfully raised his hands in defeat. "I don't doubt that for a minute, guardian angel," he said, chuckling.

Megan playfully swatted Drake's arm. Drake rested his hands back on Megan's knees and looked up at Rebecca's cardiac monitor, making a mental note of her vital signs continually flashing across the screen. He turned back to see Megan caressing Rebecca's cheek with eyes filled with love.

"When are orthopedics going to take Rebecca to the operating room to fix her left arm?" he asked.

Megan turned back to Drake and frowned. "They said they should have an available operating room in about thirty minutes. I had Rebecca sign the consent form before they gave her any morphine. I gave Dr. Schwartz, the orthopedic surgeon, Rebecca's medical history so they're ready to go," Megan explained. "I'm just waiting for Rebecca's aunt and uncle to arrive. I called them when Rebecca was en route here. They should be here shortly."

Drake looked over at Rebecca's ice-packed arm and then turned back to Megan. "The vascular surgeons are ready to take Kyle to the operating room to repair his femoral vein. He asked to see you again before he goes."

Megan took Drake's hand and guided him to stand with her as she leaned forward and kissed Rebecca's forehead. "Please stay with her, Drake. I'll let Madison and Shawna come in while I go see Kyle and Scotty."

♥ *TENDER HEART* ♥

Drake gave Megan his handsome smile and took Megan's seat, leaning close to Rebecca's ear. "So, I hear that you and your lesbian lover bought a new house together. I bet it doesn't have as many boy toys as mine does," Drake said, chuckling.

A beautiful smile curled the corners of Rebecca's lips as she slowly opened her sleepy eyes and turned to Drake. "We don't need boy toys or boys, Drake. I have everything I ever wanted in that house and in my lesbian lover," Rebecca whispered proudly.

They all laughed as Megan leaned close to Rebecca's face and smiled. "Sweetheart, I'm going to see Kyle before they take him to surgery and give him a kiss for both of us. In the meantime, I want you to ask Drake who he met in Sherwood Forest this morning."

Megan kissed Rebecca's forehead and whispered with deep emotion, "I love you, baby." They gave each other glowing smiles as Megan headed toward the door. As she was leaving, Megan heard Rebecca say in a sleepy voice, "Sherwood Forest? Where's that, Drake?"

♥♥♥♥♥♥♥♥♥♥

Megan brushed her hand across Scotty's back and eased herself onto the edge of Kyle's stretcher. He removed his oxygen mask, wrapped her in his arms, and hugged her tight. Megan leaned back and kissed him softly as Scotty stood at her knees. Megan sat back as both men asked about Rebecca and she filled them in on all the details. Tears drained from Kyle's eyes as Megan reached forward and wiped them away. "She's going to be fine, Kyle, thanks to you and Scotty. If both of you hadn't acted so quickly and realized that something was wrong, then God knows what would have happened to Rebecca today.

"Rebecca and I have been worried sick about you and Scotty in here. Drake has been relaying messages to us about what's been going on. Every time Rebecca opens her eyes she asks about you and keeps wanting to see you. I have been telling her that Superman has been temporarily grounded."

♥ TENDER HEART ♥

Megan slipped her hand into Kyle's and gave him a gentle squeeze. "How are you feeling, Kyle?"

"I'm fine, really, Meg. Considering what could have happened. I'm grateful that Beck and I walked away with our lives. A few pints less of blood, but we're still here to tell the story. Please tell my boss lady that we'll all be due for a very long vacation after this."

"You both definitely deserve a vacation, Kyle. I can't tell you how grateful I am to have you both back to me. I was terrified till Scotty called me and told me that you were both alive."

Kyle and Megan looked up into Scotty's exhausted smile. "How are you doing, Scotty?" Megan said.

"I feel like I'm in a state of numbed shock. Today has been an absolute nightmare. I can't help but feel responsible for not stopping Abbott from hurting the ones we love." Scotty reached down to touch Kyle's face as Kyle took his hand and kissed his fingers.

"You went above and beyond the call of duty protecting us from that nut case, Scotty. You didn't have anything legally binding against Abbott so your hands were tied. We're already mourning the loss of those two police officers. We can't allow Abbott to terrorize us with guilt, regrets and doubt," Kyle said.

Scotty leaned down and kissed the top of Kyle's head. "I love you," he whispered.

Megan handed them both tissues and slipped her hand into Kyle's. "I hear that Superman is going to have the tear in his cape repaired," Megan said.

Kyle and Scotty laughed for the first time in hours as Megan reached for Scotty and pulled him closer. They both dried their eyes. Kyle squeezed Megan's hand and took a deep breath.

"The vascular surgeon said it should be relatively easy to repair my femoral vein and that Beck saved my life by applying that tourniquet and pressure dressing."

Megan smiled and looked toward Kyle's bandaged thigh. "Rebecca tells me that you saved her life, so I guess you're both

♥ *TENDER HEART* ♥

even. We're going to have to throw a hero and heroine party when you both come home."

They all laughed as a beautiful smile lit up Kyle's face. "No, wait! Let's have a Superman and Wonder woman party instead," he suggested. They all burst into laughter as Megan leaned back and rolled her eyes.

"I can just see it now: Rebecca will make us all dress up like every superhero that was ever created to get in the spirit of things," Megan said, chuckling.

They all laughed together as Scotty reached forward and ran his fingers through Kyle's hair. "That would be so much fun. I always wanted to cover my body in green paint and turn into the Incredible Hulk," Scotty confided.

Megan burst into laughter as Kyle reached for his hand and gave him a seductive smile. "The Incredible Hulk has nothing over you, my incredible hunk," Kyle said affectionately. Scotty blushed sweetly and leaned toward Kyle to kiss him softly. Megan watched their loving kiss and felt embraced by their deep love.

When the O.R. crew arrived to take Kyle to surgery, Megan leaned forward to hug and kiss him one more time. She leaned her forehead against his and gently caressed his cheek. "Rebecca and I will be praying for you. You'd better hurry up and get this surgery over with because we will both be needing a big Superman hug by the time they are done repairing your cape."

Kyle closed his eyes and fought the tears that were bursting past his eyelashes. "I look forward to delivering those hugs," Kyle said, as he took both of Megan's hands in his and tried hard to control his tears. "Meg, please tell Beck that we love her and that we are praying that her surgery goes well."

Megan smiled and squeezed his hands warmly. "I sure will, Kyle. Your love means a lot to her." Megan kissed him again and stepped back so Scotty could say good-bye. She gently squeezed Scotty's hand and gave him a brave smile. "You can go with him as far as the surgical waiting room, Scotty. I'll see you there after Rebecca's surgery."

♥ *TENDER HEART* ♥

Scotty bent down and gently kissed Megan's cheek. "Thank you, Megan. For everything," Scotty said.

Megan gave him a beautiful smile and headed toward the trauma room door. She stopped in the doorway and looked back at the loving embrace between these two tender men and smiled.

"Hey, you two." They both turned to Megan with tears in their eyes. "I love you guys," Megan said.

Kyle and Scotty gave each other a loving smile as Scotty turned back to Megan. "We love you very much too, Meg. Please give Beck a big hug and kiss for both of us," Scotty said.

Megan smiled and felt her tears slip onto her cheeks. "That would be my pleasure." She gave them a gentle wave and headed toward Rebecca's trauma room.

Megan stepped in through the doors. Sharon was giving Rebecca more intravenous morphine while the other nurses buzzed around the room getting Rebecca ready for her surgery.

Rebecca's aunt Sarah turned and caught Megan's eye. Wordlessly they shared their anguish as Sarah slipped into Megan's open arms. They hugged each other tight as Sarah struggled to take a deep breath. "Tell me she's going to be okay, Megan. I really need to hear the truth from you."

"Rebecca is going to be fine. The orthopedic surgeon is going to repair her fractured left arm and then I'm going to make sure she is going to be fine," Megan explained emotionally. They held each other tight as they looked over at Rebecca holding Madison's hand and sharing her nightmare with her uncle and Shawna.

Rebecca's uncle Mitchell moved to Megan and hugged her close before taking his teary wife into his arms.

Megan stood behind Shawna and Madison, placing one hand on each of their backs. She leaned down and kissed Rebecca softly and got a huge smile in return. Her golden eyes burst with love and happiness as Megan gave her a loving wink. "Why is your oxygen mask off, young lady?" Megan said sternly.

Rebecca giggled and gave her a guilty, impish grin. "While you were away Meg, this beautiful little tinker bell fairy flew

❤ *TENDER HEART* ❤

into my trauma room and told me this terribly sad story about a severe oxygen shortage. She said that there were lots of little tinker bells that needed the oxygen more than I did. So, I was kind and generous enough to offer them my oxygen mask." They all burst into laughter as Megan gave her a beautiful scolding smile and picked up the oxygen mask sitting on Rebecca's chest.

"Oh, look. Tinker bell must have returned your oxygen mask when all the other little fairies were done with it," Megan said.

Rebecca giggled sweetly as Megan replaced the mask on her face and kissed her forehead.

"I love you so much," Megan whispered.

Rebecca smiled as her eyes filled with huge tears. "I love you too, baby."

Megan smiled and wiped Rebecca's tears away with her tissue. Madison and Shawna asked about Kyle as Megan stood tall and leaned her hip against Rebecca's stretcher. She relayed their messages and told them that Kyle was doing well and on his way to surgery. Megan looked down at Rebecca and gently caressed her cheek.

"We also decided that we're going to throw a Superhero party and Scotty is going to paint his body green and come as the Incredible Hulk." Everyone burst into laughter.

Rebecca winced and reached for her fractured ribs. "Stop making me laugh. It hurts." Megan gently placed her hand over Rebecca's fractured ribs and supported them for her as she slowly caught her breath.

Drake stepped into the trauma room and smiled. "Must I remind you, ladies, that this is a trauma room and not a party room?" They all smiled. Drake came to stand behind Shawna and Madison, and rested a hand on each of their shoulders. He looked lovingly from Megan to Rebecca and gave her a smile. "They're ready for you in the operating room, Rebecca."

Rebecca grimaced with dread. Megan caressed her head and said, "I'll be in the O.R. with you, baby, so don't be sad."

Drake looked at Megan, total shock on his face. "Megan, I won't allow you in the operating room with Rebecca."

♥ *TENDER HEART* ♥

Megan stepped towards him with an angry, stunned look in her eyes. "What?" she shouted.

Drake sighed and ran his hand through his hair. "You can't be in the O.R. with Rebecca, Megan, you know that. You're way too close to this. You're in emotional shock and you can barely think straight. The orthopedic team have a job to do and they don't need Rebecca's emotional lover in the room watching them manipulate her arm back into place."

Madison, Shawna and Rebecca exchanged a concerned look as Megan backed away from Drake and groaned in frustration.

"Don't do this to me, Drake. I want to be in there with Rebecca. I don't want to leave her side."

Drake stepped close to Megan. She saw the stern, unyielding look in his blue eyes. "Look at me, Megan, and tell me that you're going to be able to function as an unbiased, unemotional, unattached observer in that room with Rebecca," Drake demanded.

Tears rolled down Megan's cheeks as she looked down at her hands and fought to control her anger.

Drake cupped Megan's chin in his hand and brought her eyes to meet his. "I'm not trying to cause you more pain, Meg. Try and understand that. Sarah, Mitchell, Madison, Shawna, Scotty, you, and I are going to wait together for the two people we love while they are in surgery," Drake stated firmly.

Megan jerked her face away from Drake and took one step away, kicking a trashcan clear across the room and into the cardiac arrest cart. The others were shocked by Megan's anger.

Rebecca took control. "Hey! That's enough, Dr. Summers! Sit your little temper tantrum down here beside me right now," she commanded. Megan gave Drake a furious scowl as she slumped into the stool at the head of Rebecca's stretcher. Megan's tears soaked her cheeks as Rebecca gently ran her hand into her hair and rested it on the back of her head, pulling Megan's face next to hers.

"I'm so sorry for everything I put you through today, baby. I know you're scared to death, but I think Drake is right. It would

♥ *TENDER HEART* ♥

be terribly traumatic for you to watch them operate on my arm and see exactly what that monster did to me. I don't want you left with images of that for the rest of our lives." Rebecca gently wiped away Megan's tears as she rested her forehead against Megan's.

"I know you're worried sick, sweetheart, but you're going to be an emotional wreck if you come into that operating room with me. You're my wife right now, not my doctor. I need you to separate the two and just trust in the people that are going to take care of me for you. I want you with the people that I know love you and are going to take care of you for me while my orthopedic surgeon turns me into your bionic woman."

Megan smiled through her tears as she raised her eyes up to Rebecca's. She struggled to catch her breath as she gently caressed Rebecca's face. "I don't want you to be alone," Megan gasped between anguished breaths.

Rebecca smiled deeply at her loving partner and brushed away her tears. "I'm never alone, Meg. I always carry you in my heart. You and our beautiful relationship were the driving force behind my will to survive today. This surgery is going to be a piece of cake compared to the rest of my lousy afternoon." Megan and Rebecca's tears flowed as one as Rebecca pulled her in close and held her tight.

The O.R. crew arrived to take Rebecca. Megan stepped back and watched Mitchell and Sarah kiss her and hug her tight. Madison, Shawna, and Drake kissed her and wish her luck. They all hugged her and promised to take good care of Megan while she was in surgery. Rebecca looked across the room at Megan's anguished face and crooked her finger at her to come closer. Megan leaned down and hugged Rebecca tight.

"I'm going to be okay, sweetheart. You know I'm too stubborn to let some pathetic man slow me down."

Megan's breathing came in short gasps as she nuzzled into Rebecca's neck and kissed her tenderly. "I'll be waiting for you, so hurry up or your Hershey's Kisses are liable to melt in my pocket."

♥ *TENDER HEART* ♥

Rebecca laughed, then held Megan's face in her hand and kissed her softly. She looked up into the glistening emerald green eyes that owned her heart. "I love you so much, Megan Summers. Please try not to worry so much and promise me that there will be no more temper tantrums while I'm gone. Otherwise, there'll be a spanking waiting for you when we get home."

Megan smiled, wiped at her tears, and leaned her forehead against Rebecca's. "I promise to be good, but I still think I might like to collect on that spanking." They both laughed softly and held each other close. "I love you, sweetheart. I'll be waiting very impatiently for you. Tell those orthopedic surgeons to do your surgery skillfully and quickly, or I might just have to go in there and kick their shins if they keep you away from me longer than I can stand." They both smiled as Rebecca kissed Megan tenderly.

"I promise to relay that message my sweet, emotional girl."

Sharon smiled and touched Megan's shoulder. "Every things set, Megan. The O.R crew is ready to take Rebecca."

Tears swelled in Megan's emerald green eyes as she gently touched a finger to Rebecca's heart. "Remember that I'm always in your heart as you are always in mine." They kissed each other softly and whispered good-bye as the others stood beside Megan with tears in their eyes. They all stood close together watching Rebecca wave with her good arm as she was wheeled down the hall.

Rebecca blew Megan one final kiss. "I love you," Rebecca said, as she disappeared into an empty elevator.

Megan watched the elevator door close and stood in heart-wrenching anguish as she whispered, "I love you too, baby."

Drake placed his hand on Megan's back and gently guided her toward him as she melted into his arms.

"I'm so sorry, Drake."

Drake held her close as he felt her tears against his cheek. "It's okay, Meg. I'm just glad you kicked the trashcan and not me. Have you ever thought of trying out for the place kicker on

♥ *TENDER HEART* ♥

the Dallas Cowboys? They could really use you." They both laughed as Drake hugged her warmly.

"Rebecca's going to be fine, Megan. She has the best orthopedic team we could ask for in there with her. And out here, we're all here for you and Scotty," Drake said.

Madison handed them both tissues. They walked together toward the elevators that would take them to the surgical waiting room, a room where, together as a family, they would wait and pray for Rebecca and Kyle.

Scotty sat on the edge of the coffee table and talked to Drake, Madison, and Shawna. Mitchell and Sarah were on the phone making plans for someone to stay with Lindsay after school. They all watched Megan pace the tiled floor relentlessly and stop to straighten the same picture for the hundredth time.

"Megan, come have a sip of your Diet Coke. You haven't stopped pacing since we got here," Drake said.

Megan checked the painting one final time and rubbed her raw stomach. "I'm okay, Drake. I'm really not thirsty and I don't think my stomach can handle anything right now." Megan shoved her hands into the pockets of her navy blue slacks and continued on her emotionally wrought journey.

"I don't know about you guys but I'm getting dizzy watching her. Come on Shawna, if we can't beat her, let's join her," Madison said. Madison and Shawna caught up to Megan and slipped a hand into hers and watched a beautiful smile brighten her face. They stood on either side of her and joined her on her journey.

Madison gave Megan a sheepish grin and squeezed her hand. "Megan, I had a fascinating conversation with JC and Penney today when Shawna and I went over to feed them."

Megan gave her sister a suspicious look and smiled. "Really, Madi? What kind of a fascinating conversation?"

Shawna giggled as Madison tried hard not to laugh. "They tell me that it took you and Rebecca exactly three days before

♥ *TENDER HEART* ♥

you slept together and it would have been two if you hadn't been called into the hospital on day two, you little hussy, you!"

Megan burst into laughter and finally stopped walking as she turned to face Madison and Shawna. She stepped toward them with a menacing look in her eyes as they both took measured steps backwards. "JC and Penney would never squeal on me like that. Let me guess which incredible, golden-eyed woman is the real tattletale in my life."

Madison and Shawna bumped into the soda machine and stopped suddenly as Megan reached for both of them. Madison squealed as Megan tickled her side. "No, Megan. It wasn't Rebecca, I swear. JC and Penney told us everything and they even described a few delicious things they watched you do to Rebecca that Shawna and I thought we might try later, you hussy, you!"

Megan's cheeks blushed with embarrassment as Shawna and Madison grabbed her and pulled her down onto the couch with them. They burst into a laughter that invigorated their souls and brightened the light in their hearts.

♥♥♥♥♥♥♥♥♥♥

Megan, Drake, and Scotty surrounded Kyle's stretcher in the recovery room as the vascular surgeon explained the surgery in detail and told everyone how pleased they were with the outcome.

Kyle gave them all a glowing, sleepy smile as Scotty sat on the edge of his stretcher and held his hand.

Megan and Drake assessed the circulation, sensation, and movement in Kyle's left leg and were thrilled at how well he had done. Megan stood beside Kyle's stretcher and peeked under his hospital gown to have a look at the dressing on his left thigh.

Kyle watched her and squeezed Scotty's hand. "Excuse me, Dr. Summers, but are you peeking under my cape?"

Megan blushed sweetly and stood closer to Kyle. "It's your dressing I'm looking at and nothing else, Superman. Trust me,"

♥ *TENDER HEART* ♥

Megan said, as she rolled her eyes skyward. All the men burst into laughter as Megan leaned forward and kissed him softly.

Kyle reached up and caressed her face with a look of loving warmth. "Be careful, because what you might see under there could convert you to the other side," Kyle stated playfully.

Megan burst into a beautiful smile as she leaned intimately close to Kyle's beaming face. "I've never had any desire, interest, or inkling to even venture to the other side, mister. The incredible woman that tangles my bed sheets is the one and only whose cape I wish to venture beneath." All three men burst into laughter and applauded Megan's spirit.

The doors to the waiting swung open as Rebecca was wheeled in. She laid back peacefully with her eyes closed and her left arm in a cast. Megan and Drake rushed to her side and helped position her stretcher to the right of Kyle's. The two female recovery room nurses moved swiftly around everyone and hooked Rebecca up to a cardiac monitor. Kyle and Scotty were riveted on her pale, still face.

Megan quickly assessed her arm and vital signs and lowered the nearest side rail. She sat on the edge of her stretcher and gently caressed her face as the orthopedic surgeon, Dr. Schwartz, stepped into the room. Megan stood to greet him as he took her by the shoulders and gently sat her back down.

"Don't get up, Megan. I'd hate to give you the opportunity to kick my shins," he scolded.

Megan blushed sweetly as they all laughed.

He leaned forward and squeezed Megan's shoulder. "Rebecca's surgery was a huge success, Megan. We implanted a metal plate and four screws in her humerus to realign the bone. I feel optimistic that with rest and rigorous physical therapy Rebecca should regain one-hundred percent of the movement in her left arm."

Megan stood and took Dr. Schwartz's hands. "Thank you for everything you did for Rebecca," Megan said.

"I was thrilled to be here for you and Rebecca, Megan. I had only met Rebecca since this terrible tragedy occurred and I liked

♥ TENDER HEART ♥

her instantly. She is a real little spark this one," Dr. Schwartz said, as they looked towards Rebecca's peacefully sleeping form. Dr. Schwartz checked the circulation to Rebecca's hand one final time before hugging Megan and saying good-bye.

Megan carefully sat on the edge of the stretcher as she watched Rebecca slowly start to come around as she heard her mumble "Megan?" several times. She leaned closer and kissed her face as Rebecca suddenly looked at Megan, confusion and fear in her eyes. Megan held her face in her hands and spoke to her softly. "You're okay, baby. The surgery is over and you're here safe with me."

Rebecca was finally able to focus her eyes on Megan and gave her a smile of pure relief. She ripped her oxygen mask off her face and guided Megan down to her where they shared a kiss of passionate comfort. Megan held her tight in her arms as they both shared tears of joy.

Rebecca finally lifted her head off the pillow and looked around at the smiling men on either side of her. She looked back at Megan with a confused look in her golden eyes. "Meg, what are the boys doing in our bedroom?" They all burst into laughter.

Megan guided Rebecca down onto her pillow. "We're in the recovery room, sweetheart. We haven't quite made it home yet."

Rebecca looked around her and took in her new environment. The anesthetic fog was beginning to lift. She rubbed at her eyes, looked back at Megan, and laughed at herself.

Megan kissed her cheek softly and hugged her with all the love in her heart. "The only boy allowed in our bedroom is JC, and I have to talk to you about what he's been telling Madison and Shawna." Megan gave her a playful scowl as Rebecca grinned, the light slowly returning to her beautiful golden eyes.

Megan asked her about her pain and watched her assess her new cast and wiggle her fingers with glee. Megan explained the surgery to her and watched Rebecca slowly look over at Kyle.

"Kyle. You're here. How's your leg?" They all laughed at Rebecca's excitement.

♥ TENDER HEART ♥

"I've been right beside you the whole time, my Lois Lane. Do you think your Superman would ever leave your side?"

They all laughed as Megan told her all about Kyle's successful surgery. He wiggled his toes for Rebecca to see as she cheered with delight.

"After the day we all shared it certainly makes you realize how precious life is with the ones you love," Megan said.

Kyle stretched his arm toward Rebecca and took her hand in his. "Exactly, Megan. However, I did lose something near and dear to me," Kyle said.

Everyone looked into Kyle's emotionally exhausted eyes and waited for him to continue.

"They cut my Superman boxers off in the trauma room," he announced sadly.

They burst into laughter as Rebecca squeezed his hand lovingly. "Megan and I are going to buy you a lifetime supply of Superman boxers because you, Kyle Kennedy, are my hero," Rebecca announced with glee.

Everyone's eyes were moist with tears as they watched Kyle entwine his fingers in Rebecca's and blow her a kiss.

♥ TENDER HEART ♥
CHAPTER TEN

Megan closed the barbecue lid and set down her tongs. She marveled at the beautiful smile on Rebecca's glowing face as she leaned against the cedar railing. The afternoon sun bathed Rebecca in a golden hue as she stood on their raised, two tiered backyard deck that wrapped around the back of the their new home. Megan stepped around the sunken Jacuzzi pool and stood before Rebecca. Megan glided her hands along the waist of Rebecca's sleeveless white cotton sundress and openly admired her shapely legs.

Rebecca gave her a magnificent smile as she gingerly raised her left arm and slowly removed Megan's sunglasses. Rebecca set them aside on the cedar railing and ran her fingers through her thick, rich hair and pulled her intimately close.

"Happy tenth week anniversary, Dr. Summers," Rebecca purred. They both smiled deeply as their eyes met in a passionate dance and their lips met slowly, seductively until Rebecca touched her tongue to Megan's full lower lip and heard her arousing sigh. Megan opened her mouth and guided Rebecca's tongue in deeper as they shared a kiss of sultry passion.

Scotty and Kyle stopped on the top step and smiled at the vision before them. Kyle slipped his hand into Scotty's as they tiptoed closer and watched the fireworks explode before them. They watched Rebecca's hands glide across the silk of Megan's sexy, coral green sundress and entwine in Megan's hair as she guided her intimately close. Rebecca breathlessly leaned her forehead against Megan's and slowly opened her eyes. She saw the boys standing directly behind Megan in their matching Superman swim trunks and sun-bronzed, muscular bodies. Rebecca gave them an impish smile as she held Megan close.

"Don't look now, babe, but JC isn't the only boy that enjoys watching us."

Megan slowly turned around and swatted at Kyle and Scotty's arms and gave them a menacing look.

♥ TENDER HEART ♥

"Will you two please stop sneaking up on us like that? You're going to give us a heart attack some day," Megan shouted.

Both men laughed and easily stepped out of Megan's reach as Scotty stepped behind her and subdued her in his strong, loving arms. Kyle smiled as he watched Megan hug Scotty's arms close to her. He turned to Rebecca and gave her a glowing smile.

"Superman and his husband are starving, so we decided to get out of the pool and come up here and see what was holding dinner up and what do we find?" Kyle went into his hilarious Nathan Lane routine and gestured wildly with his arms. "We find Wonder woman here feasting on her wife's lips and not sharing any of her meal with the rest of us."

Everyone burst into laughter as Kyle stepped toward Rebecca and tickled her until she collapsed into his arms. Rebecca begged him to stop as Kyle guided her to sit down on the deck bench with him and held her close in his arms. Rebecca finally caught her breath and rested her hand on the long scar on Kyle's thigh.

Megan and Scotty smiled warmly and joined them on the cedar bench adorned in thick flowery cushions as Megan leaned back into Scotty's arms.

Rebecca leaned her head on Kyle's shoulder and turned to kiss his cheek.

"Ready to go back to work on Monday, Superman?" Rebecca asked.

Kyle leaned his head against Rebecca's and sighed. "It's been two months since that psycho turned our lives upside down. I think I'm ready to get back to being your slave and feeling a sense of normalcy again," Kyle said.

Rebecca gave him a beautiful smile as he kissed her forehead.

"We have both healed beautifully and the doctors have given us their okay, so I guess the vacation is actually coming to an end. However, I thoroughly enjoyed recuperating in Hawaii with

♥ *TENDER HEART* ♥

Scotty for three weeks." They all smiled and sat close together. Kyle ran his hand gently over the scar on Rebecca's arm.

"I thought it was wonderful that Megan took a month off work to be home with you," Kyle said warmly.

Rebecca looked over at her loving partner and entwined their hands. "Yes, she is absolutely incredible. It's been wonderful having my Meg home with me but I must admit I have one tiny complaint." Megan smiled sweetly as Kyle gave her a questioning look.

"What complaint could you possibly have against this gorgeous woman who treats you like a royal princess?" They all burst into laughter. Rebecca turned her smiling face up to Kyle.

"She's a grueling, unyielding physical therapist! As soon as my cast came off she got me into the pool three times a day to do a strict set of exercises and expected her royal princess to swim laps each time after." They all laughed as Megan brought Rebecca's left hand to her lips and kissed it gently.

"It always amazed me how you whined and complained throughout your exercises, but as soon as I said you were done you had no trouble getting me naked on an air mattress and spending an hour exercising both our bodies," Megan stated.

Rebecca smiled sweetly as they all laughed at their loving playfulness.

"Well, Meg. At least the exercise routine I created for you brought you incredible, explosive pleasure compared to my exercise routine."

Megan gave her a seductive wink as they rested their hands on Megan's thigh. "You never heard me whine and complain once did you?" Megan asked.

Rebecca gave her a seductive smile as she leaned close to Megan's lips.

"No, the sounds I hear from you, my lover, are far from whining and complaining." Megan blushed sweetly as both men applauded. Rebecca kissed her softly, seductively, and leaned back against Kyle's arm. Megan was left hungry for their air mattress routine. Megan gave her a lusty, wanton look as Rebecca smiled at her desire.

"Show the boys the results of all of our exercise routines, my little tease," Megan said.

Rebecca gave her a glowing smile, sat straight up, and flexed her arms in Ms. Universe-style.

"Look at my big muscles, boys," Rebecca said proudly. Kyle gently squeezed both of Rebecca's tensed arms and playfully whistled at her arms of steel.

"I have a bionic arm now, so look out, world. I am indestructible. I am woman, hear me roar," Rebecca announced. They all laughed and applauded Rebecca's spirit and emotional strength.

Megan glided her thumb down the long, white scar running down Rebecca's left arm. "You sure proved to be indestructible, my darling, however this scar will be a constant reminder to all of us of how precious life is with the ones we love."

Rebecca leaned forward and gently brushed her lips against Megan's. "I love you, Meg," Rebecca breathed.

Rebecca leaned back against Kyle's arm as he leaned toward her and kissed her cheek.

"How are your nightmares, little Ms. Indestructible?" A frown creased Rebecca's smiling face as she looked over at Megan and squeezed her hand. Rebecca tilted her face up to Kyle, sadness in her eyes.

"They're getting less and less. I'm not waking up in the middle of the night screaming anymore and scaring Meg half to death. When I do dream, I see Abbott's contorted, enraged face hovering over me and reaching out to tear at my clothes. I can never seem to get away from him. I keep fighting and clawing at him but he always manages to pin me down and I feel like I'm suffocating and fighting for my life all over again," Rebecca explained painfully. Megan reached over and gently caressed Rebecca's cheek. "Our sessions with the psychologist seem to really be helping. She's given me some mind exercises to do before we get into bed and that has helped to diminish the

♥ *TENDER HEART* ♥

nightmares." Rebecca turned her head and smiled at Megan. "Just climbing into bed with Megan is enough of a distraction to help keep my mind on healthier thoughts," Rebecca confessed.

Megan smiled and squeezed her hand lovingly. "Rebecca's nightmares are much less frequent but when we are awakened by one, we always manage to find a way to soothe her shattered nerves," she said sweetly.

Rebecca gave Megan a glowing grin as she discreetly ran her finger along the inside of her thigh. "Yes, you certainly know how to get a girl's mind off her troubles, Dr. Summers." Megan growled playfully as she slowly slid from the bench.

"I better check on our steaks before the natives start getting restless for their dinner again," Megan said, never leaving her gleaming eyes from Rebecca.

They all smiled warmly as they heard a burst of laughter erupt from the crystal blue pool below. They all stood and leaned against the cedar railing as they watched Madison and Shawna try in vain to teach Lindsay to float on her back.

"They have been at that for an hour now. Each time they try to hold her steady, Lindsay bursts into giggles and inhales a gallon of water," Rebecca said.

They all watched Madison wipe the water from Lindsay's eyes and smile at the precious girl who has become so dear to everyone's hearts.

"All right, Lindsay, that's it. From now on, the girls are going to use a snorkel to teach you how to float, otherwise you're going to drink all the water in the pool and you'll have no room in your tummy for supper," Rebecca scolded playfully.

Lindsay caught her breath and looked at Rebecca with shy disbelief.

"I couldn't drink all this water, Becky. I'd be in the bathroom peeing all night," she said innocently. They all laughed at Lindsay's sweet personality.

Drake and Stephanie stood together on the wooden bridge overlooking the tranquil goldfish pond. The pond centered around a five-foot high rock garden waterfall, adorned with

♥ *TENDER HEART* ♥

blossoming impatiens, pansies and snapdragons. Two channels extended beyond the waterfall. One ran along the edge of the two-tiered deck, and the other ran in the opposite direction beneath the wooden arch bridge, allowing the plump koi five hundred feet of swimming space.

Rebecca smiled as she watched Stephanie slip her hand into Drake's. Drake brought her hand up to his lips and kissed it gently as he pointed down to JC and Penney, hunched down on rocks near them.

"Look at those two fur balls staring into the water and dipping their furry little paws in. I think they have delusions of grandeur of catching themselves a goldfish," Rebecca said, as Megan joined them at the deck railing.

Rebecca smiled into Megan's vibrant green eyes and touched her glowing face. "Have I told you lately how much JC and Penney appreciate the huge, in-ground goldfish bowl that we had built in their new backyard?" Rebecca said.

Megan laughed and watched the cats' intense concentration. "Those two little fur balls must think they've died and gone to goldfish heaven," Megan said, chuckling. They all laughed.

Below, Stephanie melted into Drake's strong arms and guided his face intimately close as they shared a slow, tender, passionate kiss. They all shared a warm smile for Drake's happiness.

Megan shouted out, "Hey, you two. Didn't Rebecca tell you? There will be no heterosexual kissing in our new house. You guys are liable to scare the fish and we're trying to set a good example for Lindsay." Everyone burst into laughter as Stephanie turned to Drake and leaned intimately against him as they displayed a kiss of intense passion and lust.

Scotty lifted the barbecue lid and picked up the tongs and flipped the steaks. They stood close together and shared their joy over Drake and Stephanie's beautiful, new relationship. Scotty closed the lid on the barbecue and listened to Kyle tell the girls about his leg. He heard a strange noise from below the deck.

♥ *TENDER HEART* ♥

Slowly slipping around Megan, he leaned over the deck to have a look.

"Oh shit! Incoming water balloons," he shouted.

He quickly guided everyone away from the railing as a barrage of balloons splattered at their feet. Megan guided a shocked Rebecca to safety behind the barbecue as Scotty and Kyle ran down the deck steps to squeals of fright and were pelted with balloons. Megan and Rebecca bravely ventured to the edge of the deck to watch. The expressions on Drake, Stephanie, and the girls' faces changed dramatically as they quickly realized they were being counter-attacked. Scotty quickly picked up the garden hose and turned it on full blast. They heard squeals of playful fright and watched everyone dive back into the pool for cover. Scotty set the garden hose down as he and Kyle dove into the pool and sent the squeals of fright to an all-time high.

Megan and Rebecca saw everyone off and blew kisses to Lindsay sitting happily in the back of Shawna and Madison's Honda Passport. Their taillights faded down the palm tree-lined street as Rebecca slipped her hand into Megan's. She happily guided her toward their backyard and into a lounge chair at the edge of the fishpond.

The summer sun was just beginning to set as a balmy breeze blew past and caressed their bodies. Rebecca rested in Megan's arms and luxuriated in her warmth. They shared a glass of white wine and admired the lights illuminating their pond and the soothing sound of water cascading over their rock garden.

Megan wordlessly handed Rebecca the glass of wine and reached under the chair for the remote control to the sleek, model sailboat Rebecca had bought to go with the fishpond. Megan had been ecstatic with the gift and quickly learned how to maneuver it skillfully through the pond's channels.

Tonight was a very special voyage for the sailboat Megan and Rebecca had christened "Dream Catcher." Megan had strung tiny, white Christmas lights all along the deck and sail of the

♥ *TENDER HEART* ♥

boat and polished it to gleam in the moonlight. Megan's heart burst with happiness when Rebecca saw it float out from under the bridge toward them and applauded with excitement. She looked up into Megan's glowing eyes and smiled beautifully.

"Dream Catcher looks magnificent, sweetheart. She looks like a floating Christmas tree," Rebecca said joyfully. Megan laughed and carefully maneuvered the controls in Rebecca's lap to float Dream Catcher closer.

"Even though it is the middle of July, I would like us to pretend that tonight she is a Christmas tree, and you might want to see if she has a gift for you."

Rebecca gave her a smile as she watched Dream Catcher come to dock by their feet. She leaned toward the festive model boat and glowed with happiness as she looked on the shiny deck. Rebecca picked up two small, beautiful, gold foil boxes with white ribbon and a small note attached. Rebecca held the gifts in her hand and leaned back against Megan, feeling her arms wrap around her. Rebecca tilted her head back and kissed Megan softly.

"I love you, Dr. Megan Summers."

Megan smiled beautifully and guided Rebecca's lips back to her.

"I love you, Ms. Rebecca Rhodes, now and always."

Rebecca kissed her gently as their passion burned and their lips united in a kiss of fiery need and desire. Rebecca leaned back and gave her a glowing smile as she looked down at her gifts and read the note.

♥ *TENDER HEART* ♥

My Dearest Rebecca,

You are my heart, my soul and my dreams.
I love you like no other.

                        Love always,
                        Your Meg   XOXO

Rebecca looked up into Megan's glistening emerald eyes and hugged her close. Tears of joy fell onto their cheeks.

Megan wiped away her tears and looked down at the gifts in her lap.

"I believe that Dream Catcher and I are still waiting for you to see what she brought you." Megan chose one of the gold foil boxes and handed it to Rebecca.

Rebecca leaned back into Megan's arms with the smile of a child on Christmas morning. She kissed Megan's cheek, then quickly peeked into the box and squealed with delight as she looked down at two, heart-shaped chocolate raspberry truffles. She gingerly pulled one out, bit off half, and placed the other half in Megan's mouth, then gasped as Megan took her finger into her mouth and caressed the tip with her tongue. Megan slowly released her finger and watched the passion slowly dance across her eyes as she leaned closer and kissed Rebecca with burning desire and hunger. She glided her hand across Rebecca's scantily clad, slender abdomen as their tongues strained to entwine. Rebecca gasped with aching desire as Megan's hand glided higher and outlined the soft underside of Rebecca's breast.

Their kisses burned hot and wet between their thighs as Megan's fingertips found the erect, cotton-covered nipple that strained for her touch. Rebecca gasped and arched her back higher as Megan leaned down, quickly released several buttons running between Rebecca's breasts and took that straining bud deep in her mouth. Rebecca moaned with urgent need as Megan laid a trail of warm wet kisses between her breasts, to her arching throat, and finally to the lips that eagerly awaited her.

♥ *TENDER HEART* ♥

Megan held her close and struggled to catch her breath as she nuzzled into her neck. Rebecca entwined her fingers in Megan's hair and held her tight.

"You keep kissing me like that, Dr. Summers, and I'm going to make love to you right here in this lounge chair," Rebecca said breathlessly.

Megan smiled impishly and looked into Rebecca's wondrous golden eyes.

"If you do that, you'd better ask the fish to turn their fins to us. I couldn't stand having that many eyes on us. It's bad enough that JC and Penney have become a regular audience," Megan said.

Rebecca burst into laughter and leaned against Megan's chest, basking in their loving relationship.

Megan kissed her forehead and brushed away a stray strand of hair from her shining eyes.

"I do believe you have one other gift in your lap, my love," Megan informed her.

Rebecca kissed her tenderly and set the truffle box down. She reached for the second box and tore off the gold wrapping paper. She looked up into Megan's radiant face and slowly lifted the lid off the ring box. Tears blurred Rebecca's eyes as she lifted a breathtaking two-carat diamond ring from the velvet folds and held it between her fingers. She looked up at Megan in absolute shock as Megan gently took the ring from her and slipped it onto her ring finger. It fit perfectly and glimmered in the soft glow of lights. Rebecca was speechless.

"I just wanted you to know how much I love you and how thrilled I am to be married to you," Megan whispered emotionally.

Rebecca's tears trailed down her cheeks as she leaned toward Megan and kissed her tenderly.

"It's the most beautiful ring I've ever seen in my life, sweetheart. Thank you hardly seems to convey how I feel about this gift from you. I'm ecstatic to be married to you, Meg, and to wear your ring means so much to me."

♥ *TENDER HEART* ♥

Megan's eyes were moist with emotion as she pulled Rebecca into her arms and hugged her tight.

"Happy tenth week anniversary, my Rebecca."

Rebecca smiled deeply, dried her eyes, and looked down at the magnificent ring. She gave Megan a breathtaking smile and took her lips with yearning passion. They both leaned back to catch their breath. Rebecca looked over at the edge of their pond. She smiled at the porcelain little girl that sat on the edge with her fishing pole in the water and her back against a sign that read:

NO FISHING ALLOWED. TRESPASSERS WILL BE SPANKED.

Megan had been so tickled when Rebecca had the sign and figurine created for her, and together they had placed it at the edge of their pond.

Rebecca looked back into Megan's glowing eyes and smiled. "I was wondering, Dr. Summers. Have you checked to see if you've caught anything lately?"

Megan burst into laughter and gave Rebecca a shocked look. "Are you kidding? Haven't you read that sign lately?"

Rebecca giggled sweetly and guided Megan to her feet. "I do believe I saw the string bobbing just a few minutes ago. Let's go see if we've caught a goldfish," Rebecca said sheepishly.

Megan gave her a very suspicious look and took Rebecca's hand in hers. They walked toward the porcelain figurine. Megan reached for the fishing line and was shocked by the weight on the end. She gave it one good pull and raised a plastic bag weighted down with a small rock and a tiny, square, gift-wrapped package. Megan smiled and looked over at Rebecca's excited face.

"Oh goody! We caught a gift. Pull it out, Meg, and see who it's for."

Megan burst into laughter as she eased the bag toward her and smiled at Rebecca's excitement. Megan dropped the rock back into the pond and eased the gift out as Rebecca stood before

❤ TENDER HEART ❤

her, clapping with glee. Megan guided her to sit on a pine captain's bench under a bright light, excitedly unfolded the attached note and read:

My Precious Meg,

    There is no greater heaven than to belong to you and your tender heart. I love you with all my heart.

                              Always,
                           Your Rebecca   XOXO

Tears swelled in Megan's eyes as she leaned toward Rebecca and kissed her softly. Rebecca pointed at the gift with bursting enthusiasm as Megan laughed and tore at the beautiful pink wrapping paper. She held a tiny black velvet box in her hand and looked up into Rebecca's expectant eyes. They both listened as the lid creaked open and Megan stared at a breathtaking band of solid diamonds. Tears slid onto her cheeks as Rebecca took the ring and slipped it gently onto Megan's ring finger. Rebecca slowly twirled it as they both admired the perfect fit of the exquisite diamond band.

"You are so incredibly special to me, Dr. Megan Summers, and I am blessed to have you as my wife."

Megan leaned toward Rebecca and kissed her with deep passion. "I love you, my Rebecca, and I absolutely love my ring. It will always represent your unconditional love and our deep bond."

Rebecca caressed Megan's face and held her close. "I love you, my tender heart, now and always." Rebecca slowly leaned toward Megan's moist, slightly parted lips; their lips brushed together. She heard the gentle moans that ignited her passion as she leaned her body against Megan's and held her face in her hands. She teasingly brushed her tongue across Megan's upper lip and watched her close her eyes and moan wantonly.

♥ *TENDER HEART* ♥

"Wait here," Rebecca breathed in her sultry, exotic voice as Megan watched her walk towards their pool and reach down for their favorite air mattress. Within seconds she returned with a huge grin and their makeshift bed. Megan burst into laughter as she watched Rebecca ceremoniously drape a beach towel across the air mattress and guided Megan to come join her at the edge of the pond.

Rebecca's passion burned along her thighs as she gently eased herself to lie on top of Megan. She gently separated her thighs with her own knee and rested intimately against Megan, brushing her lips softly against Megan's and gently encouraging her tongue to come and play. Megan glided her hands onto Rebecca's thighs and gently floated them under her cotton sundress.

Their lips ached to devour and taste as they strained to consume each other with hungry, impatient desire. Megan basked in Rebecca's erotic groans as she felt her own desire explode in her most sensitive areas. Rebecca swayed and rocked intimately as Megan's fingers strained to lower her french cut panties. Rebecca raised herself slightly on her knees as Megan's fingers found her aching, wet center. Rebecca gasped and stared deeply into Megan's passionate eyes as she sent her desire spiraling throughout her entire being. Rebecca rocked and swayed to the gently caressing rhythm of Megan's fingertips as she felt her world spin out of control. The soothing, tranquil sounds of night quickly floated into the abyss. All Rebecca could hear was the pounding surge of passion building with each tender stroke. Weaving tension and blissful euphoria battled for control as Megan plunged her fingers deep within Rebecca. Rebecca arched her back and thrust harder against Megan's tingling touch as she struggled to sustain this ecstasy and hold off the inevitable rapture that awaited her.

Megan ached to taste Rebecca's passion as she supported her against her and swiftly rolled her onto her back. She impatiently pulled Rebecca's panties completely off and tossed them onto the grass. She glided herself between her lover's awaiting thighs and plunged her tongue deep within her wetness.

Rebecca groaned with aching desire and shouted Megan's name as she thrust against her probing tongue. The hypersensitive tingling swelled with each stroke of Megan's tongue as Rebecca glided her fingers into Megan's hair and held her tight against her straining desire. Rebecca arched her hips higher and held her breath as she felt Megan take her erect center tightly between her caressing lips. Rebecca felt her floodgates straining with each stroke as the pulse between Megan's lips beat faster and faster. Megan plunged her fingers deeply as she felt the gentle spasms hold her still within Rebecca as she felt as one with this amazing woman. Rebecca arched her neck and held her breath as Megan felt her surge with wetness and erupt in undulating spasms. Rebecca thrust one final time and gripped Megan's head tightly as she screamed her name deep into the still night air.

Rebecca struggled to slow her ragged breathing as she glided her hands into Megan's hair and gently guided her up to her. She stared into Megan's emerald eyes of passion, pulling her gently closer and devouring her lips with astounding desire. Megan gently collapsed into Rebecca's arms and held her tight as the soothing sound of their cascading rock garden permeated their satiated souls.

Rebecca gently held Megan's glowing face in her hands. Their eyes met and conveyed their burning passion and insatiable hunger. She stared into Megan's passionate, sensitive eyes as Megan ran her fingertips across Rebecca's flushed cheeks. Several minutes later, Megan wordlessly rose, took Rebecca by the hand, and guided her to her feet. Megan scooped the discarded panties off the lawn as they both smiled and took two steps towards the house.

The sound of a humming motor stopped them dead in their tracks. They slowly turned together and saw Dream Catcher float toward them, then take a sharp right, a sharp left, and move forward. They looked at each other in disbelief and then over to

♥ *TENDER HEART* ♥

the lounge chair where JC sniffed at the remote controls and occasionally swatted at the control stick.

Rebecca burst into laughter as Megan shouted, "JC, no!" JC looked up at Megan and dove under the lounge chair, trying to hide his furry body in the well-manicured grass. They both turned back to see Dream Catcher come to a slow gliding stop along the bank. Megan and Rebecca burst into laughter and held each other close. Their laughter echoed in the night air as their diamond rings reflected the passionate glow of their tender hearts.

♥ *TENDER HEART* ♥

♥ *TENDER HEART* ♥
About the Author

My name is Ana and I have been a nurse for sixteen years. Twelve of those years have been spent working in intensive care units. My nursing experience is the backdrop of my story. Nursing is a career that envelops a multitude of skills and emotions. Throughout the years I have been blessed with caring for patients that have taught me the lessons of patience, human kindness, humility, modesty, suffering, self sacrifice, love and the powerful language of human touch.

My partner of nine years and I love to travel and share new experiences. January 1995, we packed our bags and signed on with a travel-nursing agency and have worked in Florida, Texas, California and now Arizona. We have enjoyed some of the most beautiful sights and experiences that these states have to offer.

My passion for travel equals my passion to create love stories. My partner's unconditional love and undying encouragement inspired me to put pen to paper and thus my story danced across the screen of my computer. At times like a chaotic screen saver and finally like the movie in my mind.

I have been fortunate enough to experience the beauty of love between women. It is that depth of commitment and passion that resounds throughout my book and my life.

When your mind is relaxed and at ease, put your feet up and crack open the front cover. I hope you enjoy reading my book as much as I enjoyed writing it.

Sincerely;

Ana P. Corman

♥ TENDER HEART ♥

♥ *TENDER HEART* ♥

♥ *TENDER HEART* ♥